SLOW
HAND

VICTORIA VANE

sourcebooks
casablanca

Published by Sourcebooks Casablanca, an imprint of Sourcebooks, Inc.
P.O. Box 4410, Naperville, Illinois 60567-4410
(630) 961-3900
Fax: (630) 961-2168
www.sourcebooks.com

Printed and bound in Canada.
WC 10 9 8 7 6 5 4 3 2 1

For Jill.

Thank you for spurring me into the twenty-first century.

Chapter 1

THE FASTEN SEAT BELT SIGN glared like a malevolent beacon.

Clutching both armrests with clammy palms and white knuckles, Nikki diverted her terrified gaze from the sign to the window, where lightning slashed the black clouds. She then looked in panic to the seat pocket in front of her, vainly seeking the little white paper bag.

Dear God, don't let me get sick! Breathe, Nikki. Just breathe.

As if on cue, the plane took another turbulent lurch, sending bile to the back of her throat.

Was this foul weather some kind of dark omen? What would happen if lightning struck the plane? Or would they just run out of fuel while circling the blackened skies above Denver?

She hated flying. Always had. Maybe it was irrational, but she despised any situation that placed her fate under anyone else's control. On a normal day she didn't even like being a passenger in a car. Flying, however, literally put her life in a perfect stranger's hands, so she avoided it at all costs.

Until now.

But Atlanta to Sheridan, Montana, was over two thousand miles, an impossible drive with only a three-day bereavement leave.

She closed her eyes, willing away the nausea churning

her stomach, wishing she had never received the fateful phone call, and hoping that this entire episode was just a very bad dream. She didn't know why she'd felt such a strong obligation to get on the damn plane in the first place. He'd bailed out when she was only seven, after all. Followed by over twenty years of stone-cold silence.

Then the letter arrived.

It had come to her with a Bozeman, Montana, post-mark, but no return address. Still, she had known it was from *him*. She hadn't opened it, but she hadn't destroyed it either. Instead, it sat in a state of purgatory in her desk drawer—untouched for eighteen months. Well, that wasn't quite right either, for she had *touched* it often enough. Picked it up, turned it over, smelled the familiar Marlboro scent, and thrown it back in the drawer again. Everything short of actually opening it. The letter repre-sented a virtual Pandora's box of heartaches that she just wasn't willing to experience again. So, she'd buried it. Chapter closed. Until the blasted phone call with news that unleashed a gale of emotions about a man she'd hardly known.

Hours later she'd torn the letter open, devouring every line as if starved. She wished she'd never read it because then she wouldn't have cared. But she had, and she did. But now it was too late.

He was gone.

They would never get to say what needed saying. She would *never* see his face again. The letter left her with a relentless ache in the middle of her chest, a pain that she suspected would continue to eat at her until she followed this through. In the end, she'd had no choice but to suffer the motion sickness and face her near-paralyzing fear of flying.

The garbled voice of the captain jarred into her wildly rambling thoughts. Three precious words were all she understood, but also all she cared about—*cleared for landing*.

———

Nikki anxiously waited another fifteen minutes before the plane actually hit the tarmac. It had barely reached the Jetway before she flipped the seat buckle and snatched the shoulder strap of her oversized purse, the one she'd barely managed to cram under the seat to begin with. A struggle to release it ensued, eating up valuable seconds before she could escape from the flying deathtrap. One last tug and it lurched free, only to have the contents spill helter-skelter all over the floor.

"Help me, sweet Jesus," she murmured, more curse than prayer.

She scrambled to collect her cell phone, tubes of lipstick, feminine products, and miscellaneous other objects that littered the floor. By the time she'd gathered everything up and crawled out from under the seat, passengers were jamming the aisle.

Shit! With nothing else to do but stand there with her neck craned to avoid the overhead compartments, she turned on her cell phone to check for messages, but the digital clock sent her heart lurching into her throat. *Double shit!* Her connection to Bozeman was scheduled to depart in eighteen minutes! Even if she could squeeze out of this sardine can, she'd never make it across the behemoth Denver airport to her next gate. *Could this trip possibly get any worse?*

Hell yes, was the answer when she arrived, winded and flustered, at gate fifty in Terminal C to find stranded passengers camping around the counter.

———⚉———

"Please, you've got to help me," Nikki pleaded with the gate agent. "I didn't even want to make this trip to begin with, but my father has passed away. I *have* to get on this flight."

"I'm sorry for your loss, miss." The agent's gaze barely flickered up from the computer monitor. Although the words were sympathetic, the voice was anything but. "I have done all I can. The next flight is already overbooked due to the inclement weather and all the earlier cancellations. I have you on standby, but I wouldn't get my hopes up. I can confirm you on our noon departure tomorrow."

"*Tomorrow?* You mean I'll be stuck here overnight?"

The woman glanced up with an exasperated sigh. "We can provide a room and meal voucher." She gazed over Nikki's shoulder and beckoned to the next passenger.

"Wait! You don't understand! I *have* to be there."

Nikki felt a burning sensation behind her eyes. *Keep it together, Nikki. You've already made an ass of yourself in front of a hundred strangers. Don't you dare cry.*

"I'm sorry, miss." The agent's face was completely impassive, now looking past Nikki as if she wasn't there. "Next in line, please."

With eyes blurring with tears she still refused to acknowledge, Nikki spun around but found no vacant seats close to the gate. Lacking any other options, she threw herself to the floor beside her bag, fished out a Kleenex from her purse, and blew her nose loud enough to draw some stares. Well, *more* stares.

What had possessed her to break down into near-hysterics over a man she'd hardly known? She shook her head, drew in a ragged breath, and scrubbed her face with her palms. For a moment she deliberated turning back, catching the next flight to Atlanta, but that would be cowardly.

And Nikki was no coward.

She'd proven it enough times in her life. Except for flying, that is, but she'd even braved *that* horror when she'd had to. She drew another long and shaky breath in an effort at composure, glaring back at those who still gaped at her, reserving her best glower for the cowboy she'd caught staring at her ass. He was slouched in his seat with his Stetson hat and ostrich Lucchese boots, his long legs stretched out and crossed at the ankles, taking up all the surrounding floor space as if he owned it.

God, how I hate arrogant, swaggering cowboys.

She'd had a bellyful of them with their tall boots, big hats, monster trucks, Red Man, and NASCAR. It was one of the reasons for getting the hell out of Toccoa ten years ago—to avoid repeating all of her past mistakes involving no-account cowboys. At least greater Atlanta had a more diversified mix of losers and players—the only two breeds of male she'd identified so far—unfortunately, *by dating them.*

When Marlboro Man rose to talk to the gate agent, she assumed he must also be on standby. She slanted a covetous glance at his seat the moment he'd vacated, as did several other people. Well hell, if she didn't take it, someone else certainly would. She stood and slid into it, noting with surprise that it was still warm. Somehow it seemed weird to be absorbing a total stranger's body heat in such an intimate place.

After his exchange with the agent, Mr. Look-How-Damned-Hot-I-Am headed away from the gate area. *Thank God for small favors*. The jerk actually had the balls to tip his hat at her with a smirk that said *I'm God's gift to womankind*. Perhaps he'd decided to take the noon flight tomorrow, which made her wonder what the chances were—

"Paging passenger Powell. Passenger Powell, please come to gate number fifty."

―∿―

It was her ass he'd noticed first—actually, he couldn't avoid it since it was parked right in front of him at eye level. Clad in tight denim, supported by legs that went *all the way up*, it was a mighty fine, shapely, womanly ass, the kind a man liked to fill his hands with.

His interest piqued, Wade's gaze roamed higher to light brown hair that fell in waves over her shoulders. With her back to him, he couldn't see her face or judge her age, nor could he hear a word she spoke with George Strait crooning in his earbuds. Still, he was an observer by nature, and his innate ability to read body language had been further honed by his profession. Lacking any other distraction, he watched her, playing a game with himself to see how much of her story he could discern by her actions alone.

The youngish woman attached to the prime ass had a boarding pass in hand that she flapped at the apathetic gate agent whose attention appeared fully engaged in tapping on the keyboard, and staring into her monitor like it was a crystal ball. After a time, the wooden-faced woman glanced up and shook her head. Further fruitless argument ensued, at which point Wade pulled out his earbuds to eavesdrop.

Hot Ass wasn't getting on the flight.

She spun around giving Wade the first glimpse of her face. With red blotches staining her neck and cheeks, and mascara and snot streaming down her face, what a hot mess Hot Ass turned out to be. She threw herself to the floor beside her bag, a vision of pure woebegone.

"I have to say good-bye," she repeated to herself in a choked whisper.

Ah hell! Her desolate expression and pathetic words sent Wade surging to his feet with a groan. He'd been bred to do the right thing, especially where women, children, and animals were concerned, and the right thing now was to give up his damned seat—even though this was the last flight to Bozeman tonight and he had a court date in Virginia City at nine a.m.

He glanced at his watch. It was nearly six. If he rented a car, he could be on the road within the hour, and if he drove through the night, he'd hit Virginia City by six a.m. He figured he could crash for an hour in his office and still make his appearance, albeit not in his most pristine condition.

Having set his course, he stashed his iPod and earbuds, threw his carry-on over his shoulder, and approached the desk. After a few minutes of low conversation, Wade turned to leave, tipping his hat and flashing his killer smile at Hot Ass as he passed. Having appropriated his seat, she averted her face with a guilty look.

Seconds later when the garbled PA system called out her almost indistinguishable name, he couldn't help glancing over his shoulder to catch her surprise.

———∿∿∿———

An hour after leaving the airport, Wade was nursing a number of regrets about his impulsive decision. Driving from Denver to Virginia City wasn't the most inspired idea he'd ever had, but then again, he'd always been a soft touch where women were concerned, especially pretty ones in distress. Now he'd pay for it…again.

In reality, the entire trip had been a bust. He should have known the ol' man would back out of the deal. Dirk must have jumped on the opportunity to undermine Wade the moment his back was turned, or more rightly, the moment he'd boarded the plane for Denver. Not that it would have taken much work for his brother to persuade their father. Wade had been a fool to think the lure of cash would overcome four generations of fealty to the land, regardless of the pressing circumstances. Ranching ran bone-deep in all the Knowltons—*all but him*.

Still, it had come close. Closer this time than he would have expected.

Allie, of course, was pissed as a wet cat, having spent weeks brokering the deal. She'd already refused his invitation for lunch after the thwarted closing. If he'd been stuck in Denver, he wouldn't have been welcome in her bunk tonight.

He realized he was getting damned tired of her using sex to manipulate him. For nearly four years they'd played it fast and loose, which had suited him just fine. Work took up most of his time anyway, but now Allie had begun to press for commitments he wasn't ready to make. From the moment he'd met her in Denver, she'd acted like he was a bonus to the six-figure commission she'd expected—the one she'd just lost.

Hell, we've all lost out on this one—who knows when or if another offer might come along in this shitty economy.

Like most private ranches in these times, the Flying K had teetered on the brink of foreclosure for years. The Knowltons had forged on in the false hope that the next year would be better, but it never was. It was just no damn good any more. They needed to sell out while they still could, but Dirk had refused. Instead, he'd been willing to hazard everything, the ranch and his family's entire economic future, on the slim chance that his breeding experiments would pay off.

"Damn you to hell, Dirk!"

Wade was bone weary, stretched to the breaking point, but his family showed little appreciation for his efforts, and he'd worked too friggin' hard to keep them above water to watch it all go down the drain. Perhaps he and Allie could still salvage the deal? As soon as he got back to Twin Bridges he, Dirk, and the ol' man would have a serious "come to Jesus" meeting.

He had a lot of time to strategize with an eleven-hour drive ahead of him. But two hours out of Denver had him yearning for the good old days when he could have done it in about eight—the days before they'd reinstated a speed limit on Montana highways. At least the weather had cleared, and he'd left late enough to have missed the outbound commuter traffic.

As for Allie, he supposed the rift was no great loss.

Although he wouldn't be getting any for a while after this fiasco, he'd survived lengthy dry spells before — even during his marriage. Given Allie's recent change in attitude, it wouldn't hurt to put some distance between them anyway. He'd never been a player, but maybe it was time to seek out greener grazing.

His mind wandered back to the girl at the airport. He still marveled at the impulse that had spurred him to give up his seat. He wondered what might have happened had he been stranded in Denver with her. Maybe he would have offered her dinner. Maybe she would have accepted. And maybe they would have shared a room at the airport Hilton. He then shrugged it off as another lost opportunity, a sorry addition to all the rest.

Wade plugged his iPod into the audio jack of the rental car and scrolled impatiently through various play-lists in search of something to help the two cans of Red Bull keep his eyes open for the all-night driving marathon. He settled on the blaring sounds of Big and Rich.

I'm a dynamite, daddy, I'll put the rhythm in your blues, I'm not a wishy-washy boy like you're used to...

Yeah. That was the ticket. Part country, part urban madness. Much like him.

Grinning, he punched the accelerator of the Dodge Avenger. And like any good cowboy, Wade drove off into the sunset.

Chapter 2

IT WAS AFTER ELEVEN WHEN NIKKI LANDED IN Bozeman. Expecting to arrive hours earlier, she'd reserved a rental car, but after collecting her bags and proceeding to the Thrifty counter, she found it dark and abandoned. She glanced down the row of rental car desks in mounting frustration. All of them were closed. *Damn it all! What now?*

The bank of hotel courtesy phones caught her eye next. That was it. She'd just call a hotel with an airport shuttle and get the car in the morning. She was dead tired and in no shape to drive almost a hundred miles in total darkness on unfamiliar roads anyway. It would be smarter to pick up her car early in the morning and then depart for Sheridan. She could live with a few hours delay. At least she wasn't stuck in Denver.

Satisfied with this plan, she picked up the phone, reserved a room at the Holiday Inn Express in Bozeman, and settled on the bench at the shuttle pickup. Up until now she hadn't thought through many of the details and the flight delays had screwed everything up even worse. Now she had to put her mind to reordering her priorities.

The mortuary had already held his body for an entire week before anyone had tracked her down. She wondered if he would have wanted cremation or a burial. She didn't even know him well enough to say. Did he have any friends who mourned him? No one aside from the mortuary had even tried to contact her. Had he left a will? She didn't know that either. She supposed she'd have to contact the attorney's office to find out. She rolled her eyes at the prospect of dealing with blood-sucking lawyers.

First things first, Nikki. Get some sleep. Get to Sheridan. Sign whatever you have to. See him properly buried. Then, get the hell out of Montana. It seemed like a solid plan.

Nikki was the sole passenger when the shuttle pulled up in front of a brightly lit entrance to the hotel lobby. With an exhausted groan, she dragged her bags inside and up to the front desk. Surely a hot shower and a clean bed would make everything right again.

"Hi, I'm Nicole Powell." She greeted the night clerk with a weary smile. "I called a few minutes ago from the airport."

"Welcome to the Holiday Inn Express, Miss Powell," he replied. "I'll be happy to check you in. All I need is a credit card."

"No problem." Nikki plopped her purse on the counter and fished inside, but her blindly groping fingers failed to encounter anything approximating calfskin. "I'm sorry. I can't seem to find my wallet. Just another minute, OK? It's a new bag." She fully opened the mouth of the leather abyss and reached inside again, only to come up short for a second time.

With rising panic, Nikki dumped her entire bag on the counter.

Two sets of keys, miscellaneous makeup items, a cell phone, address book, Tampax, and her checkbook—many of the same things she'd collected when they'd spilled out under the seat of the airplane. *But no wallet.*

She shook the bag upside down in disbelief. *Oh shit!* She'd lost her damned wallet on the plane! With a flushed face and shaking hands, she began cramming everything back into her purse. "I'm sorry. I seem to have lost my wallet. Will you take a check?"

"Certainly. I just need a driver's license and credit card."

"But I don't have them. My license and credit cards were in my wallet."

The clerk shook his head with an impassive expression. "I'm sorry, Miss Powell. We can't accept a personal check without proper identification."

"But I need a room. Surely there's *something* we can work out."

"Is there someone you can call? A friend or family member?"

Nikki stared at him, scrambling to make sense of this situation. She was stranded at a motel in Bozeman, Montana, without a room, money, or identification. Worse, there wasn't a soul she could think of to help her in the middle of the night. Her mother was out of the question. She couldn't even remember the last time they'd spoken. Since her grandparents died, her sister Shelby was the only family member she'd maintained any contact with, but Shelby was a total screwup. There was no one.

"No." Nikki shook her head.

"Do you have any business associates, perhaps?"

"Look, I only have two numbers, the Sheridan

mortuary and a law office. Do you really think either one is going to answer the phone at this time of night?"

His smile thinned. "I'm sorry, but we can't accommodate you without payment. This is a hotel. We are in business to sell rooms."

Overcome with a growing sense of helplessness, Nikki turned away to dig desperately inside her purse for her cell phone. Not putting much stock in the mortuary, she decided to try the lawyer. Finding the number, she punched it on a whispered prayer.

—⁓—

Wade's lids were drooping, and his vision blurring when the sound of his tires bumping the road reflectors jarred him fully alert. He swore aloud and shook his head to clear away the cobwebs. Where the hell was he anyway? Wyoming? Yeah, now he remembered. He'd just passed through Casper—the halfway point. The caffeine had already worn off and he still had a good five hours to go.

By now he was cursing both Hot Ass for provoking his stupid act of chivalry and his Momma for raising him to be a gentleman. Would he have given up his seat if the girl had been old or ugly? Yeah, on the first account anyway. His grandma would roll over in her grave if he'd let some elderly woman get stranded. But ugly was a matter for debate. Attractive women made fools of men.

The vibration of his phone suddenly jolted him. He jerked it out of his holster, noting the unfamiliar area code with a scowl. Who the devil outside his family, or maybe Allie, would be calling him at this ungodly hour?

"Wade here," he growled, half expecting a wrong number.

"Excuse me?" a female voice responded. "I was try-ing to reach Evans and Knowlton Law Firm."

"This is Wade Knowlton of Evans and Knowlton."

"Thank God!" she answered with a near-sob.

"Look, ma'am, this is my private line and it's after midnight. I suggest you call me back tomorrow during normal business hours." He paused. "How did you even get this number anyway?"

"Your office had a recording to call this number in the event of an emergency. This *is* an urgent matter."

"It had better be life or death," he warned. His re-sponse was ill-tempered and lacked his normal courtesy, but he was dog tired.

"It is." She paused. "Well, death anyway."

"All right, you've got my attention. Now what are you going to do with it?"

"I have an emergency."

"I thought we'd already established that, Miss—"

"I'm so sorry—I thought I said. This is Nicole Powell."

"Powell? Sorry. Doesn't ring any bells."

"My father is…was…Raymond Powell. He just passed away. You were recommended by the Sheridan mortuary."

The first rays of understanding in this bizarre con-versation had begun to dawn. "Ah. Then you wish me to handle the probate."

"Yes, I suppose so."

"Then I once more suggest that you call back in the morning. There's nothing I can do for you right now."

"But there is—"

Given his fatigue and foul mood, Wade made no attempt to restrain his sarcasm. "You have my sincere

condolences for your loss, Miss Powell, but I fail
to see how this is an emergency…given that he's already dead."

"But it's not him. It's me that needs your help, Mr.
Knowlton. I've just arrived in Montana and I've lost my
wallet. I have no money. No ID. No room for the night.
I'm so sorry to burden you, but aside from the mortuary,
your office was the only number I had. I just found it on
a scrap of paper in my purse. Please, is there anything
you can do to help me?"

"I'll do what I can," he replied, his ill humor somewhat dissipated. "How do you suggest I assist you?"

"I need a short-term loan, maybe a few hundred dollars, until I get my ID and credit cards back."

"Look, ma'am. While I don't wish to appear hard-
hearted, I don't know you from Eve."

"But surely my father must have left some cash or
something of value I could borrow against."

"I have no clue about your father's state of affairs and
am nowhere near my office even to find out. And while
I don't wish to make either of our lives more difficult, it
isn't as easy as all that anyway. You have to understand
there are legal waters to navigate in cases like this."

"Please." He detected a quaver in her voice. "I am
truly in a bind."

Her tone of desperation struck a nerve. Remembering
the woman in Denver, Wade pinched the bridge of his
nose with a sigh. *Twice in one night? Incredible.*

Giving up his airline seat had already cost him time
and money, two hundred dollars with the extra fee
charged for the one-way car rental. He knew nothing
about this woman, yet he was already damn close to

offering his own credit card, but there were limits to his generosity to strangers—even female ones. Still, he couldn't refuse her request for help.

"Where are you, Miz Powell?"

"In the lobby of the Holiday Inn Express at Bozeman. I couldn't get a room without my credit card. I'm going to have the same problem getting a rental car. I'm stranded here." He thought he heard a muffled sniff. *Aw hell*. The tears were about to fall. The last thing he needed was to deal with a hysterical woman on no sleep.

"Where are you headed?" he asked.

"To Sheridan."

"Then it's your lucky night, darlin'. I'm going to Virginia City and Sheridan isn't too far out of the way. I'm on my way to Bozeman right now to pick up my vehicle as I've been out of town on business. I'm still several hours away, but if you can hang on for a while, I'll pick you up."

"Really? Thank you so much. I truly appreciate your help, Mr. Knowlton."

"Don't worry 'bout a thing, Miz Powell," he offered in the most soothing tone he could muster. "It's been a rough night for both of us, but everything looks brighter in the light of day."

"I never could have imagined getting into a situation like this. It's a horrible feeling."

"I think in a few hours you'll see that your situation isn't near as dire as you thought."

"Why's that?"

"I'll be there to treat you to a Starbucks by six."

—◆◆◆—

Nikki stared dumbly at her phone. Starbucks? Was that his answer to her troubles? On top of all that, he'd disconnected the call without even saying good-bye. First the cocky cowboy in Denver and now her would-be attorney? Did all men out West have to get the last word? With a huff of exasperation, Nikki stashed her phone, irritation now supplanting her despair.

The clerk greeted her with raised brows as she approached the check-in desk again. "Any luck?"

"Yes…and…no," Nikki replied with a forced smile. "There's someone who's going to pick me up, but it's gonna be a while before he gets here. Please, if you won't give me a room, can I just crash in a chair for a while?"

The clerk made a face.

"But I have nowhere to go. You know my circumstances," Nikki pleaded. "I promise I'll be gone in a few hours. I'll even pay you once my ride gets here." She hoped he wouldn't accept the offer. It would be humiliating to hit Knowlton up for money.

The clerk rolled his eyes on a sigh. "That won't be necessary, Miss Powell. Just promise me you'll be gone before our guests begin checking out."

"I promise. No one will see me. Thank you so much for understanding."

Nikki slinked off to take possession of an overstuffed wingback chair by the lobby fireplace where she set her phone alarm for five thirty, and then shut her eyes hoping she'd wake up to discover it was all just a crazy dream.

Chapter 3

HAVING MADE GOOD TIME TO BOZEMAN, WADE dropped off the rental car, picked up his truck from the long-term lot, and arrived at the Holiday Inn at twenty after five. He approached the desk with a question hovering on his lips. "Miz Powell?"

"You must be the ride?" the night clerk asked.

"Yeah," Wade replied.

"Over there." The clerk jerked his head toward the fireplace where a brunette slumbered in a wingback chair. He approached quietly, hesitant to wake her.

Although her head was cocked to the side and several locks of hair hung in her face, what he could see of her wasn't half-bad. She was young. Midtwenties likely. She was also lightly snoring. His gaze fixed in fascination on the strands of hair ebbing and flowing in rhythm with her puffs of breath. He couldn't suppress an amused smile…until his gaze settled on those softly parted lips. She had a gorgeous mouth, the kind of mouth a man liked to see wrapped around…

Hell, what's wrong with me? Has it really been so long that my brain's now stuck in low gear? His conscience also stabbed him for not getting her a room. Too late for that now. He'd just have to do what he could to make it all up to her.

He reached down to wake her, only to startle at the sudden blast of rap music sounding from her phone.

She jolted upright, looking wildly about until her gaze met his. Her eyes were a stormy shade between blue and green that widened and darkened as recognition dawned.

"Well, I'll be damned." He felt the corner of his mouth kick up and then the full irony of the situation took over. It was all just too much for Wade. He threw back his head with a roar of laughter while the rapper on her phone droned on.

The crease between her eyes deepened as he palmed away the tears of mirth. She silenced the phone with a glower that she then directed at him. He could hardly blame her. The last twenty-four hours hadn't been the smoothest sailing after all.

"*You* are Wade Knowlton of Evans and Knowlton?" It was more accusation than question.

"Yes, indeed." He doffed his hat. "At your service, ma'am."

"But you can't be!" she protested. "*You* were the obnoxious cowboy in Denver!"

"Obnoxious?" He raised a brow. "That's mighty ungracious when I gave up my seat to you and then drove all night long."

Her expression softened infinitesimally. "I thought you'd decided to take the later flight."

"Nope." He shook his head. "It was purely an act of chivalry on my part. I couldn't fly in good conscience after watching your little meltdown."

"Then I suppose I owe you an apology." Her gaze wavered from his. "And a thank-you."

"Apology accepted and no thanks are needed, although it seems my sacrifice was in vain since I find you stranded all over again." He flashed a teasing grin. "Does misfortune follow you everywhere, Miz Powell?"

"Not normally." She pursed the lips that he found increasingly fascinating. "Why do you ask?"

"Because I'm thinking it might be prudent for me to increase my insurance before I drive you anywhere."

Her brows gathered in another scowl. Even sleep mussed and growing pissed, she was a looker—with a great ass to boot. His day was definitely looking up.

"Mr. Knowlton, I'm hardly in the mood for jokes. I'm only here because my father died and I need to settle his affairs. And quickly so I can get back home."

"And where is that?" he asked.

"Excuse me?"

"Home. Where do you hail from, Miz Powell?"

"Georgia," she answered. "Born in Toccoa but I live in greater Atlanta now."

He cocked his head. "You don't sound much like a Georgia peach to me."

"What? Do you think we all talk like Scarlett O'Hara?" she fired back with unveiled sarcasm.

"She wasn't really a Southerner, you know. In fact, she wasn't even American."

"Scarlett O'Hara? But she's an American icon."

"Sorry to burst your bubble, darlin' but *Vivian Leigh* was British."

"You're kidding." She regarded him with skepticism. "How would you even know that?"

"*Gone with the Wind* is Mama's favorite film. She's an endless fount of trivia on it."

"Well, I'm sorry to disappoint you. I was once

Southern-fried with milk gravy, but I've worked very hard to lose the drawl."

His puzzled look forced her explanation.

"It's how Southerners eat *everything*. Fried with gravy." She studied him with a perplexed look. "Actually, I think you sound more Southern than me."

"I blame my Mama for that, too," he replied. "She was an old-time rodeo queen from Amarillo, Texas. She homeschooled me and my brother Dirk until high school, so the Texas twang kinda stuck. Now as for Georgia, I find it a real shame you'd want to get rid of it. I find a woman with a soft Southern drawl incredibly sexy."

"Tell you what, when I decide I want to be sexy for you, I'll be sure to turn it on full force."

She was a real firecracker, this Georgia girl. He liked that.

He answered her with a grin. "I'll look forward to it."

"In your dreams, cowboy," he thought he heard her mutter under her breath.

He cocked his head. "What was that?"

"Coffee?" She smiled wide. "If I recall, you promised me Starbucks."

It had taken Nikki years to rehabilitate herself from a mortal attraction to cowboys. After being burned about a dozen times, she thought herself finally impervious—until this one flashed his irritatingly irresistible grin. She reminded herself that she was immune to his kind of rustic charm— but crystal-blue eyes and a chin dimple. *Holy crap!*

Why does my would-be lawyer have to be an incredibly hot cowboy?

When he pulled around in a dinged-up old F-150 and jumped down to grab her bags, Nikki noted he'd lost the coat and tie. The more casual look certainly agreed with him.

"I'll have to put your bags in the truck bed, I'm afraid." He gave her an apologetic look. "I didn't want to leave the Lexus at the airport."

"A Lexus? Yeah, right." She laughed.

He shrugged, threw her two bags in the back, and then rolled up his sleeve to check the time. Nikki noted his TAG Heuer with surprise. The timepiece was worth more than his heap of a ride. "We'd better hit the road now," he said, helping her into the truck. "We've a good ninety-minute drive ahead of us and you're no doubt anxious to start making calls about your lost wallet."

"I can take care of that on the drive. My cell battery is fully charged."

"Make the most important calls first," he advised. "Your phone will only last about thirty minutes—if you're lucky."

"What do you mean?"

"Look around you, Miz Powell. This ain't Atlanta. People come here to get away from it all. Which is a good thing, given how the mountains are such an effective barrier to outside communication."

Nikki took in her surroundings for the first time. She'd arrived last night in near-blackness, but now the sun was rising, casting rays of pink, yellow, and orange over a majestic backdrop that stole her breath. There were no skyscrapers marring the horizon or blocking the sun—only the wide open sky and countless snow-capped mountains. The September air was crisp, clean, and invigorating. She inhaled in deep appreciation. "It's incredible."

"Yellowstone is eighty miles in that direction." He pointed south. "Barely more than twenty as the crow flies. You need to see it."

"I'm not a tourist, Mr. Knowlton. I don't have time for sightseeing."

His gaze narrowed, the morning light revealing crinkles at the corners of his fascinating crystal-colored eyes. "Some things, Miz Powell, are worth *making* the time for. This is God's country. It's unique. There is a lot here you may never get another chance to see."

"We have mountains where I come from too, you know. Atlanta is only fifteen miles from Stone Mountain." She sounded more prickly than she'd meant to, but everything about him seemed to elicit an overreaction from her. She wondered why.

"Just like an Easterner," he mumbled with a deprecating head shake. "Always making mountains out of molehills."

Nikki bristled. "What about the Appalachians? I hiked a segment of that trail when I was in college."

"Darlin', you ain't *seen* a mountain until you've been to the Rockies. Come on now. Time's a-wastin'. At least you can admire this scenery all the way to Virginia City." He put the vehicle in gear and pulled out onto the highway.

"Virginia City? I thought you were taking me to Sheridan? I have to see to—"

"Sweetheart, you won't be able to see to anything until you get your ID. I can promise you that. You might not want to hear this, but you're in a bit of a catch-22 pertaining to your father."

"What do you mean?" she asked.

"By Montana law you can't authorize disposal of his remains without a certified death certificate, and can't obtain the death certificate without proper ID."

"You're kidding! I came all the way up here and can't even *bury* him?"

"'Fraid not." He shook his head. "But I'll do what I can to help you get it straightened out. Just be aware that this is likely to take some time."

"How *much* time? I don't have time!"

"I can't rightly say. Do you by any chance have a passport?"

"No. I've never traveled out of the country. Until now, I've never even been north of the Mason-Dixon Line. Not that I haven't wanted to travel. I'd love to go to Mexico or take a cruise someday."

"That's mighty unfortunate."

"That I haven't a passport or that I haven't traveled?"

"Both." He cast her another sideways look. "It seems you need to broaden your horizons, Miz Powell."

She wondered what he meant by that remark. He was obviously trying to help her, but everything he said put her on edge. She could only conclude her churlish reaction to him was caused by a feeling of dependency that she despised. She wasn't used to relying on anyone for anything, but now she had no choice.

"My horizon seems pretty broad at the moment," she shot back, jerking her head toward the wide open landscape.

"You'd better start making those calls," he advised.

"I suggest you begin with the airline to see if your wallet's been recovered. If it hasn't, you'll need to notify the Denver police."

"I've already called the airline," she replied, "but why the police? It wasn't stolen."

"Should anyone get their hands on your credit cards and ID, you'll want to have a report on file for fraud prevention. You should also alert the credit reporting companies."

"Thanks." She offered a grateful smile. "I wouldn't have thought of that."

"My office in Virginia City is on the way to Sheridan. You can use the phone there while I get showered and changed."

"You have a shower at your office?" she asked with a hint of longing.

"And a pullout sofa. I've been known to crash there. At one time, more often than I preferred," he added dryly.

Was that a look of regret? "Are you a workaholic?" she asked.

"Something like that," he hedged. "You're welcome to the office, the shower, and the pullout, at least until we get things sorted."

"Thank you. That's generous...but where will *you* stay?" she asked warily.

"I've no shortage of options. I've got a place in Bozeman where I live most of the time. On my few court days in Virginia City, I crash at the office if I don't feel like driving, and most weekends I spend at the family spread outside Twin Bridges."

"Spread? You mean a ranch?"

"Yeah. My family has had a working cattle outfit since the Civil War. It was a profitable operation for four generations, but the past decade it's been more like a sinkhole. I've been trying to persuade them to sell out, but my obstinate brother is convinced he can save things."

"How?" she asked.

"Thinks he can create a superior cattle breed. Ever heard of Wagyu cattle or Kobe beef?"

"No, but that doesn't say much, I don't know jack about cattle."

"Wagyu cattle come from Japan. Kobe is one of these Japanese varieties and is the most highly prized beef in the world—goes for up to fifty dollars an ounce at the better steak houses."

"Over five hundred bucks for a T-bone? Holy cow!" Nikki exclaimed.

"No, that would be India," Wade corrected with a grin.

"So what does this have to do with your ranch?" Nikki asked.

"Dirk seems to think breeding a hybrid Wagyu-Angus herd is the answer to all our troubles."

"Why? What's the big difference between the Japanese and American cattle that they command such a high price?"

"Dirk could go on ad nauseam about it, but suffice it to say there's a difference in the composition of the meat, mainly in its marbling, that makes it more tender and gives it a different taste. There are a handful of ranches in the U.S. producing what they call American Kobe by crossing the Japanese breed with our own cattle. Dirk has jumped on that bandwagon."

"Sounds like a great opportunity," Nikki remarked. "So why are you opposed to the idea?"

"Because it could take years to establish a herd, and there's no guarantee of the payoff. Maybe the market is hot now, but all that could change. I'm not willing to forfeit my entire future for something so chancy. My brother sees that as disloyalty. He accuses me of lying down without a fight, but I just see things differently. I don't believe ranching is viable anymore, but my brother's as bullheaded as his damned stock." His gaze appeared focused on the horizon and his hands looked tight on the wheel. "'Sides, I always wanted to do something else with my life. Maybe leave something behind besides my blood, sweat, and tears in the ground."

"But you're still here."

"Yeah. I've stuck around. But that doesn't mean I like it."

"If you feel so strongly why do you stay?"

"I dunno. Wish I did." He shrugged. "Probably obligation mixed with guilt."

"But you resent it?" she suggested.

"Yeah, I do," he said. "I want to live my own life. I'm damned tired of playing second fiddle to big brother."

"I find it really hard to imagine you playing second to anyone."

"Why thank you, ma'am. That sounded damned near complimentary."

She wished he'd stop flashing that irresistible crooked grin. "Regardless of your differing opinions, it still sounds like you hold your brother in pretty high regard."

"Does it?" he asked.

"Yeah. It does."

A muscle tightened in his jaw. "Maybe I do," he confessed. "But Dirk's always been a tough act to follow. He won a full rodeo scholarship to the Ag College at MSU. Won overall Champion at the collegiate rodeo finals and could have gone on to pro rodeo but joined the Marines instead. He did two tours and lost half his right leg."

"Wow. I can't even imagine what that must be like." Nikki shook her head. "I'm so sorry."

"Don't be," he added dryly. "Dirk's sorry enough for all of us. And his disability hasn't slowed him down much."

"Really?" she remarked in surprise. "What does he do now?"

"He runs the ranch."

"By himself?"

"Not completely. The ol' man does what he can and I still help out when hands are short."

"But you said you hate ranching."

"It's a damned hard way of life, thankless, and never ending. What's not to love?" He smirked. "I don't really *hate* it, but it doesn't run thick in my blood like it does with Dirk."

"You talk more about your brother than about yourself," she remarked.

He shrugged. "Not much to tell. Raised here then studied law at the University of Colorado."

"That was surely the *Reader's Digest* condensed version," she remarked dryly.

"What else do you want to know?"

"Why did you choose law?" she asked.

"Seemed   practical...and   more   profitable than ranching."

"Has it been?" She wondered given the vehicle he drove.

"I do all right." He shrugged. "But I would have done a lot better had I stayed in Denver or gone east. I was offered a job with a big firm in Boston, but like an idiot, I came back home."

"Why did you turn the job down? Were you homesick?"

"Dirk's injuries had a lot to do with it, but I s'pose you can take the man out of the mountains but can't take the mountains out of the man."

"But you've just said you want to sell out. If you didn't wish to settle here, why'd you come back at all?"

He stared straight ahead and seemed focused elsewhere. "Not all folks are meant to settle down."

True enough. In her experience cowboys were notoriously unreliable, generally unfaithful, and rarely capable of settling at all. Wade was past thirty and she hadn't seen a ring, or sign of one on his left hand—*not that she had any interest*. Looking was simply a habit she'd formed after a nearly disastrous mistake. His name was Clint. Tall, lean, and swaggering with piercing gray eyes like his Hollywood namesake. They'd lived together for six months before she'd discovered he had a wife and kids. Cowboys seemed to have a franchise on two-timing.

"Besides," he interrupted her mind's ramblings, "there's no reason for me to stay here once I've convinced them to unload the ranch."

"What then? What do *you* want?"

His gaze left the road and roamed over her with a look that heated her insides. "Right now? I can think of lots of things. Unfortunately, none are compatible with driving."

She scowled. "It was a serious question."

"What makes you think I'm not serious?" His gaze returned to the road.

"What makes *you* think I'm interested?" she rejoined, intently studying his profile.

His mouth tugged up at the corner. "You are. I feel it and you do too. It's why you've been so riled up from the very start. You don't like that you're attracted to me."

"Keep on dreaming, *cowboy*."

He laughed, a warm sound that reverberated through her.

Nikki snorted. "I don't go for players."

His smile vanished. "I'm not a player. A flirt maybe, but not a womanizer. There's a huge difference."

She set her jaw. "I'm neither convinced nor interested."

"Give me time and I'll change your mind. You'll see. No woman can resist my charm. I'm a legend."

She snorted. "In your own mind maybe." He *was* pretty hard to resist—except that he knew that too. His presumption served to shore up her defenses.

"You're just fighting yourself right now, which only makes the prospect even more enticing. Men *always* like a challenge."

Her throat felt suddenly thick. He was right. Taunting him was reckless as hell but for some reason he made her feel a bit reckless. "This conversation isn't going anywhere."

"We can take it wherever you want," he replied. "I aim to please."

Given that cue, Nikki abruptly changed the subject.
"You still didn't answer me. If you don't want to be
here, what do you plan to do?"

"That's a damn good question that I'm still trying
to answer. I don't know. I may move back to Denver.
There's an expectation that I'll eventually take over the
firm there."

"You mean from Evans?"

"Yeah. He only practices part-time in Bozeman,
commuting as needed for the biggest clients. He
only comes up for the big ranch deals his daughter reels in. I hold down the fort here the rest of the
time and handle the smaller stuff. He's looking to
retire altogether in a few years." He glanced in her
direction. "Hungry?"

The mention of food made her stomach growl, an em-
barrassing reminder that she hadn't eaten since lunch the
day before. "I am as long as you're buying," she replied
with a cheeky grin.

———

They pulled into a truck stop on Highway 287 just into
Madison County. Wade stopped her as Nikki reached
for her door. "No, wait, Mama would have my hide."

"And they say chivalry is dead?"

"Not if your mother's a Southerner born and bred."

"I promise you'd still be a novelty where I come
from." She laughed as he helped her step down from the
truck, but secretly luxuriated in his attentiveness.

He gave her that heart-stopping grin. "Are you
referring to my old-fashioned manners or my legend-
ary charm?"

She didn't reply, but couldn't suppress a half smile. Wade's conversation was easy and his boyish grin was disarming. Gradually she began to relax. They made more small talk inside the truck stop during a hastily scarfed egg and hotcake breakfast.

When they got back into the truck, Wade reached over her to open the glove box, brushing his shoulder against her breasts. Although accidental, the sudden intimate contact made her breath catch and her nipples pebble against her bra. Their gazes met, intense physical awareness once more electrifying the air between them.

"Sorry." He broke the sudden tension. "You know that wasn't intentional, don't you? I was just hunting a notebook for you."

"Yeah." She gave a nervous laugh and willed herself to breathe again. "You hardly seem the type who needs to resort to covert tactics to cop a feel."

He retrieved a small pad and pen and closed the glove box. "Thought you might want to jot some things down while we drive. There's much you'll need to do when we get to Virginia City."

"Right. Thanks. That's thoughtful of you." She was glad he'd shifted the conversation back to a business level.

"By the way," his husky voice broke into her thoughts, "if I *was* inclined to make a move, you're right that I'd do it without pretense."

"So you aren't inclined?" She bit her lip the moment the words were out, wishing she could pull them back. He learned toward her, bracing his arm on the back of her seat, studying her face with an intensity that made her shift in her seat.

"I was always taught that a gentleman waits for an invitation."

She fixed on his mouth, wondering what it would feel like. Would his lips be firm or soft? How would his tongue feel? How would he taste? She wet her lips, telling herself it was just a nervous reaction.

"That's close enough for me," Wade murmured and made his move.

Cupping her face, his mouth came over hers with smooth and well-practiced confidence. His kiss was an unhurried exploration, his lips sliding warm and firm over hers. Slanting his head, he added tiny, teasing flicks of his hot tongue and then toe-curling nips of his teeth until he caught her lower lip between them. He slowly released, staring into her eyes as if waiting for her to protest, but Nikki was too overcome to make any sound.

When she made no sign of resistance, he claimed her mouth again, but this time he was more demanding, his tongue probing the seam of her mouth until she parted her lips. The first contact of his tongue jolted her senses. Shutting her eyes and stifling a moan, Nikki curled her fingers in his hair, losing herself in the sensation of their tangling tongues. *Holy shit! This man knows how to kiss. Too well.* It took all she had not to melt into the seat beneath him.

That thought was enough to jar her brain and kick her protective instincts back into gear. She pressed her hands against his chest, but he was first to break the kiss.

"I didn't invite that," she insisted, knowing it was a lie.

"I think you did, but don't worry. I won't do it again until you ask."

"What makes you think I will?" she challenged.

He turned the key and started the engine. "Because you enjoyed that every bit as much as I did. I dare you to deny it."

She couldn't. The kiss promised dangerous things. It had been a long time since she'd felt attraction this strong. Maybe never, but Wade Knowlton was everything she'd sworn off—all in one big hot cowboy package. *Shit*. Very bad word choice. Her gaze instinctively drifted southward to his crotch. She shifted it quickly away. She definitely didn't need her mind to go *there*.

Another silence ensued, longer and less companionable than the ones before. "Do you mind if I turn on some music?" she asked, eager for any distraction.

"Be my guest, though I warn you there aren't many choices."

Intent on replacing the tension that permeated the air with music, Nikki reached for the radio dial. It was then she noticed the lack of an audio jack or even a CD player. "How old *is* this truck anyway?"

"I'd guess it's about a 1980 vintage, which makes it about as old as me," he said.

"Really?" She laughed nervously. "I don't think I've ever ridden in a vehicle that was older than I am."

"And how old is that," he asked.

"Twenty-eight last month," she said.

"You seeing anyone?" he asked.

The question, posed out of the blue, took her by surprise. "Not presently. It's been a good six months since I've dated anyone seriously." She turned the dial, flipping absently through static-filled stations. Finally hitting a station with a decent signal, Nikki quit fumbling with the radio. The upbeat tempo of Rascal Flatts's "Life is a Highway" filled the air. Country. *Argh*. She *hated* country. The music was a reminder of all too many mistakes she'd made.

"I'm guessing it was a bad breakup?" he said.

"Yeah." She gave a dry laugh. "You might say that. Why do you ask?"

"I'm just wondering why you seem so gun-shy."

"I have a number of good reasons to be—most of them with first and last names."

"We're not all assholes, you know, so you shouldn't hold it against every man you meet. You can trust me when I say I'm here to help you, not to hurt you."

"Why?" she asked. "Why have you gone out of your way for me like this?"

He grinned. "Technically speaking it isn't that far out of my way."

"I'm not talking about the drive. I mean the airport, picking me up, feeding me, and giving me a place to stay."

"Maybe because it's the right thing to do...or maybe it's because I like you."

"Like me? You don't even know me," she insisted.

"I know enough"—he shrugged—"and I like what I see."

Ditto, cowboy. She'd been taking a subconscious inventory of him from the moment she'd met him and was hard pressed to find anything *not* to like. On top of all that, one kiss had scattered her wits to the four winds. Her attraction to Wade was growing worse by the hour. Some way, somehow, she needed to get away from him. Nikki closed her eyes, drifting off on those dangerous thoughts.

"Here it is," Wade announced. "Don't blink or you'll miss it all."

Nikki opened her eyes to find they'd arrived in Virginia City. She almost gaped when they drove down the center of town. Lined with false front buildings with clapboard siding, it looked like the set of *Gunsmoke*. "This is it? There isn't even a traffic light."

"Nope." He chuckled. "The onetime capital of the Territory of Montana, and now the seat of Madison County, has fewer than two hundred full-time residents."

"It's surreal. I'm half expecting to see horses and stagecoaches...and a saloon."

"All that happens in the height of summer when the town becomes a living museum. If you're looking for the saloon, the Pioneer's right over there." He jerked a thumb to indicate a building beside the old Opera House. "This community thrives on the tourist trade now. The rest of the time it's still pretty much a ghost town. I only come here when business requires, generally no more than once a week, sometimes less. Hard to believe this was once a thriving metropolis."

"What happened? Was there some kind of disaster?"

"You might say that. It was all built up around a single gold strike, the biggest one ever recorded in the Rockies. Within a week of the discovery, hundreds of prospectors and nine mining camps cropped up along the fourteen-mile stretch of Alder Creek. The first real settlement was built up here at the midpoint of the Alder Gulch. The town grew to ten thousand within months, but when the gold dried up so did the local economy."

"Why is it named Virginia City? It's nowhere near Virginia."

"The original name proposed for the new town was 'Varina,' after the wife of Confederate President Jefferson Davis, but the territory's judge was a staunch Unionist and refused to approve a charter with her name. He crossed it out and wrote in 'Virginia' instead."

"Wow. I had no idea of the Old West history here."

"There's tons of it. We even have a boot hill. If that kinda thing interests you, I'd be happy to give you the ten-cent tour later."

"Yeah." She smiled. "I think I'd like that."

He parked the truck on the street, hopped out, and came around to offer his hand to help her step down from the truck. For a moment she hesitated. She couldn't recall the last man who'd opened a door or helped her with anything. Even in the South, chivalry seemed a rare commodity these days. She found his old-fashioned manners flattering, although peculiar.

"My office is right here." He inclined his head to the false front building. "It was once Miss Ruby's boardinghouse."

"Boardinghouse or bordello?" she asked.

"Probably one and the same." He grinned. "Half the reason I signed the lease was that I liked the irony of practicing law in a former bawdy house."

She stepped up onto the ancient-looking wooden boardwalk and gazed down the neat row of authentic nineteenth-century buildings lining both sides of the street. He opened the door with Evans & Knowlton,

Attorneys at Law etched on the glass, and gestured for Nikki to precede him inside.

"Mornin', Iris," he greeted a plump middle-aged woman. "This is Miz Powell. She's up from Atlanta and will be using the office to take care of some personal business. Please allow her free rein to the computer, fax, et cetera…"

"Sure thing, Wade." Iris smiled at Nikki. "Nice to meet you, Miss Powell."

Nikki extended her hand with an apologetic look. "I'm sorry to impose on you like this. I'll try not to get in your way any more than necessary."

"Get in the way? A little bitty thing like you?" Iris waved her hand with a chuckle. She then gave Wade an assessing once over, her brows meeting in a frown. "You look like you could use some coffee."

"That rough, eh?" He rubbed his bristled jaw. It was a particularly nice jaw, strong and square with the sexiest dimple in the middle of his chin. Why did he have to have that? She was such a sucker for dimples. Nikki wondered what the ones above his ass looked like. She'd noticed that part of him too but acting on her physical attraction to him could only lead to trouble.

What was wrong with her? One moment he was aggravating as hell and the next she was checking out his ass? Her intense reactions to him bewildered and annoyed her. She'd been around a number of hot cowboys before—more than she cared to remember and certainly none worth wasting brain cells thinking about. What made this one any different? *He's your lawyer, nothing else*, she reminded herself.

"Now, I didn't actually *say* that," Iris replied. "I'd be

happy to run down to the café while you get cleaned up. The usual?" she asked.

"Just coffee," Wade replied.

"Anything for you, Miss Powell? Coffee?"

"Yes. Please," Nikki answered. "I could use the pick-me-up. It was a long night and will surely be a full day."

"How do you take it?"

"Extra cream, no sugar. Thank you."

Wade hung up his hat, and then came behind the desk to glance over Iris's shoulder. "What's on the docket this week?"

"Not much. Just more disputes over grazing rights."

"Grazing rights again! I'm damned sick of environmentalists and special interest groups sticking their noses into our business. Give 'em an inch and they'll take it all, not giving a damn that the majority of people here are just trying to eke out modest livings." Wade raked his hand through his sandy hair with a curse. "Damned vegan tree-huggers will destroy our entire state economy."

Iris rolled her eyes as if anticipating a full-blown tirade. "Be back in a jiffy." She winked at Nikki as she slipped out the door.

Nikki grinned. "I take it you're not a card-carrying member of the Green Party?"

"No." His gaze narrowed and brows pulled into a frown. "You're not one of them I hope."

"Who me?" Nikki shook her head. "No, sir-ee, I'm a live-and-let-live Libertarian and a longtime omnivore. My grandparents had a chicken farm in Lavonia. I betcha didn't know Georgia is the country's biggest chicken producer."

"No, ma'am." His shoulders visibly relaxed. "I didn't, but then I'm not a big chicken fan myself."

She let her gaze travel over him in a slow appreciation of his tall, lean, muscular frame. She guessed he stood at least six-three in his boots. "I suppose not," she said. "It would be only prime grass-fed beef and Idaho potatoes for you."

He crossed his arms over his broad chest and leaned on the door frame studying her. "Miz Powell, if I didn't know better, I'd think you were undressing me with those pretty blue-green eyes of yours."

A guilty flush infused her face but she refused to give him the advantage. She opted for a strong offense instead. "So what if I was? Weren't you quite fixated on my ass at Denver airport?"

He raised a sandy eyebrow. "You noticed that, eh?" His confession came with a shameless grin attached.

She jutted her chin. "*Quid pro quo*, Counselor. What do you say to that?"

He approached her slowly, the smile in his eyes transforming in a blink to a wicked gleam. A gleam that promised very bad things. His reply sent a warning signal to every nerve in her body. "I'd say, why just use your eyes?"

Dear God, he was trouble with a capital T.

He closed the space between them in two long strides. Instinctively, Nikki backed up as many steps—but her ass hit the desk. Before she realized what he was about, he'd caught her hips and lifted her onto it. He held her hostage with his gazed locked on hers, his arms braced on either side of hips. "There's something real interesting going on here," he remarked at length.

Nikki swallowed hard, her gaze wavering. "I already told you I'm not interested. I don't do casual hookups."

"You think that's what this is about?"

"Isn't it?" she asked, intentionally blithe.

He shook his head. "Hell, I don't know. Maybe. I'd be lying if I said I didn't feel a damn powerful attraction to you."

She'd never had such a strong reaction to another man either. All he had to do was *look* at her to get her pulse racing and her insides quivering. And right now he was too damned close for comfort. She shifted backward, trying to create some distance, but there was nowhere to go.

"Don't you have to be in court soon, *Counselor*?" she reminded him in a voice that came out breathless.

"Yeah, I do," he replied. "Guess I got a bit side-tracked. You're turning out to be a big distraction, you know that?"

She bit her lip. "I'm sorry. I didn't mean to be such an imposition."

"I said a distraction not an imposition. There's a big difference. I didn't realize until now just how badly I've needed such a distraction." He stepped away with a reluctant sigh.

Her pulse still hammering in anticipation, Nikki exhaled the breath she hadn't realized was trapped in her chest.

Wade spun toward his office. "Help yourself to the phone and anything else while I get cleaned up." He paused again on the threshold. "Of course, you're welcome to use my office if you need greater privacy," he added over his shoulder with a look of devilment.

"Or in the event any wild impulse overtakes you while I shower."

He went to work on his shirt buttons. His collar was soon wide open revealing a generous show of muscular chest that make her hands itch to rip it off him. She diverted her gaze and curled her itchy hands by her sides.

"Have no fear, cowboy," Nikki replied in a tone meant to disguise the warm flush that had come over her. "I corralled all my wild impulses long ago."

"Did you, now?" He still stood in doorway, head cocked. "Somehow, I think you may have missed a few strays."

"Maybe I need to make myself clearer. I have an aversion to cocky cowboys."

Just keep telling yourself that, Nikki. Maybe if you repeat it often enough it'll become true.

"Is that so?" His brows flew upward. "I can't say I ever met a woman with an actual *aversion* to me."

"Don't take it personally. It's nothing against you in particular, but to your type."

"And what do you *think* you know about my *type*?"

"Since I don't have a pole handy, enough to keep you at arm's length. Besides that, this whole line of conversation is entirely inappropriate in light of professional ethics, don't you think? You are my attorney, after all."

"Well, darlin'"—he scratched his unshaven jaw—"there's a little hitch to that."

"What do you mean? You said you'd help me."

"And I will, but you can't engage my professional services until I know who you are."

"I've told you who I am!" she insisted.

"Sweetheart, I'm a lawyer, and according to the law, your claim don't weigh without authentication."

"Authentication?"

"Proof."

"So what are you saying? That you don't believe me?"

"I'm not saying that at all. Only that our *professional* relationship will commence once you get your ID. In the interim"—his gaze slid over her in a way that threatened to melt her insides—"you'd best find yourself a nice, long, sturdy pole."

———

Nikki opened her mouth, but Iris's return with the coffee meant he'd got the last word once again. Wade closed the door with a chuckle, and then shrugged out of his clothes. He didn't know what had come over him to goad her like he had. She was prickly as a porcupine but it was also clearly a shell of self-defense. He'd already seen hints of humor and glimmers of smiles that she fought to suppress, all of which only increased her appeal. He wanted nothing more than to see her let it all loose and laugh.

It was probably just the novelty of the chase, of having to work for it for a change—something he'd rarely had to do where women were concerned, but that wasn't all. There was something different about her. Something that drew him to her at a visceral level. Maybe the whole damsel-in-distress thing had brought out dormant protective instincts, but then again, protecting her wasn't exactly first on his mind—not unless it involved getting real up close and personal.

He hadn't intended to kiss her in the truck, and knew

he shouldn't have, but the impulse was too strong to deny. A moment ago he hadn't really planned for anything to happen either. He'd only meant to yank her chain—until he'd registered that unmistakable flash of desire in her pretty eyes. It had invoked another powerful urge but it wasn't the time or place to act on it. Had they been anywhere else he might have been tempted to test her resistance.

He looked forward to another chance to do just that. If she looked at him the way she'd been looking a moment ago, all bets were off. She could deny the attraction until the cows came home, but he'd felt it pass between them—like lightning to lodestone. Just like that moment in the truck when he'd opened the glove box. The knowledge that he'd made her nipples harden had nearly the same effect on his dick. *Hot damn!* But it had struck him hard.

He'd only known her a short time, but the lust smoldering between them seemed to be increasing by the hour. At this rate it wouldn't take much for it to combust into an inferno. He'd felt it almost from the first moment they'd spoken—and she had too, though he suspected she'd choke before admitting it.

On top of the physical attraction, he was also enjoying the hell out of their verbal sparring. Given his obvious advantage of arguing for his bread, she'd done a damned good job of holding her own. All in all, they were well-matched, which only begged the question of how well they might suit in other ways—something he was mighty inspired to discover.

Hell, yeah. He looked down as he soaped himself. *He was damned inspired.*

Chapter 4

HAVING MADE HER REPORTS TO BOTH THE AIRLINE and the police, Nikki phoned the Georgia Department of Driver Services, but hung up in frustration after holding for more than twenty minutes. "Is there a computer I could use?" she asked Iris. "The recording said most services are available online. Maybe I can request a duplicate license that way."

"Be my guest." The older woman smiled and vacated her seat. "I have some filing to do anyway."

"Thanks."

Only a moment later Nikki cried out with increasing aggravation, "Damn it! I can't believe this! I feel like a dog chasing its tail! The website says I can only request a duplicate license with a credit card, and I've already canceled my credit cards!"

"Is there anyone you can call?" Iris asked. "Do you have a family member who might allow you to use their card?"

"My mom and I aren't exactly on speaking terms and my half sister doesn't have a credit card. Too irresponsible." Nikki shook her head on a sigh of frustration and despair. "What am I going to do?"

"Don't fret, sweetie." She patted Nikki's hand. "Wade'll help you get it all sorted out. It's what he does."

"Professionally you mean?"

"Yes, but more than that," Iris said. "He carries a great deal on those broad shoulders."

"How so?"

"He's the only thing that's kept his family's ranch afloat these past three years. Under those good looks is also a real good man—a man who should settle down, if you ask me, but he's burning himself out working all the time like he is. Trying to make up for lost time I s'pose, but I still hate to see it."

"Really?" Nikki said. "He hardly strikes me as the workaholic type with all that charm and swagger."

Iris shook her head. "You should have known him before. But it's been even worse on his brother Dirk. He isn't the same man at all."

"Before what?" Nikki asked. "I'm not following you."

"Before the accident—"

"Iris, you worry too much," Wade's baritone voice interrupted the exchange.

He stood in the doorway knotting his necktie. He was now clean-shaven, with his wet hair slicked back. To Nikki's chagrin, the lack of beard growth only accentuated the damned chin dimple. "I already have a mother, if you recall, and don't need two. Besides, I'm certain Miz Powell has little interest in my personal history." His rebuke over the gossip was kind but real, delivered with a steely-eyed smile.

"Sorry, Wade." Iris flushed, visibly cowed. "I just think you should take some time off and enjoy life a bit before it all passes you by."

"I just returned from two days in Denver," he said.

"A working trip," she argued. "Hardly a vacation."

"When the ranch is sold, maybe I'll take some time off. Perhaps I'll go to Mexico or try a cruise—*if* I can find an interesting traveling companion." He slanted Nikki a sly look.

What game was he playing by repeating her earlier wishes to go to Mexico or take a cruise? Every comment he made seemed loaded with innuendo.

When Iris went back to filing, he added in an undertone, "My, my, Miz Powell. All charm and swagger, am I? That's quite an improvement since I left the room. Words like that are sure to turn my head."

Nikki's gaze locked onto his teasing one, and she felt another flush coming on. "I hardly meant it as a compliment." *Hell no*. She'd been a fool for his type too many times before. She didn't believe his earlier denial either. He was a player of the most dangerous kind—a damned hot *cowboy* player. She didn't trust him. But, being honest, she trusted herself even less.

After Wade left for court, Nikki opted for a shower as well. When she entered the bathroom, the pungent scents of cedar and spice mixed with man struck her senses like a two-by-four. In his hurry, Wade had left out his shaving gel and deodorant, neither of which was heavily fragranced. Men like Wade rarely wore fragrances to mask their natural scent. She'd always preferred guys like Wade to the perfumed and overgroomed metrosexuals. Wade's lingering essence was heavenly. She closed her eyes and breathed in a lungful before turning on the shower.

Nikki wet her hair and picked up the soap, feeling a

moment of hesitation. It was soft and sudsy from his use. It seemed almost obscenely intimate to use the same bar he'd used to lather the most private parts of his body—obscenely intimate and incredibly arousing.

She'd had a teasing glimpse of his bare torso earlier. Now her imagination painted a portrait of his entire naked body, all big and hard, sinewy and sudsy. She soaped herself, and then applied his shampoo to her hair. Shutting her eyes to rinse, she imagined sharing not only the soap with him, but the shower, too. *Dear God, Nikki! Get a grip.*

It had been too long. That was her problem. Six months was far too long to go without sex. Maybe that's what was making her nuts. And there was an easy enough cure for that. The shower was equipped with an adjustable shower massager. She switched the setting to pulsate and adjusted the angle, and then braced herself against the wall, parting her thighs and letting the pulse of hot water work its magic. It didn't take long to get off—not once she shut her eyes to more fantasies about Wade. She shut off the water with wobbly knees, but flying solo always left her dissatisfied…and bitchy.

She wondered briefly if giving in to her attraction might be a cure of sorts. Maybe it would balance her scales. She'd felt completely off-kilter since leaving Atlanta. She knew a lot of women who wouldn't bat an eye at the thought of a short-term fling.

Yeah, that's right, Nikki, let's just start grasping at straws now. Let's see if we can fabricate any reason at all to jump into bed with a hot cowboy.

She'd never needed much reason beyond pure lust in

the past. Tight jeans, broad shoulders beneath button-down Western shirts, boots, and hats still combined to make her crazy, but she'd finally learned her lesson after Clint. Yes, she had. *Thank you very much!*

She then reminded herself how often she'd been disappointed with cowboys in bed—far more often than not. Kinda like anticipating a full night of rodeo only to have it end with the eight-second ride.

After her shower, Nikki spent the next three hours making calls to the mortuary, her bank, and several credit card companies—all just spinning her wheels. She was almost in tears by the time Wade returned.

"Care for some lunch?" he asked.

"No thanks. Iris already brought me something."

"Which you didn't eat." He nodded to the unfinished sandwich. "From the Star Bakery, too. Best homemade bread around."

"I just wasn't hungry," she replied. "Help yourself."

He parked his ass on the corner of the desk and picked up the other half of her sandwich. He took a big bite. "Has Iris gone home?"

"Yes. She left a few notes on your desk."

"I'll take a look in a minute." He surprised her by taking a swig from her Coke. It was a thoughtless act, but struck her once more as too intimate. Drinking after another was something you only did after kissing—with tongue. She recalled with a flush that they'd actually passed that marker already.

She'd fixed her gaze on his bobbing Adam's apple as he swallowed and even found that part of him sexy.

This wayward pattern of her thoughts was getting out of control.

"Any progress to report?" he asked.

She shook her head and massaged her temples. "Not much. I managed at least to get my driver's license number from my insurance company, but I can't get a replacement without a credit card. And even then, it could take up to seven days before I receive it. I don't *have* seven days! I called to request a longer leave from work but my boss is a coldhearted *be-atch*. I've managed to get the rest of the week off by using up all my vacation time, but if I don't clock in the following Monday morning, I'm canned for job abandonment."

"But then you won't be working for the coldhearted *be-atch* anymore." His crystal-blue eyes twinkled with humor. "You see, darlin'? Every cloud has a silver lining."

Nikki couldn't help herself. For the first time in days, she laughed. Maybe it was just a substitute for despair, but she let it rip, a long, spastic belly laugh that made no sense at all when crying was so much more appropriate. Was she hysterical? By the time her eruption of mirth finally petered out, he looked like he was wondering the same thing.

"I'm sorry." She sobered. "Please don't think I'm unhinged."

He grinned wide. "First impressions are mighty hard to dispel."

"If you're referring to Denver, it's unfair of you to throw *that* meltdown in my face. You have to understand how much I hate to fly. Even in *good* weather. It terrifies me, Wade. It's just not natural to defy gravity

like that. I'll never understand how those hulking tons
of metal stay in the sky. Then after all that stress, to find
the next flight full, it was all just too much to handle."

"Let's just say your extreme reaction was enough
to move me to give up my seat. Matter of fact, I seem
to be developing a weakness for helpless and hysterical women. It seems you now have me at your complete mercy."

"I'm really sorry about that—for putting you in
this position."

"Don't be. I wouldn't have met you otherwise,
and you are most definitely worth the trouble, Nicole
Powell." He gave her a slow smile that warmed her to
the toes. "Good thing too, since you carry so much of it
around with you."

"I'm not normally like this," she protested. "I have
it together. Really. My life is very quiet, orderly, and
uneventful. And I really like it that way."

"Speaking of carrying things…" He ignored her re-
buttal. "You might want to grab your bags. My business
here is done. I'll take you to Sheridan now, but I'd rather
not come back this way until morning. I'd like to head
out to the ranch tonight instead. There's an important
matter I have to discuss with my brother, one that's best
done in person. I think you should come with me."

"Why?" she asked. Time away from him was exactly
what she needed.

"I don't think you should be alone," he answered,
"especially not knowing anyone."

She despised her feelings of helplessness, vulnerability, and being out of control. It was as if the moment
she'd arrived in Montana, someone had pulled the rug

out from under her. Worse still, Wade made her *want* to trust him, and *that* was really treading treacherous territory.

"Your concern is kind but unnecessary," she said. "I can take care of myself. I'm a grown woman after all."

He gave her another slow perusal. "Don't think *that* has escaped my notice, but like it or not, you're stuck with me, since no other cowboy's come along in his gleaming white pickup to rescue you."

"It doesn't gleam. *At all*."

"It's nothing a coat of wax…or ten…won't fix." He chuckled and flashed her that contagious grin again. She couldn't help smiling back.

"If you really prefer it, I'll bring you back here for the night, but you'd be much more comfortable bunking at the ranch."

Although she hated the thought of being alone, his suggestion spelled "danger" in blazing neon.

"I don't think it's such a good idea," she said. "It's one thing for me to stay here at your office, but quite another to intrude on your family."

"Look. It ain't like that here. We have one of the sparsest populations in the country. We embrace strangers. In fact, Mama will probably try to move you in. It's not often she gets to have a hen party, outnumbered by men as she always is."

She gnawed her lip. "I don't know." She'd be a fool to spend any more time alone with him, but being truthful with herself, she didn't really want to be by herself in a strange place either.

"It's not a problem," he insisted. "They're already aware I may be bringing a guest."

Wade's offer seemed genuine. When Nikki weighed her options, she found she really had none. It would be pointless to stay in town when she still had no money and no transportation. Stifling the frantic neon flash in her brain, she replied, "If you're really certain about this…"

"Yeah. There's nothing to entertain you in Virginia City."

"What about that ten-cent tour you promised me?"

"Oh that? I guess it slipped my mind. I'll make it up to you when we come back through. Tell you what, I'm feeling generous. I'll throw in Nevada City for free."

Chapter 5

"HOW FAR IS IT TO SHERIDAN?" SHE ASKED.

"About twenty miles. Are you sure you're ready for this?"

"Ready? What do you mean?"

"Have you ever *seen* a dead body before?"

She licked her lips. "I've been to a few funerals."

"This isn't the same. It's not like a viewing in a casket. He hasn't been embalmed and the body will be in a refrigerated holding area. It's not going to be a pretty sight. Although there should be minimal decomposition, you need to prepare yourself."

She swallowed hard but it did nothing to alleviate the sudden dryness in her throat.

He turned toward her, placing his large warm hand on her knee. "I just want to be sure you understand that. Are you sure you want to go through with it?"

"Yes," she whispered. "I need to do this."

"All right then." He released his hand from her leg with a nod and then started the engine.

They drove to Sheridan in silence. Wade threw her occasional assessing glances, but seemed to understand she needed the quiet to compose herself. When they arrived, she hopped out of the truck before he could even open his door.

"Don't you want me to go with you?" he asked.

His offer took her aback more than she wanted to

admit, but she had to do this alone. She was strong enough to handle it. "No, I don't think so," she said. "You didn't even know him, after all."

The smile left his eyes. "I'm not offering for *him*, Nicole. I'm offering for *you*."

Nikki didn't know how to respond to that. She could deal with the flirty cowboy, but this sudden protective turn threw her for a real loop. "Why?"

"I don't know." He shrugged. "Just seems like the right thing to me."

Oh, that was all. She deflated. He was just being the gentleman his Southern-bred mama raised him to be. "That's kind of you, but I'm really OK. I shouldn't be long."

The moment Nikki entered the morgue, she realized she wasn't ready at all. Although Wade had tried to warn her, nothing could have prepared her for the reality. It was so cold her teeth chattered, and the sickly sweet smell of decay drifted faintly through the air. Her head reeled and her stomach churned, as nausea and light-headedness dueled for supremacy. She wasn't sure if she wanted to faint or puke, but when the attendant opened the drawer to reveal the body, she forgot everything else.

Time suspended as she gazed upon a grim, blue-tinged replica of the father she once knew. His hair had thinned and receded and his body was at least thirty pounds heavier than she remembered. Her gaze focused on his face, wrinkled around his eyes and more deeply grooved around his mouth. Set in harsh lines, it was nothing like the smiling face she recalled in her memories. Desperate to replace this ghoulish version with the father she remembered, Nikki closed her eyes and dug into the deep recesses of her mind.

Although the memories had grown a bit hazy over twenty some years, she recalled his warm hazel eyes beneath the battered straw Stetson, the faded jeans, and the pointy-toed boots that he always wore…and his big, slightly gap-toothed smile. All of these things she associated with the happiest years of her childhood—before the bad times got worse. Before the divorce. Before he disappeared from her life for good.

Even in those early days when it was just the three of them, life was an emotional roller coaster. She remembered weeks at a time with him gone. Her mother's tantrums and fits of depression. The good times when he'd come home sober, tossing Nikki into the air and calling her Sweet Pea. And the frequent bad times he came home staggering and reeking of booze.

Arguments always followed. Accusations and curses were screamed back and forth. Four-letter words that Nikki was too young to comprehend tainted the air. More often than not, there'd be shattered glass or holes punched in the walls. Nikki would huddle out of sight and pretend to be invisible while the storms raged. Once or twice she'd even seen the flashing blue lights of a police car, but the aftermath was always the same. Noises of another sort altogether—from behind a locked bedroom door.

Her existence virtually forgotten, Nikki would retreat to her own room. The routine was pretty much the same until the night she woke up to a trailer filled with smoke—the night they'd lost everything.

Only now could she even begin to understand the true fire-and-gasoline dynamic of having an alcoholic father and a histrionic mother. It was a destructive relationship in every way.

But there were a few good memories—like her sixth birthday when he'd surprised her with a trip to Cleveland, Georgia, to buy her a Cabbage Patch doll. She'd wanted one for Christmas. All of her friends had them, but the stores couldn't keep them on the shelves. Knowing her disappointment, Daddy had taken her to Babyland General. She'd seen Mother Cabbage beneath the Magic Crystal Tree and watched the birth of the cabbage babies. She even got to pick the one she wanted. After signing the oath of adoption for Zora Mae, she took her doll home. It was one of her fondest childhood memories, and she still had the ugly damned doll.

Nikki opened her eyes and reached out her hand, forcing herself to touch him, but recoiled at the contact with flesh that was as hard and cold as stone. Her throat grew thick, her vision blurred, and her chest ached with raw regret. He was gone, and only this frigid, hollow shell remained.

She fingered the tattered letter in her pocket—his last words to her, which she'd nearly memorized. It was written in a shaky, near-illegible scrawl and filled with excuses, apologies, and pleas for forgiveness. Words penned following five years of sobriety. They both opened and salved the old wounds.

"I'm sorry, Daddy, so very sorry. I never gave you a chance to make things right when you tried."

She wasn't sure how long she stood there. It could

have been a minute or an hour, or anything in between. When she thought she'd lose it altogether, when she longed for a strong shoulder to lean on, Wade was suddenly there beside her.

"For what it's worth, I'm sorry for your loss."

His deep voice and solid presence offered comfort that she was almost desperate to claim, yet she held back. "What loss?" She almost choked on the lie. "I hardly even knew him."

His big warm arm came around her. "Wanna talk about it?"

"Not particularly," she sniffed. She never talked about her screwed-up family. "You don't want to hear about my childhood any more than I want to talk about it."

"Sometimes it helps just to get it out, Nikki. When did your parents split?" he gently prompted.

"Before I started first grade. When I was a kid I didn't understand why Daddy packed up and moved out. When I asked my mom, she just said he was a drunk and a cheater, and that he never loved us, which was why he was never around."

"She said *that*?"

"Yup. 'Course, I didn't understand what it all meant. I was only seven, but the truth is that his work took him away for weeks at a time—and *she* was the cheater."

"Did he know that?"

"Yeah, after a while. It's why he finally walked out. My mom was already pregnant before the divorce, which meant she'd been stepping out on Daddy for quite some time. I was too young to put it all together at the time, but I did later when I discovered Shelby's birth certificate."

"Shelby?"

"My sister. Well, half sister. Her father was my *first* stepfather."

He looked surprised. "*First?* How many did you have?"

"Three. They were all pretty much the same—drinkers and freeloaders—just different names and faces. It was the type my mom was attracted to. She was a real magnet for losers."

"Shit, that musta really sucked growing up like that."

"Yeah. It did. I left as soon as I was old enough. Packed up the day after my seventeenth birthday and moved in with MeeMaw and PawPaw."

He smirked. "*MeeMaw and PawPaw?*"

She frowned back at him. "My grandparents."

"The ones with the chicken farm?"

"Yes. They're the only reason I didn't self-destruct. Some of my best memories are from those couple of years at the little farmhouse. I might have stayed on indefinitely if not for PawPaw's heart attack. He never recovered and MeeMaw had to sell the farm to pay for his medical bills and nursing care.

"She had a stroke shortly after that. They died within months of one another." She rubbed her eyes and sniffled. Her throat felt terribly raw.

Wade's arm tightened around her. "That happens a lot when couples have been together a very long time like that."

"I miss them, Wade. They were good people and did what little they could to be a stable influence. After they passed, I was pretty much on my own. I went a little wild for a time... I made a lot of stupid mistakes."

"We all make mistakes," he said with a sympathetic look. "The trick is to learn something from 'em."

She sighed. "Well, that's just rubbing salt in the wound, 'cause I keep making the same ones over and over." She refused to acknowledge that the big warm cowboy beside her might be another one ready to happen. "So you see? I still don't even understand why I came here. He didn't even raise me. I hardly saw or spoke to the man for over twenty years."

"It still hurts though, doesn't it?"

"Yes," she confessed. She'd tried to deny the welling of emotion, but he must have seen it in her face. "I keep thinking it shouldn't, but it still does. Am I irrational? Have you ever experienced that?"

A muscle worked in his jaw. "Yes. I know how it feels to lose someone when there were important things that shoulda been said."

"I feel so lost, like a whole hunk of my life wasn't really what I thought it was. Do you know what I mean?"

"Yeah." He nodded slowly. "I know exactly what you mean."

"How did you deal with it?" she asked.

"Not very well, I'm afraid." His expression went grim, color flushed his high cheekbones. But he didn't elaborate. "Are you ready to leave now? Not that I'm trying to rush you or anything."

"You're not rushing me, and yes, I'm ready."

"Then, c'mon. Let's get you outta here."

With a steadying arm about her waist, he guided her out of the morgue. Once outside, Nikki dragged in a great cleansing lungful of fresh air. And then another in an effort to purge the scent of death. Nikki wasn't even aware of the tears streaming down her face until he brushed a thumb over her cheek.

"Are you OK?" he asked.

"Yes. No. I don't know. I thought seeing him would give me closure, but it hasn't. I only feel worse." She couldn't keep the quaver from her voice. "You were right, Wade. I wasn't prepared."

"No one is." He fished a handkerchief out of his pocket.

"I didn't know anyone still carried handkerchiefs." She accepted it and blew her nose.

"They come in useful at times. Most of the ranch hands carry them. It's not uncommon to need a makeshift bandage when mending barbed-wire fences."

"Do you really do that?" she asked. "Mend fences?"

"Yeah. I still do my share of ranch work," he said.

"On top of lawyering?"

"There's many folks in these parts who wear two hats. Partly because it's so hard to make a living ranching full time."

"So why don't they do something else?" she asked.

"Because this is Montana and people here are proud of their heritage—often to the point of stupidity."

"Your brother?" she suggested.

"Yeah. My brother. It's what I have to talk to him about and it's not gonna be pretty."

"I shouldn't be there then. It'll be awkward."

"It'll be fine. If it gets too nasty, we'll take it outside."

"Surely, you don't mean that *literally*."

"Won't be the first time my brother and I settled a matter with our fists." He shrugged. "I figure it won't be the last."

"But that's ridiculous! You can't resolve issues like that with violence!"

"Sure we can." He laughed. "Men aren't like women, Nikki. We don't think and feel the same way you do. Sometimes things between us are *best* settled by forceful means. It's ugly as hell, but when it's over, it's over."

"So what happens now?" she asked. "About my father I mean."

"You can't do anything until you have a certified death certificate."

"Which I can't get until I have my license."

"Exactly. Once that happens you can dispose of the remains and then start settling the estate."

"*Dispose of the remains?*" she repeated with a frown. "That's my father."

Wade flushed. "I'm sorry. That was mighty insensitive of me. I guess I'm just a bit hardened to this process after so long. It's a hazard of the job when you handle probate."

"Apology accepted," she replied.

He steered her toward the parked truck.

"How does probate work?" she asked. "I don't know anything about it."

"It's mostly a bunch of paperwork," he replied. "Your first priority will be to post notices of death in all the area papers. Then outstanding debts and taxes need to be paid. You especially don't want the IRS knocking on your door."

"Taxes? Debts?" A huge knot formed in her stomach. "I hope to God he didn't leave any behind. I don't think I could deal with that on top of everything else."

She hoped he'd left sufficient funds at least to cover

the burial and prayed she wouldn't be saddled with any of his outstanding debts. She had more than enough of her own, barely keeping her head above water with a dead-end job she despised.

"You won't need to worry about any of that," Wade reassured her.

"How would you know?" she asked.

"Because I looked into a few things earlier today. There's no harm in telling you that his affairs are in pretty good order *and* he left a will. I had Iris check with Evans on the off chance there might be one."

"Why would he have made a will?"

"It's smart to plan for the unexpected."

"Spoken like a true lawyer," she replied dryly. They stood beside the truck, she spun to face him. "If you knew all this, why didn't you tell me before?"

"I didn't know. He filed the will six years ago when he first established Montana residency—before I was in practice here. I didn't mention it earlier today because I wanted to wait until we had your ID straightened out, but I figure there's no harm in setting your mind at ease. You need to understand that I can't disclose anything more to you at this juncture. You can rest assured, however, that there's no debt burden for you to carry."

"Well, I guess that's a relief anyway. So what now?" she asked.

"I was going to take you back to the ranch, but I think maybe a change of plans is in order. Can I buy you a drink? You look like you could use one."

"You just might be right about that too," she replied with a shaky laugh.

"C'mon. I know just the place. The Pioneer's the best watering hole in the entire Ruby Valley."

———∿∿∿———

The bar reminded Nikki of an old-time Western saloon, with its cedar shingles and siding, and the old-fashioned wooden placard outside. It felt even more like one when she followed Wade inside. The paneled walls were dark, with numerous mounted antelope, elk, and bison heads as well as an array of faded black-and-white framed photos from the turn of the century. The backbar was crafted of deeply stained, hand-carved oak with a huge counter-length diamond dust mirror.

Wade tipped his hat to the barkeep, and then to several waitresses who seemed to light up in response to him. She guessed he must have that effect on lots of women. He was certainly no stranger to the place, but then again, this area was his stomping ground. He propelled her to a corner table, pulling out her chair before taking his own.

"Come now," she chided. "The gunfighter seat?"

"Force of habit." He chuckled.

He'd no sooner doffed his hat before a brown-eyed bottle redhead appeared wearing a low-cut top that displayed attributes that would put the Hooters girls in the shade.

"Hey, Wade." She flashed him a huge smile. "Been a long time."

"Janice? I'll be damned. I didn't know you were back in town."

Her smile flickered for just a moment. "I never thought I'd set foot back here either, but I had nowhere else to go with my kid and all."

"I was sorry to hear about all that…" Wade shook his head. "What a gruesome way to go."

"It was." She shrugged. "But he knew as well as anyone that it was bound to happen sooner or later. With the bulls it's never a question of *if* you're gonna get hurt—it's just when and how bad. Least he didn't suffer much, being that he never gained consciousness."

"I'm glad Dirk gave up rodeo, though the way it turned out for him, maybe joining the Marines wasn't the best choice either," Wade said.

Her expression grew troubled. "I haven't seen him around. How's he doing?"

Wade shrugged. "As well as can be expected, I guess, but he hardly leaves the ranch. You know about his injuries, don't you?"

"Yeah, I heard."

"He's changed a lot from what he was before."

Her brow wrinkled. "I'd expect as much." She bit her lip, then asked, "He seein' anyone?"

"Dirk?" Wade shook his head. "Not to my knowledge."

"Think he'd mind if I dropped by?"

Nikki had watched the exchange with a mild feeling of resentment until she realized it was Dirk and not Wade that Janice was actually interested in. Did she and Dirk have a history? She eyed the other woman with renewed curiosity.

"Don't know," Wade replied. "But I think he could use some old friends—as long as you aren't put off by his surly, badass behavior."

Janice grinned. "You're kiddin', right? I ain't thin-skinned. Could never afford to be. You don't know what it's like to be a woman working the chutes with all those bulls and rough riders. For the record, I can give every bit as good as I get." She paused. "Maybe I will call on Dirk one day."

"Forgive me, Nikki," Wade said. "This is Janice—"

"An old friend," Janice supplied smoothly and extended her hand. "I grew up here and just recently moved back."

"Nikki Powell from Atlanta." Nikki briefly shook Janice's hand.

"Welcome to Montana. First time?" Janice asked.

"Yes, and likely my last. Wade's helping me with some personal business. My father passed away here."

"Oh," Janice replied, looking uncertain. "My condolences."

"We just came from the mortuary," Wade explained. "I thought she could use a drink."

Janice smiled. "Then you came to the right place. Whatcha gonna have?"

"The usual for me. The bartender knows." Wade looked to Nikki. "Sorry, I don't know your poison."

"I'll take a shot of Patrón."

"Salt and lime?" Janice asked.

"Of course," Nikki said.

"What?" she answered Wade's querying look. "You thought I'd order some girlie umbrella drink?"

"Yeah, it was pretty much what I expected, more than straight tequila."

"This seemed like a tequila occasion," Nikki replied.

"You are full of surprises." Wade chuckled as Janice hustled away to fill their order.

Their drinks appeared within minutes—a foaming beer in a frosted mug, and a shot glass sporting a paper

umbrella that Janice set it in front of Nikki with a wink
for Wade.

"I suppose this is a joke?" Nikki said.

Wade laughed, a low, warm rumble that ceased the
second she licked the back of her hand to apply the salt.
Meeting his gaze, she slowly licked off the salt. He
locked on her mouth, his pupils flaring big and black.
She took the shot, downing the tequila in a single choking swallow, then bit into the lime with a grimace.

"That bad?" he asked.

"The salt is supposed to reduce the burn, but I don't
think it works."

"Would you like something else?" Wade asked.

"No, I don't think it's a good idea to mix liquors. I'll
stay with my friend Patrón."

He nodded at her empty glass. "You want another?"

You know better, she told herself, staring at his dangerously tempting dimpled chin. *He's made no secret
about what he's after. The last thing you need is to let
your guard down.* Ignoring the voice of reason, she
smiled back at him. "Sure. Why not?"

Two shots later, Nikki felt a sweet lethargy, the kind
induced only by drink or sex. Since they were still in
the bar, she had a pretty good idea it was the drink. She
ordered a third and took her sweet time licking off the
salt. She rarely drank tequila and had ordered it purely to
tease him. From his expression, it was working.

"I think we need some music," she said.

"Why? You wanna dance?"

"Maybe," she answered coyly.

"Too bad there's no band tonight. The one that usually plays here packs the house."

"Are they good?" she asked.

"If you like a mix of blues and rock in your country. Ten Foot Tall and Eighty Proof. They play all around the area. If you stick around long enough, I'll bring you back to hear them."

"Do you dance, Wade?"

"Not really, but if *you* feel like dancing"—he patted his lap—"knock yourself out."

"Keep dreamin'." Nikki rolled her eyes with a snort. She then idly flipped through the playlist attached to the old-timey jukebox on the tabletop. "Got any quarters on you?"

"Why? You got a favorite song?"

She flashed him a dazzling smile. "I got *your* song, Wade."

"*My song?* Really? What is it?"

"You'll see." With a throaty chuckle, Nikki dropped the coins he gave her into the machine, and then made her selection. The sultry tones of Carrie Underwood filled the air. "See?" She laughed. "I've totally got your number, Wade."

"'Cowboy Casanova'?" He speared her with those amazingly clear and sexy light blue eyes. "Is that what you think I am?"

"Yeah, I do. A big-time sexy cowboy player, but I don't do players and for damned sure not sexy chin-dimpled cowboys."

"Sexy?" His brow kicked up. "You think so? Then, I'm confounded to understand this aversion of yours."

"It's been acquired by experience," she replied, carefully enunciating her words with lips that felt warm and a bit numb. "Every damn time I've fallen for one it's bitten me in the ass."

"So you think one bad apple—"

"One?" She laughed outright. "I've tried a whole crate full of apples, Wade. All bad. Worm-infested and rotten to the core, every last one of 'em." She struggled a bit with the *l* but thought she managed to keep the slur out of her reply. Even her toes felt warm and tingly now.

"Sounds like a real challenge to overcome such a fierce dislike of *apples*."

"Yeah. No more apples for me. *Ever*."

"Ever?" He cocked a brow. "Maybe you just need to try a hybrid variety."

"A hybrid? You mean like a Honeycrisp?"

"Not quite the analogy I was aiming for. Maybe we need to progress from fruit to the animal kingdom."

"Whadya mean?"

"I told you my brother Dirk has been crossing Japanese bulls with Angus cows to create a superior breed. I like to think I'm kinda like that."

"Like a *bull*?" Her gaze dropped to his groin. "That's quite a boast."

He grinned back at her. "Not *exactly* what I meant, but I'll go with it. Then again, maybe I'll let you be the judge."

She frowned. "Not likely, cowboy. You see, you've already got a third strike against you."

"Three now, eh?"

"Oh yeah. 'Cause I don't like lawyers either. Never have. So three strikes means you're out."

"Only in baseball, darlin'. But we're mixing far too many metaphors now. I think we need to go back to your classification system. It's flawed."

"Whadya mean?"

"You ignore the fact that sometimes crossing two different breeds can result in the best combination of both."

"Or the worst," she interjected.

"I argue the proof's in the puddin', darlin'. I think that's what you need, Nikki, a man who's the best of both—one who knows how to *act* domesticated and when to be wild."

"*Act* domesticated?"

"Well, yeah. With men it's only an act anyway. We aren't meant to be domesticated. But a woman wants one who knows how to fake it, how to be tender and sensitive when she needs it."

"Is that so?" She placed her hand on his arm and leaned in real close. "And how well do *you* fake it, Wade?"

"You really want to know?"

"I do. I really, really do," she insisted.

Damn. Why had she gone for the tequila? She should have settled for a beer. Maybe it was a subconscious sabotage. If he got her drunk, she could hardly blame herself in the morning for tumbling headlong into his bed. The more she drank, the less complicated the issue seemed. She deserved some fun for a change—and why not a bit of Wild West Wade?

He leaned in closer still, murmuring hot and low in her ear. "How? By giving her slow and easy, when what I really want is hard and fast."

She ran a finger leisurely around the rim of the glass, and then stuck it in her mouth, slowly sucking off the salt residue. She released it with a pop, then leisurely licked the remaining salt from her lips. His Adam's apple visibly bobbed as he tracked every flick and dart of her tongue. He shifted in his seat. Torturing him like this tickled the hell out of her.

She met his gaze with a mischievous smile. "What makes you think every woman wants slow and easy?"

Holy shit. She'd given him a hard-on with a simple question. It wasn't the wording as much as the *way* she'd posed it—with a challenge. Her body language said *gimme what you got, cowboy,* loud and clear. He suspected the tequila had a lot to do with it, but the hungry look in her eyes made him want to give her hard, fast, and furious right there on the table.

It was definitely time to go.

"Are you ready, Nicole?" he asked, already grabbing his hat.

"What's your hurry, cowboy?" She gave him a sloppy grin that pricked his conscience.

He hadn't set out to get her drunk. That was her doing, but he certainly hadn't discouraged it either. He'd enjoyed the hell out of watching her inhibitions vaporize and wondered how many, or better yet, how few, still lingered. He wondered if she'd be passive or bold in bed. He was mighty eager to find out.

"C'mon." He took her by the arm and gently coaxed her from her seat. "You've had enough for one night. I'm taking you home."

"Home?" She cocked her head at him. "Home where? If you think you're gonna sweet-talk my panties off, you got another think coming, Wade. I already told you how I feel and you haven't changed my mind. No indeed-y. I got your number."

"Do you now?" He threw some money on the table and guided her to the door.

"Yup. Sure do, after seeing how those waitresses were all eyeballing you like a herd of hungry sows waiting at the feeding trough."

"A herd of sows? That's not a pretty picture you paint."

She gazed up at him in earnest. "I was simply making an ob-obzervation, Wade."

"Sure you were."

He let her babble on until they got to the truck, where he was struck by an overwhelming impulse to silence her—with his mouth. He managed to restrain the urge until he reached around her for the door and found himself thigh to thigh with Nikki, her breasts pushing against his chest and her arms entwined around his neck. She looked up at him all soft and warm and welcoming.

Damn, but it was just too much!

He pinned her to the door, expecting at least some token resistance after the way she'd been sounding off, but instead, she laced her fingers in his hair, pulled his face down to hers, and then licked his chin! He jerked his head back "What the hell was that?"

She giggled drunkenly. "That dimple of yours is driving me crazy. I've been dying to do that since I first saw you."

"Oh yeah?" He grinned back at her. "You can lick any part of me you like, darlin', as long as you let me reciprocate in kind."

Her brow wrinkled. "Really? You *like* that kinda thing?"

He was taken aback by the question. "Hell, yeah. Find me a man who doesn't."

"I've found plenty of 'em," she replied dryly.

"Is that so? Then I'd be more than happy to make amends for all those selfish bastards."

"Are you for real?"

"Do I look like I'm bullshitting?" He clasped her hand and brought it down between them, pressing her palm against his engorged prick. "Here's your proof, sweetheart. The thought of putting my mouth on you has me rigid as rebar."

Her eyes widened.

"Why so surprised?"

"Because I never met a man who wanted to give it before he gets it."

He shook his head with a *tsk*. "Then you've been with *boys*, sweetheart, not men. A *man* takes care of his woman. While I'm a firm believer in equality, I was also raised to be a gentleman. The rules of gentlemanly conduct are pretty damn clear—ladies always come first."

She slumped against him with a muffled moan.

It was an invitation he couldn't resist. He dipped his head to claim her mouth, but this wasn't the leisurely exploration he'd conducted earlier. He was hungry as hell. All that roundabout talk had his mouth watering to taste her—all of her.

His mouth eagerly melded with her soft and supple lips while his hands cupped her ass. He palmed it with both hands, just the way he'd fantasized about from the first time he'd laid eyes on her, giving it a good hard squeeze, and loving the soft and firm feel of it. She had a great ass.

She ground herself into him, sending a surge of blood straight to his cock. Growing needier by the second, he thrust his tongue into her mouth and tasted—tequila.

Shit.

He couldn't do it. Yeah, he wanted her in a bad way—in an aching-balls way—but not bad enough to take advantage of her. He'd be the worst kind of heel to take advantage of a grieving woman who'd had too much to drink. As much as he wanted her, she was too boozed up and vulnerable to think straight.

He'd experienced that vulnerability himself. It was how he'd gotten involved with Allie. He'd been hurting like hell and she'd taken advantage of his shaky state. He'd been too damned out of his head to resist, but with Allie the attraction was never more than skin deep, and any comfort he'd gained from her had long worn off. Now she was more of a habit than anything else. He'd felt that way even before Nikki arrived on the scene, but now the thought of being with Allie again was about as appealing as wearing a pair of boots a size too small.

Allie was like a diamond—mighty fine to look at but just as hard. Nicole, on the other hand, was soft in a way that stirred an age-old instinct to claim, to protect, to brand as his own. Only a minute ago he'd debated not driving out to the ranch, but returning instead to his office where they'd have privacy, but even as the devil tempted him with a night of sin, he knew he couldn't do it—not now. Not tonight.

Shutting his eyes on an inward curse, he released her mouth, although he lingered a bit longer on letting loose of the ass, he was dying to put his mouth and his mark on. Dismissing that thought with another muffled oath, he reached for the door handle. "C'mon, darlin'. I'd better get you to bed."

She resisted with a frown when he attempted to herd her into the truck. "About that, Wade. I know I gave you mixed signals, but you need to know I'm still very conflicted."

"Conflicted, eh? There's no need to be."

"Why not?"

"'Cause nothing more's gonna happen. That's why. Not tonight anyway."

"*Nothing?*" she repeated blankly. "After all you just said? Y-you can't just leave it at that! It's like the female equivalent of blue balls!"

"Sweetheart, I assure you, there ain't no female equivalent of blue balls. Nothin' even close. It's a uniquely masculine condition, and one I think I'm going to suffer with for the next couple of hours."

"B-but you don't have to—"

He couldn't help a chuckle at the note of frantic frustration in her voice. "Darlin', if you weren't three sheets to the wind, I promise I'd already have you on your back in the bed of this truck."

She glanced over her shoulder. "It doesn't look very comfortable."

"I assure you *comfort* would be the furthest thing from your mind."

And based on the tightness of his jeans, it sure as hell was the furthest thing from his.

Chapter 6

NIKKI AWOKE TO FIND HERSELF IN A LARGE CHERRY four-poster bed, with sunshine streaming through brightly curtained windows of a room she didn't recognize—a room with split log walls.

A log cabin? Where the hell am I?

Montana!

She was in Montana. She remembered arriving in Bozeman the night before last and then driving to Sheridan with Wade. She'd seen her father and then... then...her throat tightened.

Oh shit! She'd gotten totally wasted!

Why had she gone for tequila? It always made her do crazy things. Stupid things—like sleeping with hot Montana cowboys. With her pulse racing in panic, she forced herself to breathe and take stock. No. It was OK. It must be. One: she was in a very unmasculine bedroom. Two: she was alone. Three: she still had her clothes on—the same ones from last night. *Thank God!* But that still didn't ease her mind about where she was or how she got there.

The last thing she recalled from the night before was Wade's tongue in her mouth. Well, that wasn't quite it either, more like the very abrupt and disappointing *removal* of his tongue from her mouth, followed by the *departure* of his big, warm hands from her ass. That part, unfortunately, she recalled quite clearly.

But what had put him off? That she'd been drunk? That would be a first—a man who didn't want her drunk as a skunk. She supposed she should look at the bright side. Even as trashed as she was, at least Wade hadn't taken her for some skank who'd give him a blow job without even buying her dinner first. Not that she'd ever sunk *that* low before. Not with anyone. Not even in high school. Well, there was the incident in the horse trailer at the Toccoa rodeo, but she'd been wasted then, too.

But Wade had revealed a number of things that made him different from other men. She flushed all over and squeezed her thighs together at a particular revelation. *Oh yeah!* She remembered *that* part of their conversation vividly. Of the half-dozen guys she'd slept with in her life, *none* had ever initiated oral sex. At best it was a halfhearted afterthought…and felt like it too. Something told her that Wade would have put his best foot forward. *Damn it all! Now I'll never know.*

She wondered—if he hadn't stopped things, if they would really have done it in the bed of his truck? She was afraid to answer that question. Last night she wasn't exactly herself. She hadn't been from the moment she'd landed in Denver. She seemed to have lost all common sense along with her ID. How was she ever going to be able to look him in the eye again after he'd seen her shit-faced? Her whirling thoughts threatened to make her dizzy.

You aren't gonna get any answers lying in this bed, Nikki. Might as well buck up and face the firing squad. She sat up too abruptly, making her aching head spin and her stomach churn.

Oh God! Bad mistake, Nikki!

She drew a few slow, deep breaths, waiting for the return of her equilibrium. Once the dizziness had eased up, she took a better look at her surroundings. The room was large, airy, and comfortable. A thick, brightly patterned quilt on the bed matched the curtains. There were framed prints on the walls too, but it lacked any truly personal touches. *Must be a guest room.* He'd mentioned the family ranch. Had he taken her there last night? If so, she'd surely be meeting his family.

Shit. In her present condition, she'd *rather* face a firing squad.

Intent on testing her legs, she swung them over the side of the bed, and then lowered her feet to the gleaming heart-of-pine floor, before gingerly pulling herself upright. She thought she might actually be OK until she took a step. Her stomach seized, sending a surge of bile upward into the back of her throat. She clutched the bed post with sweaty hands. *Please no! Not in his family's house.*

A rap on the door sounded softly. "Nicole? Are you all right?"

"No," she croaked. "Please, just go away!"

The door flew open. Then he was there looming over her, all big and strong and looking concerned, when it was *his* damned fault to begin with. "As bad as all that?" he asked, wrinkles grooving his forehead.

She choked back her reply and gave a brisk nod, praying she wouldn't hurl on his boots.

"Come on, sweetheart. The bathroom's this way."

He half carried her across the hall—just in time for her stomach to let loose a series of crippling spasms. Supporting her body with one strong arm, he held her hair back with the other as she heaved her guts out. *Could this get any worse?* She couldn't see how.

When the convulsive retching finally ceased, he dropped the toilet lid and sat her down on it. She watched dumbly while he filled a Dixie cup from the faucet. She wondered if her humiliation had hit bottom yet, or if there was still more fun to come.

"The morning after really sucks, doesn't it?" He offered her the cup with a sympathetic half smile. He wet a wash cloth and handed her that too.

"Yeah," she said, avoiding his gaze, mostly for fear of catching her reflection. She didn't want to know what a mess she was right now. "Where are we?" she asked.

"The old homestead. The Flying K."

"Why am I here? Why didn't you bring me back to town, especially given the shape I was in?"

"Thought you'd be more comfortable here, and I certainly wasn't going to leave you alone in the shape you were in."

"But that's just it. You did leave me alone when you probably could have had your wicked way with me."

"Don't take me for a saint, Nikki. I'd be lying through my teeth if I said I wasn't tempted."

"Last night maybe." She gave a deprecating laugh. "But I think I've probably cured you of that affliction for good."

He grinned. "Don't be too sure about that. I've got a hearty constitution." He opened the drawer to the miracle of a brand-new toothbrush. "Here, this might make you feel better. I also brought your bag up. It's right outside the door. I'll go get it."

"Thanks again, Wade."

The minute he turned his back, she loaded up the toothbrush with mint paste and stuck it in her mouth. Her first glance in the mirror almost made her shriek. She had pillow lines on her left cheek, her hair was a virtual rat's nest, and the makeup smears around her eyes made her resemble a raccoon. "Dear God!"

She splashed her face with cold water and frantically rubbed at her makeup shadows. She was clawing her fingers through her tangled hair with one hand and nearly brushing the enamel off her teeth with the other, when he reappeared behind her right shoulder. Great! Just in time to see her spit! She debated swallowing the mouthful of toothpaste, but decided against chancing fluoride poisoning just for vanity. Instead, she covered her mouth with one hand and dipped her head low to the sink.

"You have shitty timing, Wade!"

"Don't be embarrassed." He placed his big warm hands on her shoulders with a chuckle. "I've worshiped at the porcelain throne more times than I could count. Besides, I'm much to blame. I should have taken you home sooner."

"Why didn't you?" she accused.

"Truth?"

She nodded.

"Because I wanted to see the real you, that's why. I wanted to know what you're like with your hair down, wanted to hear you laugh."

"You got all that and a bag of chips, didn't you, cowboy?" Had they stayed any longer she'd likely have given him a tabletop striptease.

His laugh rumbled from deep in his chest. "Don't

underestimate me, darlin'. I can handle whatever you dish out."

Nikki had no reply. That seemed to be happening far too often lately. What had happened to her self-possession? It seemed to have evaporated the minute she met him.

Shit. She had it bad.

He pulled back the shower curtain and turned on the tap. "A hot shower will do you a world of good. I'll wait until you're done and then take you down to breakfast." He glanced at his watch. "Or maybe I should say brunch."

"Is it really that late?"

"Almost ten, which is practically dinnertime on a ranch. You'd better get a wiggle on it if we're to get to the bank in Sheridan. They close at noon on Saturday."

"The bank?"

"I thought of it last night. You said you need a credit card to get a duplicate license, so we'll go get you one of those prepaid Visa cards. I don't know why it didn't occur to me yesterday."

"But I have no money."

"I can spot you a couple of hundred for the card until you get things sorted out."

"Are you sure?" She chewed her lip. She hated to be even more indebted to him, but what choice did she really have? "I'll pay you back, of course."

"Don't fret about it," he scoffed. "Let's just get the card and then we'll go back to my office where you can get online and take care of things."

"Don't you have a laptop with you?"

"Sure I do, but it won't do you any good without an Internet connection."

"What do you mean? You don't have Internet here?"

He shook his head with a laugh. "Hell, we only got a satellite dish a few years ago. Mama believes too much TV rots the brain."

"You actually grew up like that?" Nikki was incredulous. "With no Internet or cable?"

"That's right. We never had much idle time anyway after the work was done around here."

"It was probably for the best," she said. "You got into law school and I barely graduated high school—a fact I'll gladly blame on MTV. Took me five years to finally get my act together."

"And how did you do that?"

"I enrolled in college after I moved in with my grandparents, then waitressed my way through school. Took me six years to get a bachelor in business administration. Now I have a glamorous job processing insurance claims. Not exactly the dream career I'd hoped for." She sighed. "But then life is all about settling, isn't it?"

"Is that what you think? That you have to settle for less than what you really want?"

"I do now," she said softly. "I've come to realize what I really want will always be out of reach, so I am trying to be content."

"That's too bad, sweetheart." He squatted down beside her, meeting her eye to eye. She swallowed hard. He had the most beautiful crystal-blue eyes framed by thick, black lashes. And that chin dimple. *Sweet Jesus.* He was temptation on a stick.

"Maybe you're just looking in the wrong direction." He grasped her chin, staring deeper into her eyes, inciting sparks low in her belly. "I've found that what I *really* want is often right under my nose." His gaze dipped to her lips.

She knew he was waiting for her invitation. Her pulse raced wildly, but this time she looked away. Who knows where another kiss could lead. The situation was growing far too dangerous.

"After all this?" She swallowed hard. Was he playing with her? He'd just held her hair while she puked. "You can't possibly mean that," she protested.

"But I do," he insisted. "In Denver I thought you were a hot mess. Now I think you're about the hottest mess I've ever seen." His hands dropped to her shoulders and rested there, still waiting for her to initiate the next move.

She didn't know whether it was the steam from the shower or the look in his eyes but it was getting hot as Hades. If she were truly the brazen type, she'd have stripped down and asked him to join her in that shower, but she was only bold in her fantasies. Unfortunately they'd already begun to include him—like in the shower just the day before. She'd wanted him then all right... and now here he was. She suspected he'd be a helluva lot more satisfying than that shower massager.

Her gaze darted to the shower. *Stop it, Nikki!*

"It's getting really steamy in here, don't you think?" He wiped the damp strands of hair from her brow, his crystal eyes holding hers captive. He still made no move to leave.

Breaking eye contact once more, her gaze trailed over his big, strong arms. How easy it would be to just let herself fall into them. Right here. Right now. In this moment he'd be there to catch her, but later? She just couldn't take that kind of leap—not while stone sober and thinking straight.

"Yeah. It is," she agreed. She stood with a nervous laugh. "And I'd hate to waste any more of that glorious hot water."

"You need anything else?"

She wondered what *anything else* implied. Scrubbing her back, maybe? She suppressed the impulse to ask.

"Maybe just a towel?" she suggested.

"Sure thing." He opened a linen cabinet and pulled out two thick terry towels. "That all?"

She took the towels. "Yup. I'm fine. I promise I won't be long."

She flicked a glance to the door. This time he took the hint, but paused after two steps, raking his eyes over her over again and turning her insides to jelly. "I'm patient, Nikki. I'll be here…whenever you're ready."

What the hell did that mean? She stared after him, feeling a pronounced thud in her chest. Swagger and a silver tongue to boot? *Shit! Nikki Powell, you are a goner.*

Chapter 7

ONCE SHE'D SHOWERED AND CHANGED, NIKKI FELT like a new person, and far more prepared to deal with the challenges the day would bring. Foremost, she intended to quash the impression that she was easy game. *No, indeed-y.* He could look and lust all he wanted, but Nicole Powell of Decatur, Georgia, was off-limits to hot cowboy lawyers. There was no way in hell she was going to return home with her tail between her legs all because she'd let him put *his* there.

Wanting to look hot but not wanting to *look* like she'd tried, Nikki donned a pair of tight low-rise Wranglers and a clingy sweater over her fifty-dollar Victoria's Secret add-two-cup-sizes Bombshell bra, last year's Valentine's present to herself. She pulled on a denim jacket and a pair of well-worn Justin Ropers, remnants from her old honky-tonkin', boot-stompin' days.

She went light on the makeup and pulled her wavy brown hair into a loose braid that hung over her shoulder. It was a casual, girl-next-door look that she carried off well. It was also one that men liked—at least men like Wade.

She made up the bed, grabbed her bag, and opened the door to find him leaning on the jamb. The effect, the sheer and virile maleness of him, nearly bowled her over.

"Feel better?" he asked.

"Yes. I do. Thanks."

"You look much improved."

His eyes drifted over her, his sexy mouth quirking at one corner. She was fascinated by that mouth. His kisses had turned her inside out. She remembered that too.

She gave a dry laugh. "I'm not sure if I should take that as a compliment."

"Believe me, it is. C'mon. Breakfast is waiting."

She clutched her protesting stomach. "Maybe just coffee for me."

She followed him to the staircase leading to a huge vaulted living room. The floor to ceiling windows revealed a breathtaking vista of countless mountains etched in shades of blue and gray, capped by crowns of pristine white. She paused on the landing to take in the view.

"I can't believe all *that* sits right outside your door!"

"The ranch is in the heart of the Ruby Valley," Wade said. "We're surrounded by seven mountain ranges and have some of the best grazing lands around. I guess I've come to take the landscape for granted."

"I can't believe you want to sell," she remarked incredulously.

"Stupid as hell, isn't he?" replied a gravelly baritone from below.

The body attached to the voice came into view as soon as they descended the stairs. He wasn't as tall as Wade, but bigger, more weather-beaten, and doubly imposing. Maybe that last part was due to his expression—as hard and rugged as the mountains in the backdrop.

Wade's head jerked in his direction. "Mornin', Dirk."

She noted that neither of them smiled, but she'd been forewarned about their mutual hostility.

"Mornin'? Hell, it's closer to noon. *Some of us* actually work around here. The ol' man and I have been moving cattle for the past five hours while you've been lazing in bed." He raked over Nikki with a disapproving stare.

"Hold it right there," she blurted. "I'm not his *girlfriend* if that's what you think. I'm a client." She looked to Wade, "Or will be as soon as I get a few things straightened out."

"*A client?*" Dirk's mouth twisted on the word. "Since when did my little brother start bringing clients out to the ranch?"

"Since they needed a place to stay," Wade replied. "Miz Powell's here because her father recently passed away and she lost her wallet on the trip up here. Nikki, this rude asshole is my brother, Dirk."

Dirk's expression softened at Wade's explanation. He tipped his hat with a look of chagrin.

She stepped forward and extended her hand. His gaze met hers. It was then that Nikki noticed he and Wade had the same beautiful eyes. She also noticed the ugly burns on the right side of Dirk's face. It took an effort not to stare.

He accepted her hand with a brief squeeze of his own. "Sorry for your loss, Miz Powell. Welcome to the Flying K."

"Please, just call me Nikki."

Dirk grunted something unintelligible before turning back to Wade. He'd resumed the look of a pit bull preparing for a fight. "The only asshole is the one who would give away the family farm."

"Seven point eight mil' is hardly a giveaway."

"You can't put a price on four generations of blood, sweat, and tears. You've got no friggin' loyalty, Wade."

Wade's expression darkened, his lips compressed. The testosterone levels were rising as palpably as the flush invading Nikki's cheeks.

"Save it for later, will you, Dirk? Nikki doesn't need to witness our family feud."

"Why's that?" Dirk challenged. "Don't want her to witness your shortcomings in our pissing contest?"

Wade met his brother's glare, fists clenched at his sides. "I said this *isn't the time*, Dirk."

Silent seconds ticked by making Nikki feel like a participant in a Wild West showdown. Just when she was certain violence would erupt, Dirk backed down.

"We're not done talking, li'l bro—not by a long shot."

"No. We're not done," Wade bit back, "but it'll have to wait."

Another grunt followed and Dirk disappeared, leaving Wade staring down at his boots and shaking his head. After a time he exhaled an exasperated breath.

"Is it *always* like that with you two?" Nikki asked. They were so different from one another, he and Dirk—like oil and water—and seemed to mix about as well.

"Yeah. Pretty much. A real lovable type, my big brother."

"What's the story anyway, Wade? Why are you and he at each other's throats?"

He gave a crooked grin. "Noticed that, did you?"

"Yeah. Kinda hard not to."

"Yeah. I s'pose it's a combination of things. Dirk's problem is mostly disillusionment. He isn't the man he was before he joined the Marines, either physically or emotionally."

"But you said his disability has hardly slowed him down much."

"That's true when it comes to the ranch, but how many one-legged rodeo cowboys have you seen?"

She had no answer to that.

Wade continued, "Dirk's still struggling to adjust to life in general—and not making it easy on any of us. Deep down he knows things can't go on like they used to in the old days, partly because *he* can't go on like he did before. The ranch isn't the same either, but he's not ready to accept that and let it go."

"And your father? What does he say?"

"He's torn, of course. He knows how it is, but he and Mama so desperately want the old Dirk back, and the old life, that they keep hanging on, too. In the meantime, I keep dumping money into the place."

"I can understand why. So what will you do now?"

He gave her a grim look. "Whatever has to be done. I hate to see the place go but I'm a pragmatist. I'm not going to hold on to a losing operation out of misplaced pride. We had an offer on the table. It was a decent offer. We may not get another one. I'll try to reason with my brother, but if it comes down to it, I may have to beat some sense into him."

"You're joking, right?"

He shrugged. "Let's just say all the options are on the table."

"Really? Then what happens if he kicks your ass?"

"Wouldn't be the first time." Wade rubbed the bridge of his nose.

Nikki was incredulous. "*Your brother broke your nose?*"

"And a few ribs, but he had two good legs then. I figure we're more evenly matched now." Wade cocked a grin. "But then again, I'm a lover not a fighter."

Nikki laughed, relieved to see him returning to equilibrium. "I kinda had that part figured out already."

"Told you I'd be happy to back up my words."

"You missed your chance, cowboy. There won't be another."

Although she'd already seen enough to know he wasn't like the others she typically went for, she still suspected he'd play her in a heartbeat if she gave him a chance—well, a *second* chance, given that she'd already given him the first one last night.

"You know what they say; all good things come to those who wait."

"Never is a *very* long time to wait."

He chuckled. "There's a lot to be said for delayed gratification, you know. Given half a chance, I'd delay yours for a very long time—hours maybe."

"That's quite a boast, cowboy. You know what they say about the ones that *talk* big…" She let her gaze trail over him, allowing her shrug to speak for itself.

"It's no boast, sweetheart." His voice was lower. Darker. Inciting ripples in her belly. "And I'd be happy to prove it to you."

"I hope you know you're setting some impossible expectations."

"So you're thinking about it?"

He had her there. "I didn't say that!"

"But you implied it. And that's mighty encouraging."

He took her by the elbow before she could rebut him. "C'mon now. Mama's likely in the kitchen. The only thing that would have brought Dirk inside this time of day would be grub."

———⌇———

Flour up to her elbows, Wade's mother greeted Nikki with Wade's same crystal-blue eyes, and a gleaming toothy smile. "So you're the Georgia peach Wady's been telling me about." She spoke with a distinctive Texas twang.

"*Wady?*" Nikki almost laughed aloud.

"No one calls me that," Wade scowled.

"Except your mother," Nikki said. "Do you have any other pet names for your sons, Mrs. Knowlton?"

Wade's mother made a face. "I'd prefer you call me Donna. Mrs. Knowlton was my dear-departed mother-in-law."

"All right, Donna. I'm Nicole, but I always go by Nikki."

"*Always?*" Wade asked.

"Yes." Nikki shot him a grin. "Except with big, swaggering cowboys, but I think you're trying to distract me. I'd love to know what other names she calls you and Dirk."

Donna's forehead wrinkled in thought. "You know, I don't recall that I ever gave Dirk a pet name. What about you Wade? Did you ever have any nicknames for Dirk?"

"Plenty of 'em, Mama, but none of 'em bear repeatin' in polite company."

"You!" She playfully swatted at the side of his head.

Wade dodged her with a grin. "What brings such a pretty Southern girl so far north?" Donna asked Nikki.

"My father passed away. He retired up here some years back."

"Oh." Her expression softened. "I'm so sorry to hear that, sugar."

"It's all right. I really didn't know him all that well. My parents divorced when I was very young and I never saw him after that. Still, I'm his only kin, so I came."

"And you're only staying a few days?"

"Yes. That's all I have time for. In fact, we really need to leave here soon."

"Leave? But you just got here," Donna protested.

"I'm sorry, Mama," Wade replied, "but we really do need to head back to Sheridan. Nicole has a number of things to take care of."

"Well, you can't go on an empty stomach," Donna insisted. "I've got some stew and biscuits here."

"Just black coffee for me, please." Nikki grimaced in an effort to suppress her queasiness while Wade filled up a big bowl from the pot on the stove.

"Sure thing." Donna poured her a cup. "Are you coming back?" she asked Wade, who was already stuffing a biscuit into his mouth. "Dirk was counting on your help to move the strays off the mountain to the south pastures."

"Was he? Funny he didn't mention it just now."

"You know he'd never *ask*, Wade, but I'm sure he expected it the minute he saw you."

"He'll manage without me. I've got other things to see to today."

"Sure he'll *manage*," she scolded. "But that don't

mean he should. He's killin' himself to prove he doesn't need your help and I don't like it a bit."

He groaned. "Look, Mama, if I go out there today it won't be pretty, and I guarantee you'll end up carrying one, if not both of us, to the hospital. Then who will move the damned cattle?"

"Well, I won't see your father stepping in and having another heart attack over this. Even with the ATV, he can't do like he used to."

"All right. All right. I'll drop Nicole at my office and then come back to round up strays. Does that satisfy you?" Wade sighed and then shoved another biscuit into his mouth.

"It would be a start." Her smile held more than a hint of triumph. "You and Dirk need to work this out between you, you know."

"Yeah. I intend to. And sooner rather than later. It might not be too late to salvage the deal. The buyer was pretty hot to have this place."

"Did you ever find out who this anonymous buyer was?" she asked.

"Yeah. I met him."

"And?" she prompted. "Who is he?"

"Brett Simmons."

"You don't mean *the* Brett Simmons? The quarterback?"

"One and the same. And he was really pissed when the deal fell through. I almost gave him Dirk's number, in hope he'd pound some sense into him. He's big enough."

"Pshaw!" Donna waved a flour-coated hand. "I'd still put my money on Dirk—one leg and all."

Watching the exchange between mother and son, Nikki marveled at the tightness of their bond. Internal squabbling and all, she could still feel the warmth and strength of their relationships. It was something she'd never had, but had always longed for. Her own family was a dysfunctional disaster.

After her parents divorced, Nikki had had three stepfathers—and just as many new siblings, although she hardly knew the younger ones. She'd hightailed it out of Toccoa as soon as she was old enough and never looked back.

She wondered what Wade's father was like. If he was anything like his sons, Nikki could understand why the Texas rodeo queen had followed her cowboy from Amarillo to the wilds of Montana.

She sipped her coffee while Wade wolfed down his food and then set his bowl in the sink.

"Later, Mama." He kissed his mother unabashedly on the cheek, then turned to Nikki. "Ready?"

"Yeah." She swallowed down the rest of her cup. "Thank you, Donna."

"You're welcome anytime, sugar. I hope you'll come back soon."

"Thank you, but I don't think that's too likely. I'm leaving as soon as my father's affairs are settled. Wade's helping me with that."

Donna smiled big and white. "If I know my son, I don't think he's gonna be in any big hurry to see you go."

Wade looked embarrassed. "Like she said, Mama, this is just business."

"Of course it is, sugar." Donna winked. "You *both* just keep telling yourselves that."

———

"Don't mind her," Wade said as they left the house. "She's hankering for grandkids in the worst way and thinks I'm her best chance. She doesn't place much hope in Dirk since he returned."

"Why do you say that?"

"Because he's mean as hell and seems to have lost his sense of humor along with his leg."

"Maybe he just needs the right woman to find it again—his humor I mean."

"Maybe just getting laid would be a start for him, but he almost never leaves this place. Then again, what woman would be crazy enough to take him on?"

"Plenty of them, by the look of him."

He scowled. "You're not saying that *you*—"

"Found him attractive? Maybe," she teased then laughed. "No, Wade. He's a bit too intense for me. *Genus broodus hulkus* is definitely not my type, but I'd hazard Janice at the Pioneer would be willing to take him on. She seemed pretty interested in news about him."

"Janice? You really think so?"

"Yeah, I do. If you didn't pick up on that, maybe you don't know women quite as well as you think you do."

"What about you, Nikki?" he asked. "You've made it clear that you've ruled out cowboys and lawyers, so what exactly *is* your type?"

"I don't know. Haven't discovered it yet. But based on my experience, most men fall into two undesirable categories—bottom-feeding leeches and players. Still, I keep hoping there's a whole new undiscovered species somewhere out there."

"Or maybe your classification system needs work. I believe we touched on this last night."

"Did we?" She frowned. "I don't seem to recall that."

"No? What parts of last night *do* you remember? How about the part in the parking lot?"

She recalled his soft warm lips and hungry hands vividly, a thought that sent heat flooding into her face. "Yeah. I seem to remember a little bit about that, but believe me when I say it never would have gone that far if I hadn't been drunk. I'm not that kind of girl."

"Never thought you were."

"I don't hop into bed with men I hardly know."

"Never said you did."

She paused. "I guess I should thank you for not taking advantage of me."

"Sweetheart, don't attribute too much altruism to my motives. I didn't press things only because you'd had too much to drink, but don't count on me passing up any future opportunities."

Nikki digested that remark in silence. Part of her was annoyed he thought she'd give in to him but the other part of her was flattered at his persistence.

She thought she'd broken the cowboy habit for good—until she'd met Wade, but he wasn't like any of the others she'd dated. Hell, he wasn't like any other man she'd ever known. He was a devoted son, kind and generous to strangers, and responsible almost to a fault. Admittedly, he'd surprised her last night, and even more this morning. It seemed her early presumptions about him were evaporating at every turn; nevertheless, she clutched tightly to the few that remained.

She stole a long look at the rugged and awe-inspiring

scenery. "It's gorgeous out here," she remarked. "How far does your family's land go?"

"The homestead's a little under five thousand acres, but we also lease some federal lands for rotational grazing."

"*Five thousand acres?*" she repeated with incredulity.

Wade shrugged. "It's a modest spread by Montana ranching standards."

"Now that I've seen it, I don't understand why you want to sell this place so badly."

"Because there's no future in private ranching. And I want to get the hell out of it and live my own life."

"What's stopping you from living your own life?"

"The shackles of guilt. You can see how it is."

"Yes," she admitted. "I guess I do."

"Let's go," he said abruptly. "I'd rather not talk about it anymore."

"Where's your truck?" she asked, noting the absence of the beat up F-150. In its former place was a gleaming Lexus LX570.

"My father drove it out to the north pasture. I was going to take mine anyway."

"Yours?"

He produced a key fob from his pocket and clicked it. The Lexus responded with a happy chirp. "I don't like to park it at the airport. The door dings hardly make any difference to the farm truck, but I'd rather avoid repainting this one."

"I can certainly understand that," she said.

Once more he opened her door for her. Climbing inside, Nikki sank into the supple seat, luxuriating in the rich smell of new leather. She'd never ridden in a Lexus

or even owned a brand-new car, for that matter. Maybe
it was shallow, but she liked it. A lot.

He joined her inside, filling the cabin with his presence, with his scent. She studied his every move as he
started the SUV and put it in gear. He wore a faded
denim shirt with the sleeves rolled up to expose strong
forearms, sun-bronzed and dusted with dark hair. His
straw hat was pulled down close to his brow, shading
his eyes against the autumn sun. Dressed as he was, he
should have looked out of place behind the wheel of the
Lexus, but he looked damned good. He'd looked good
in the beater too.

Hell, he just plain looked good. Good enough to eat.
She finally admitted it. She wanted to taste him in a very
bad way. *Damn it, Nikki! Sure, he'll show you a great
time. And then when he's done, he'll break your stupid,
cowboy-lovin' heart.*

Chapter 8

THE BUSINESS IN TOWN DIDN'T TAKE LONG. AFTER getting her prepaid Visa, Nikki was able to get online at an Internet café. Another phone call ensured that the processing of her new license would be expedited and sent by express mail to Wade's office in Virginia City.

"It should be here by Monday afternoon, but then I'll need to get the death certificate before they'll let me take care of my father, right?

"That's correct." Wade nodded.

"Can you at least tell me if his will says anything about what he wanted? I don't even know if he desired to be buried or cremated."

"I'm sorry, Nikki." Wade shook his head. "Until I see your ID, I'm not at liberty to disclose anything more about Ray Powell's will."

"After I get my license and the death certificate, how long will it take to settle things?"

"Montana probate law is relatively uncomplicated, but there's still a process that needs to be followed. It will take several weeks at least, and could even extend to a few months to close the estate. I can't be any more specific until I examine the will and catalogue everything."

"But I've already requested the last of my vacation days, and that only takes me through Friday. If I'm not back home by next weekend I'll lose my job."

"That's almost a whole week away," he reassured. "A lot of things could happen between now and then."

She rolled her eyes. "Yeah, right. Like maybe I'll find an untapped vein of gold?"

"Stranger things have happened here. Do you know how that gold was discovered over in Alder Gulch?"

"Of course not. I never even heard of Alder Gulch until yesterday."

"It's a perfect illustration of how unexpectedly life can change."

"All right, cowboy, I'm all ears."

"In the spring of 1863, a couple of prospectors—most likely Civil War deserters—made camp along Alder Creek. They were looking for a spot to picket the horses and decided to prospect a section of exposed bedrock. One of the guys joked that with any luck they might score enough gold to buy some tobacco. As it turns out the lucky bastards hit one of the richest gold deposits in North America. It was like winning the lottery. So you see, Nikki? Life can change in the blink of an eye."

"Did you know that most people who win the lottery end up bankrupt?"

"I think you're missing my point," he said.

"No I'm not," she replied. "It's all about self-control, isn't it? Letting things happen *to* you, instead of taking charge. What happened to those two guys anyway—the gold prospectors?"

"I don't know what happened to the first guy, but Fairweather pissed away all his money, and drank his way to an early grave. He didn't even leave enough behind to bury himself."

"You see! He had no self-control and look how it turned out. Every time I've let my emotions get the upper hand, it's ended in disaster."

"Trust is always a gamble, Nikki. But it sometimes pays off."

Nikki snorted. "I don't buy into that fallacy. Las Vegas is proof that most gambles *don't* pay off."

He shook his head on an exasperated sound. "Damn, but you're the most cynical woman I've ever met. Don't you ever let your guard down?"

"Did last night, didn't I? And look where that almost led."

"You sound like it would've been a bad thing, but I promise you, darlin', you'd have awakened with a smile on your face. I know I would've."

She let that one go unremarked. "Was that prospector story part of the ten-cent tour you promised me?"

"It'll have to be the sneak preview because I'm promised back at the ranch."

"To help the brother who looks like he wants to break your face?"

"To help my *father* who's still recovering from a triple bypass. Dirk can go straight to hell for all I care." He looked at his watch. "Time's a-wastin.' I'd better get you back to Virginia City now."

"You're taking me back to your office?"

"Yeah. I'll be back in the morning. Although the accommodations aren't plush, at least they're free. 'Sides, I figure you probably had some phone calls and such you'd like to make. I'm sure you've got family and friends who are worried about you."

"None that I can think of," she remarked dryly. "My

family's not like yours, Wade. Truth be told, I'd rather go with you."

He regarded her quizzically. "Back to the ranch? First you didn't want to go there and now you don't want to leave?"

She nodded. "Yes. Don't you know? Women are fickle that way."

He scratched his chin. His hesitation made her feel strangely deflated. He was right to be confused by her mixed signals. She didn't seem to know what she wanted from one minute to the next. But the thought of spending the rest of the day alone in his office, and sleeping on a pull out sofa was singularly unappealing.

"So you don't want me to come?"

"It's not that I mind," he answered. "It's just that I can't entertain you, Nikki. I have work to do and don't know how long it'll take or when I'll be back. 'Sides, if I bring you back, Mama's sure to get some false notions about you and me. Remember what I told you about her yen for grandkids?"

"I already told her I'll be gone in a few days."

He chuckled. "Don't make any difference. She's a typical woman and sees what she wants to believe."

Nikki scowled. "I resent that remark."

He smirked. "The truth hurts sometimes."

Nikki restrained the impulse to swat his arm. "Can't I help you with the cattle?"

"What do you know about cows?"

"Nothing," she confessed. "But what am I going to do alone in Virginia City? There must be some way I can make myself useful to you."

He considered her with pursed lips. "All right," he

conceded at last. "I'm sure if I chew on it long enough I'll come up with something. Besides"—he grinned shamelessly—"it will piss Dirk off to no end when I show up with you in tow."

—∾∾—

It was almost two o'clock when they got back to the ranch.

"Damn!" Wade cursed as soon as they pulled into the yard.

"What's wrong?" Nikki asked.

"The pickup and ATV are *both* gone. I was hoping the ol' man would've come back by now, but he must still be out moving cattle with Dirk. I'd best get out there before Mama skins me alive for letting him overtax himself." He shot her an apologetic look. "You don't mind, do you? I hope to be only a few hours. Mama will be only too happy to bear you company. Just don't let her jaw your ear off about me."

He grabbed his hat, a pair of leather gloves, and a Sherpa-lined denim jacket from the backseat. After helping her out of the truck, he started briskly toward the barn. Nikki almost had to skip to keep up. "I thought I was going *with you*," she protested.

"That was before; when I thought we'd have use of the ATV. As it stands, I've got to do this the old-fashioned way." He jerked his head in the direction of the pipe corrals.

"You mean with horses?"

"Yeah."

Nikki could hardly contain her excitement. "Let me come along. I won't slow you down."

He regarded her skeptically. "Do you ride?"

"Yes. I ride. For the record, Wade, I can't stand tobacco-dipping, beer-swilling, swaggering cowboys. I never said I held it against the horses. In fact, I never said jack about horses. I happen to be very fond of them. I've ridden since I was a kid. I even had a pony that my Grandpa kept for me."

"On the chicken farm in Lavonia?"

"Yes. Until I outgrew him. After the pony, I used to muck stalls at a riding stable just to ride the horses."

"A working cow horse is a whole different animal from a show pony, Nikki."

"I know my way around a horse," she insisted. "I'll prove it to you. If I can't keep up, you can send me right back."

"All right, you win. I don't have the time or the energy to argue with you. We've got a couple of old geldings in the herd that are good babysitters. Redman or Copenhagen will take care of you…just don't fall off and break something."

"Thanks for the vote of confidence," she replied.

"What about your clothes?" he asked. "There's no time to change."

"What's wrong with my clothes? They're comfortable jeans and I'm wearing sturdy boots."

He eyed her backside. "You aren't wearing a thong are you?"

She spun her ass away from him. "What business is it of yours what kind of underwear I have on?"

"Because a thong'll likely rub you raw in very *delicate* places."

"Why don't you worry about your own *delicate*

places, cowboy, and let me worry about mine?" Nikki snapped. The implication, that he'd taken other thong-wearing women out on long rides, was what really chafed her.

"Suit yourself." He shrugged. "But don't come crying to me later."

Wade spun toward the barn and disappeared into a huge tack room with walls adorned with saddle and blanket racks, and miscellaneous bridlery. Following him inside, Nikki drank in the old familiar scents of oiled leather and horse sweat.

He pulled a fleece-lined oilskin drover off a coat rack and tossed it to her. "Here. It's Mama's. Might be a little big, but best take it."

"It's at least seventy-five degrees, clear and sunny."

"The weather here can change at the drop of a hat and the temperature plummets once the sun goes down. Even in summer it can hit the forties." He handed her a pair of leather gloves. "This time of year it can get even colder, well below freezing in the high country."

"You expect us to be out that long?" He took a rifle down from its rack. Nikki frowned. "What's that for?"

"Out here you have to anticipate anything and everything." Suddenly all business, he turned toward the saddles. "Do you know how to tack up?"

"It's been a while, but I'm sure I can manage." Nikki looked at the saddles with consternation. "Which one should I take?"

He grinned. "Whichever you think you can carry."

Nikki scowled at him and then grabbed the horn and cantle of the first one she could reach. One strong tug pulled it free of the rack—and nearly knocked

her on her ass. "Good golly! How much does this
sucker weigh?"

"I'd say close to half of what you do. It's a roping saddle, designed to stand up to the rigors of working cattle.
You'd best let me take it." He tossed it over his shoulder
with ease, and then jerked his chin toward the opposite
wall. "You can get the halters, bridles, and blankets."

She gathered up the ones he indicated, following him
out to the pipe corrals where about two dozen horses
were penned. She hung up the bridle, took the halter
in hand, and climbed up and over the rails. A pretty
palomino mare caught Nikki's eye. "Look at you!" she
crooned. "Such a pretty girl."

"How'd you know it was a mare?"

"I have eyes, don't I? It's pretty obvious she's missing some vital male anatomy." She stroked the horse's
muzzle. The animal nickered back. "What's her name?"

"Sunshine."

"I'll take her."

"I don't know about that, Nikki." He pulled on the
brim of his hat with a frown. "Mares can be—"

Her hackles instantly rose. "Hormonal? Touchy?"
She arched a challenging brow. "Bitchy? Is that what
you mean?"

His mouth kicked up in that taunting kinda way. The
way that made her want to slap him and kiss him all at
the same time. "I was about to say *sensitive*."

"Oh." She instantly deflated.

"And don't let that one fool you. She's worse than
most. She's grown spoiled and lazy."

"Why do you keep her then?"

A strange look passed over his face. "I don't know.

Maybe because she's bred up the wazoo…maybe because she was born here. Dirk originally trained her and then gave her to…a friend."

"Dirk trained horses?"

"Yeah. He used to be one helluva bronc rider too, but that's all over now."

"I s'pose he can't ride at all anymore, huh."

"Not true. He rides when he *has* too, but he avoids it because it's a bitch for him getting on and off. On top of that, the prosthesis tends to throw him off balance. Still, when he wants to, he can ride circles around most anyone." He threw a halter on a big sorrel gelding. "Redman's not so flashy, but he'll suit you."

"But she likes me, Wade." She regarded the mare wistfully. "We've already bonded."

"Women and horses." He shook his head with an exasperated sound. "Just trust me on this, Nikki. I know what I'm about. Sunshine hasn't had a saddle on her back in four years. You'll ride the gelding or you don't ride."

She jutted her chin as if to challenge him, but thought twice. It wasn't worth fighting him just to fight. He *was* right after all. She hadn't been on a horse in several years and even then, she had ridden English rather than Western. Still, how different could it be?

Two hours later, he proved right about something else—the thong she'd chosen that morning just in case he honed in on her backside again. It chafed like hell between her butt cheeks.

After riding fence for miles, they finally caught up with Wade's father and brother in the north pasture, surrounded by countless lowing cattle. "I've never seen so many cows. How many are there?" she asked in amazement.

"At last count, around four hundred head, but Dirk could tell you for sure. At one time we ran almost a thousand, but had to scale back substantially a few years ago when prices bottomed out and we had to let some hands go."

"Do you have any extra help now?"

"Dirk and the ol' man handle most of it with my help on the weekends, but we also hire a couple of part-timers during calving and branding seasons."

"And how many horses do you have?" she asked.

"Only about thirty now, also a fraction of what we used to keep in the old days when Dirk also worked them to sell. He gave it up when he lost his leg, but then again, horses aren't as profitable as they used to be either. Now he mostly uses the ATVs to move cattle—except when we have to push them up into the mountains for summer grazing. We still have to use the horses for that."

"And to bring them back down again?"

"Yeah, like now when they don't all come down on their own."

At their approach, the older man looked to Nikki and tipped his hat. Wade made the introduction. "Nikki, this is my father, Justin Knowlton."

She dismounted, and extended her hand. "Nice to meet you, sir."

A broad smile broke his craggy face. "Pleasure's all mine, miss…"

"Nicole Powell, but please just call me Nikki."

"Just like Wade to avoid all the work and show up for the party," Dirk mumbled.

"It's hardly done," the older man said. "There's at least a dozen strays still out there if I counted right—unless the damned wolves got to 'em."

"*Wolves?*" Nikki felt her eyes bulge.

"Yeah," Dirk said. "The damned Wildlife Service reintroduced them to these parts ten years ago and now they prey on our stock like it's a friggin' buffet table. And if you shoot one of the sombitches, you're likely to face an inquisition."

"Not that that's ever stopped you," Wade said.

"Hell no," Dirk replied with a grin. "Only good wolf on *this* ranch is a dead one."

"Where do you think the strays are?" Wade asked.

"Spotted a few up toward Bulldog Mountain." Dirk scowled up at the sun. "Not much daylight left. Late as it is, we'll probably need to overnight at the spike camp and drive 'em down in the morning."

"Spike camp?" Nikki asked.

"It's a cabin a little farther up into the mountains," Wade explained. "We mostly use it now for hunting elk and big horns, but it's handy when we have to recover cattle from the mountain. Dirk and I'll go up there. You can go back to the ranch with the ol' man."

"Why can't I go?" Nikki protested.

"We're not talking a vacation chalet," Dirk said.

"He's right, Nikki," Wade agreed. "It's just a rough shelter with a couple of cots. It keeps the bears and wolves out, but that's about it."

"Bears and wolves?" she repeated, wondering if he was pulling her leg.

Dirk smirked. "You ain't in Georgia anymore, Peaches."

Wade gave his brother a warning look, and then explained to Nikki, "It's also going to be pretty cold up there tonight. I doubt you'd enjoy it very much."

"But I've camped out before," she protested. "I'd really like to ride up that mountain with you. You said yourself that I should see some of the sights while I'm here."

"It's gonna be rough going," Wade cautioned.

She jutted her chin. "I haven't slowed you down yet, have I?"

—◊—

Wade regarded her for a long, thoughtful moment. In truth, she really hadn't slowed him *that much*, which had actually surprised him. They'd left the ranch at a good clip. He'd pushed a bit harder than he maybe should have, given she wasn't used to it, but after two hours of hard riding, she hadn't complained. She had a halfway decent seat on the horse, too. He'd enjoyed making *that* observation.

Although common sense should have told him to leave her behind, Wade couldn't deny the temptation of having her alone for the night. The ride up the mountain would be slower going and treacherous in places, but Redman was as surefooted as a bighorn sheep.

"Got overnight gear?" he asked Dirk.

Dirk inclined his head to the packs in the bed of the ATV. "Everything we need, but we'll have to take a pack horse to get it all up there." He jerked his head toward the mountain.

"You really think you can rough it?" Wade asked Nikki. "Once we set out there's no turning back."

"Yes, I can," she insisted. "I've camped out before and can even cook over a fire. I make a mean pancake breakfast."

"Using my stomach against me is mighty close to blackmail," Wade drawled.

"Whatever it takes." She shrugged and grinned back at him.

"Just listen to this shit," Dirk mumbled to his father.

Wade ignored the remark. "All right, just don't say I didn't warn you about the cold, the spiders, and the lack of amenities."

"I can handle it," she insisted.

"Three's a damned bit crowded for me," Dirk interjected.

"That's just fine, big brother," Wade retorted with a big smile. "'Cause I don't recall inviting you."

Chapter 9

NIKKI DIDN'T KNOW WHAT HAD POSSESSED HER TO RIDE into the mountains alone with Wade. Was it a moment of madness? She told herself from the moment they'd met that she'd sworn off cowboys, but now she was going to spend the night alone in a cabin with one. Had she lost her mind?

Perhaps she was just intoxicated by the sheer beauty of her surroundings. She hadn't recalled ever feeling so at peace with nature. The white-capped peaks to the northwest, and the sweeping grassy vista below, broken only by the snaking and shimmering Ruby River, were nearly as stirring to her senses as her cowboy companion. The going was treacherous in places on the narrow cow path, but the horse never faltered and Wade stayed close.

By the time they arrived at the cabin the sun was already dipping like a red-gold ball of fire below the blue-tinged mountain peaks on the western horizon. The experience was *almost* enough to make her forget her raw backside—at least until she dismounted. Her legs protested as well, turning suddenly to rubber, and nearly giving out when her feet touched down. She cast a critical eye over the crude structure that was little more than a shed. "Is *this* the camp you were talking about?"

"I warned you it would be rough," Wade replied without apology. "It was put up for cattle gathering and hunting, not for recreation. There's two cots and a small wood stove. That's about it." Wade pointed to a place higher up the mountain where the cattle appeared as no more than black dots to Nikki's eyes. "It's too late to do anything about them now," he said. "So we might as well just get settled for the night and bring them down at sunrise."

Decision made, they unloaded and picketed the horses.

"What about water for cooking and washing?" Nikki asked.

"You'll find an artesian fissure spring in the back—the main reason we chose this location. If you need to bring water inside, there should be a few bottles and buckets. I'll carry these in." He untied their saddlebags, and then slung them over his shoulder. "If you want to unpack whatever's good to eat, I'll see about gathering some wood to put your cooking boast to the test."

Their exchange was interrupted by a long and eerie echoing cry that sent a shiver rippling down Nikki's spine. It was high-pitched and sounded like a cross between a shriek and horn blast.

"What the heck was that?" she exclaimed.

Wade smirked. "*That* was the mating call of a bull elk. The sound is called bugling and means that rutting season has officially begun." He withdrew the rifle from his saddle holster. "Know how to use one of these?"

"Not really. I've never fired any guns," she confessed. "To be honest, I've never liked firearms of any kind."

"Like 'em or not, a gun can save your ass. You should at least learn how to use one."

"I've never felt the need for that kind of protection before."

"That's only because you've never stared down a wolf, mountain lion, or grizzly bear. The minute you faced any one of those, I promise you'd be pretty damned thankful for a loaded gun."

She glanced at the rifle with a nervous laugh. "Then Dirk wasn't joking?"

"No. He wasn't. You thought he was?"

"I thought he was just trying to intimidate me into staying behind. He seems that type, rather chauvinistic, I mean."

"You'd be right about that part." He laughed. "But it's too late now for me to take you back. It would be dark before we even got off this mountain."

"Don't misunderstand me. I didn't ask to go back."

"But you're sorry that you came?"

The elk bugled again. She looked from Wade to the rifle and back again.

"Not as long as *you* know how to use that thing." When he cocked a brow Nikki couldn't resist the urge to add, "Just 'cause you've got the tool, doesn't mean you know how to use it."

"Don't worry, sweetheart," he replied with a dangerous look. "I know good and well how to use *all* my tools. But if you need convincing, I'm happy to demonstrate."

"They aren't dangerous too, are they?" she asked with growing unease. "Aren't elk just another kind of deer?"

"Big-ass deer, with very large antlers. And aggressive as hell when in rut. A bull elk has only one thing on his mind this time of year, and will charge a man, a horse, cattle, even a damn motor vehicle if he feels threatened."

"You're kidding."

"Not at all." He laughed at Nikki's grimace and unlocked the cabin door where he dropped the supplies.

"I thought you said you'd camped out before."

"Well yeah, I did. Sort of," she confessed with a pang of guilt. "I once spent a week at a Girl Scout camp on Lake Lanier."

"*Now* you tell me? This ain't the Girl Scouts."

"I didn't want you to leave me behind."

"Well, sweetheart, you're stuck here now whether you like it or not. You'd best stay inside until I get back. I'll take the rifle in case I get attacked by a horny elk…or find something better to eat than the Spam or jerky that's probably in those packs." He left her with a shit-eating grin on his face and the rifle propped on his shoulder.

—⁓—

Unfortunately, Wade hadn't exaggerated the cabin's lack of amenities, the jerky, or the Spam. The structure was small, a single room with only a rudimentary kitchen—a wooden cupboard for food and dishes, and a small wood-burning stove. The furnishings were the bare basics as well, a roughhewn wooden table, two bench seats, and two cots. Clearly, the place was never intended to be recreational.

She found the artesian spring and filled a couple of buckets. There was already a small stack of wood beside the stove, enough to start a cooking fire, but not enough to burn through the night. She found matches and gathered enough kindling to get it started. To her immense satisfaction, she had a nice blaze going before Wade returned.

As for food, Nikki had searched the cupboards for

anything palatable to complement the dried and canned meats she'd found in the saddlebags but only discovered such gastronomic delights as expired biscuit mix, pinto beans, and Vienna sausages—not exactly the makings of a banquet—but enough to survive on, she supposed. Before she'd completely despaired, however, she found two cans of cling peaches and a half bottle of Jack Daniel's.

"Your poison?" she asked when Wade came back in with an armload of wood.

"No." He glanced away. "I don't touch the stuff. Must be Dirk's. He spends more time up here than I do."

"Alone?" Nikki asked.

"Yeah. He disappears every now and then. You can always tell when the walls are closing in and he has to get away. Enough about my brother." He dropped his hat on the table and came up behind her sniffing the air. "What have we got to eat?"

She laughed. "Are you really sure you want to know?"

His brows kicked up in question.

"There seems to be a surprising variety of cuisine choices." She elaborated. "We have Spam Classic, of course, but if you care for a bit of Cajun cuisine, there's Spam Hot and Spicy with Tabasco, or if Tex-Mex better suits your palate, we even have Spam Jalapeño."

She tossed the three cans at him with a grimace.

"Have you ever eaten it?" he asked.

"Spam? Are you kidding me?"

"Don't knock it till you try it. Billions of cans have sold worldwide. It's even considered a delicacy in Asia." His mouth formed that cocky heart-stopping grin that made her idiot pulse speed up.

"I'll stick with the peaches, thank you kindly."

"*Peaches?*" He cocked his head. "I never tried peaches with Spam before."

"The peaches are mine, Wade." She clutched the two cans tightly to her chest.

His grin faded. "You don't intend to share?"

He set the Spam on the table and advanced slowly toward her, circling with a dangerous look, one that reminded her of the wolves that very likely sat right outside the door. She shook her head and hugged them even tighter, licking her lips with growing anticipation.

"I don't think so, Wade. Finders keepers and all that."

"Come now," he cajoled in a honeyed voice. "I'm mighty fond of peaches."

She found her back to the wall with his forearms pinned on either side of her head, his body looming over her all big and hard. She breathed him in with a sense of fullness in her chest. He smelled faintly of horse and leather... and something else that made her go tingly all over.

He just stood there looking down at her, his gaze sliding slowly down her body, making her skin prickle in its wake. Every nerve ending suddenly sounded an alarm. She knew she'd only egged him on. Was he going to make another move?

He dipped his head to murmur darkly in her ear. "As a matter of fact, I can't think of anything I love better than sucking on a ripe, juicy peach."

He sure as hell wasn't talking about the canned variety. Nikki bit her lip. The cans slipped right through her fingers as a ripple of raw lust ripped through her. The first thudded to the floor, thankfully missing her foot. He must have caught the second.

Oh dear God. Here we go again!

She'd been ten kinds of fool for thinking she could resist him. Nikki closed her eyes and parted her lips on a sigh of surrender—but the claiming she both longed for and dreaded, never came.

"Thanks for the peaches, sweetheart. Now all we need is a can opener."

She opened her eyes to his mocking grin. *Damn him!* He'd played her like a virtuoso, effortlessly turning her into a hot and quivering mess.

No way in hell was she going to let him have the last word yet again!

"I'll make you pay for that, Wade. I promise before this night is out, you'll pay *dearly*."

"I don't think so, darlin'. I wasn't lying about my love of peaches…though I'm especially eager to try the ones from Georgia."

His expression was taunting and playful but his blue gaze was searing hot. Though he tried to play it cool, his little game had him just as fired up with lust as she was. She pursed her lips and shook her head, determined not to let him hold the upper hand.

"I'm afraid I can't help you out there, Wade. Now if you'd said you were partial to nectarines…"

"Nectarines?"

"Yeah." Her mouth twitched. "You know. They're a lot like peaches…sweet and succulent…only without the annoying—" She gifted him with a seductive smile.

In sudden understanding his pupils instantly flared big and black. Nikki's gaze flickered to his crotch. She certainly had his attention now.

"Shit," he mumbled and shifted his stance. "I've never eaten a *nectarine* before."

"Then I guess you've got something new to add to your bucket list." Her smile widened in triumph. "Payback's a real bitch, isn't it?"

Chapter 10

IN THE END, THEY'D FRIED UP THE CANS OF SPAM AND shared the peaches. It was hardly the best meal she'd ever had, but Nikki didn't taste it anyway. Her senses were far too overloaded by Wade. The tiny cabin virtually vibrated with sexual tension. She wondered what the night would bring, but also knew it was up to her. He'd made his desire known in no uncertain terms, but he'd also made it clear he wouldn't take without an invitation.

She knew coming up here with him was stupid and reckless, but her life had been dull and empty for so damned long. After moving to Atlanta, she'd worked her way through at least a half-dozen loser boyfriends— hoping to find the elusive Mr. Right. Once she'd given up cowboys, she'd thought she'd find a decent guy, but any decent ones she'd dated were as dull as dirt.

At twenty-eight, she'd thought she'd be settled down by now, but instead she'd just plain...settled. Every day was the same routine, punching the time clock, meeting a few friends in the cafeteria for lunch, talking smack about their respective bosses, and then clocking out at the end of the day. No dates. No cowboys. No crazy passionate sex.

She'd never felt the lack of intimacy in her life more deeply. She had little doubt she was getting ready for a big fall. She was more than half there already, but sleeping with Wade could only lead to heartache. No good could come of getting involved with him—well, that probably wasn't true. She had a feeling it would be *damned good*—just not the aftermath.

That would be a train wreck.

She'd never been able to detach her emotions from sex. When she gave herself, it was always the whole enchilada—*that* was her problem. Sex always equated to love but men weren't wired that way. Wade had already admitted he had no desire to settle down. Given his age, and single status, he wasn't likely to change.

She continued this internal debate while sitting in front of the fire sipping Jack Daniels from the bottle. She'd used the excuse of seeking warmth, but what she really needed was its numbing qualities. She'd never been this wound up. She took another choking swallow that scorched all the way down her throat but so far it had done nothing to quench the desire burning low in her belly.

He cocked a brow at her. "You sure you can handle that?"

She took a bigger swig, hoping it would work some magic on her nerves. She offered him the bottle.

He raised a hand. "I don't drink that stuff…not anymore." When she would have asked why, he shook his head. "I don't care to talk about it."

"Fine, be that way," she snapped, her nerves ever tighter.

How the hell was she ever going to get through this night? Stillness followed, punctuated by pops and sparks from the fire. She scooted closer, wishing she'd brought warmer clothes. The temperature had dropped at least thirty degrees since they'd arrived and Wade had warned her it could get well below freezing before morning.

Wade had settled his length on the floor, crossing his booted ankles, one hand propped under his head studying her. The silence lengthened, thickening the air until she felt compelled to break it again. "How do you entertain yourselves up here with no TV, Internet, or even a radio?"

"Usually we're too tired to think about anything besides food and sleep."

"It *is* a hard life, isn't it?"

"Ranching is a damned hard way of life. People kill themselves just to get by, but they're just as proud as they are tenacious."

"And close-knit too, aren't they? Like your family."

"Yeah. I guess we're pretty tight."

"I always wished for that kind of family."

"Did you?" He grimaced. "It isn't always what it's cracked up to be."

"You just take it for granted because you've never known anything else."

"I s'pose you're right. What else do you wish for, Nikki? What do you want out of life?"

"I don't know," she replied. "I guess maybe that's part of why I came to Montana. Not just to say good-bye to Daddy, but to figure it out."

"I'm sorry this trip has turned into such a mess for you."

"It hasn't been all bad." She darted a gaze at him and then took another sip from the bottle. "I have to admit there've been a *few* redeeming moments."

His mouth twitched. "Are you sure you want to drink

any more of that? Seems to me you got to feeling pretty raw the last time you drank."

"I overdid it because you encouraged me," she accused.

"Yeah, well, that's debatable, since you ordered the shots. Either way I'd rather you kept a clear head tonight." He sat up and took the bottle from her hands.

"Why's that? Are you implying I can't trust you?"

"You can trust *me*, sweetheart. I'm just wondering if you can trust yourself."

"Why you deluded jackass! If you haven't noticed, I've managed just fine to keep my hands off you," she uttered the bold-faced lie. In reality, it was all she could do to keep her hands off him.

"Is that so? Then why'd you come up here with me?"

The directness of his question threw her off balance.

"I—I had lot of reasons—the scenery, riding the horse, the nature experience."

"Is that all?"

"Yes, that's all," she insisted. "And now all I want is a warm bed. You said we'd be getting up early, right?"

"Yeah. Before sunrise."

"Then I'm going to turn in." She nodded to the cots. "Which one's mine?"

"Take your pick," he replied.

She dragged the nearest one closer to the fire, and unrolled her sleeping bag thinking she'd soon be snugly and safely cocooned but knew she wouldn't sleep. She was strung so tight she thought she'd snap, but her agitation worsened when she realized she had to answer nature's call.

"Wade, where are the…er…facilities?"

"Facilities?" He shook his head with a chuckle. "I'm sorry, Nikki. I know it's a bit rough on a woman, but you'll just need to pick a spot out behind the cabin and squat—unless you want to use a coffee can inside."

"No, thank you! Do you at least have a flashlight?"

He rose, got one from his pack, and handed it to her. "Do you want me to come with you?"

"No. I can manage," she answered tersely.

"All right, but stay close by, OK? I wouldn't want you to meet up with any new four-legged friends."

Her throat went dry. "You mean *wolves*?"

"Wolves, bears, coyotes, or maybe a mountain lion. There's lots of nocturnal prowlers up here."

"Maybe I can hold it until morning, after all."

"Don't be ridiculous. C'mon." He took her by the arm and guided her to the door.

"But I have a shy bladder, Wade. I won't be able to go if you're standing nearby."

"I won't be. I need to answer the call too. I'll just stay close enough to hear you if you need me."

He opened the door and the night air hit them like an arctic blast. "Looks like the first frost of the season," Wade remarked, his breath forming a smoky white vapor. "Snow will come early."

"Great. Just great," she mumbled as she walked past. "I get to pee icicles."

"Look on the bright side..." He chuckled. "It's too cold for any snakes to bite you in the ass."

"Snakes! You never said *anything* about snakes!"

"Don't worry, darlin'. There's only one venomous species up here and they're all probably hibernating by now. Besides, you're unlikely to get bit unless you step on one."

"But it's dark! How could I help stepping on one?"

"You want me to hold that light for you?"

"Yes! No! Can you at least check for snakes?"

He made a sweep of the entire area behind the cabin, and then handed her the flashlight with an obnoxious grin. "I'll be close by."

Although Nikki made quick business of it, her thin Southern blood was frosted by the time she finished. Once she got back inside, she wondered how much she should undress for bed. She pulled her arms out of her coat sleeves with chattering teeth. "Wade, I'm f-freezing my ass off."

"Now that would be just plain criminal."

He came behind her, cloaking her in his big, surprisingly warm body. His hands slid down to anchor at her hips. "It's a damned fine ass, by the way. I've been studying it from all angles." He dropped his mouth to the tender spot behind her ear. "Why don't you just pull that cot up beside mine?"

He rocked his hips into her backside, ensuring that his interest, *his arousal*, was evident.

Her thighs tightened with the tremor of desire that snaked through her. Her body thrummed with want, but she swore she wouldn't give him the satisfaction of knowing it—certainly not after what he'd done to her with the peaches. "What? Fend off the wolves outside just to offer myself up to the one inside?"

He chuckled, a low and husky rumble that reverberated through her back. "I'm only trying to ensure your comfort, sweetheart, and I can't think of any better way than to warm you from the inside out."

She was already feeling warmer. Part of her wanted

to sink into him and take everything he offered, but her wiser half prevailed. "No thanks. I'll pass on that." Forcing herself to step away from his glorious heat, she spun out of his grasp. "You see how easy that was? Maybe you're not quite as irresistible as you thought."

His gaze narrowed. "You're playing with fire, you know that?"

She licked her lips, prepared to spout off another re-buttal but he muffled her—with his mouth. His searing kiss was like a branding iron, melding his lips to hers. There was nothing tentative or exploratory about this kiss. It was possessive, commanding, and demanding a response she couldn't deny. She stiffened for only a second before surrendering to the sinful sensation of his hot tongue. He grew hungrier, more demanding, stoking the embers had been smoldering deep in her belly for hours.

Nikki sank into him as if liquefied. Clutching his shoulders she lost herself in the wet and wild tangle of tongues that fired ripples through her with every slick stroke. Her nipples tingled and her thighs clamped to-gether against the agonizing ache. It had been ages since she'd been kissed like this. Hell, she wondered if she'd *ever* been kissed like this.

Only minutes ago, she'd been quivering with cold, but now she burned with want. If this was playing with fire, she wanted nothing more than to throw herself into the flames.

Moaning into his mouth, she took his collar in a death grip and ground against him with wicked abandon. *God, he felt so damn good—all hard aroused male*. But it wasn't enough. Feeling like a lit torch on a puddle of gasoline, she ripped at his shirt buttons and yanked at his clothes, desperate for the feel of flesh on flesh.

He broke from the kiss looking as lost in lust as she felt. "Holy shit, sweetheart. Just hang on one minute, OK?"

Shedding his jacket and shirt with amazing speed, he dragged the two sleeping bags off the cots and zipped them together on the floor. He settled his long frame on the floor, stretching his hand out to her in invitation. The whole process had only taken him seconds, but the brief lull was enough for her stalled brain to kick back into gear. *What are you doing, Nikki? Are you crazy?*

When she made no move toward him, he came to her, his breathing ragged and desire flaring in his hungry eyes. Cupping her face, he kissed her again, long and deep and seductive, releasing her slowly, reluctantly.

"You're reading too much into it, sweetheart," he murmured. "You're freezing cold and I'm burning up. Why not let the ends justify the means?"

Once more, he'd left it to her. Sleeping with him would be like skydiving...without a parachute. The free fall would be intoxicating, exhilarating—but the landing? She didn't even want to think about that! But as much as much as that thought terrified her, it would be nothing compared to the regret she'd suffer a month from now, wondering what *might* have been.

"Just let go, Nikki." His tone was coaxing, his argument convincing...almost irresistible. He drew her against him, this time enticing the seam of her mouth with more tantalizing flicks and darts of his tongue that obliterated reason. *Just let go.*

Slanting his mouth over hers, he deepened the kiss.

His hands mapped over her body with slow and deliberate caresses until coming to rest on her ass. His kiss grew more demanding, his thrusting and retreating tongue inciting a gush of liquid heat between her thighs.

Almost mindless with want, she broke from the kiss, dragging in a desperate lungful of air. "Promise me one thing, Wade."

"Just name it, sweetheart," he replied low and husky. "Right now, I'm likely to swear to just about anything."

"Then swear you'll make this so damn good I won't regret it in the morning."

His mouth molded into that sexy, dimpled grin. "Darlin', the only thing you're going to *regret* is putting me off for so long."

"That's enough talk, cowboy. Time to put your money where your mouth is."

<hr />

Wade had a raging hard on, but still wouldn't press her any further if she didn't want it just as much as he did. He studied her intently, his blood roaring in his ears, until she gave him that cute little chin jut and dropped another gauntlet. *Thank you Jesus*. He exhaled in prayer and hauled her hard against him.

"Sweetheart, I'd rather put my mouth—"

He never got to finish. She silenced *him* this time, softly biting his lower lip and sucking it into her mouth. His shirt was already off and her hands were everywhere. His were too, except where he wanted them most. He lowered them both to their knees and slid his hands beneath her sweater. Her skin was smooth, soft, and cool to his touch. His thumbs strummed over her lacy bra, tantalizing her nipples as he dipped his head to the junction of her neck and shoulder, breathing her in, tasting her sweet skin on his tongue. She shivered.

"I promise you'll be warm real soon," he murmured thickly.

"That one wasn't from cold, cowboy. Don't stop what you're doing."

He drew her onto his lap and pulled off her sweater, cupping her breasts, and lowering his head to root for a beaded nipple even as he unhooked her bra. Once freed from the bra, he suckled her harder. "God yes," she whimpered.

With a sound of impatience, she pushed him onto his back, straddling his thighs, and finding his chest with her mouth. She worked her way down his body with feverish desperation, yanking his belt free and fumbling with the button fly of his Wranglers. Shit! Why the hell hadn't he worn a pair with a friggin' zipper?

Giving up, she slid a hand deep inside his jeans. He sucked in a breath to give her more room as she wrapped her fingers around him. She kissed and licked and suckled his belly while stroking inside his jeans, sending him into a near frenzy to release himself into her greedy hands. Wade pulled her back up to his mouth as he tore at his buttons and then hers. Never breaking completely free from the hot and heavy bites and kisses, they yanked, wriggled, and squirmed out of their remaining clothes.

He stroked his hands over her hips to her cool butt cheeks. Sure enough, she was wearing a lacy thong. "How's your ass feeling?" he asked with a chuckle.

"Chafed raw," she confessed. "But maybe you could kiss it and make it all better?"

"Hell, yeah, darlin'. I've been dreaming of licking that sweet ass of yours since the Denver airport." He laid her down, working his mouth down her body with the intention of peeling off her panties with his teeth. *Shit!* He cursed in frustration. For hours he'd been hard as a sledgehammer from tantalizing images of *nectarines* knocking around in his head, and now it was too dark to see a damned thing.

"What's wrong?" she asked breathlessly.

"Nothing the morning light won't fix."

"I don't want to think about morning."

She shivered again. Violently. He looked up to find her lips turning blue from cold.

"C'mon. I promised to warm you up." Abandoning his quest, he dragged her into the snug confines of the sleeping bags, kissing her and warming her body with his. Taking his time, he moved down her throat once more to her breasts, loving the shape and feel of them in his hands and mouth. She squirmed beneath him, removing her panties, and then guiding his hand over the soft, smooth plain of her belly, then southward to a place equally smooth. Wade skirted his hands over her baby-soft skin to slip his fingers deep inside her. So warm and wet.

Writhing beneath him with whimpered impatience, she wrapped her fingers around his prick, coaxing him toward the source of her wet heat. She was wide open, slick as sin, and begging. "I need you inside me. *Now*."

"Just hold that thought, darlin', and I'll be happy to oblige." Extricating himself with a supreme effort, Wade groped in the dark for his crumpled jeans, sighing with relief when he found the foil packet. He quickly rolled on the latex and returned to Nikki, fisting her hair and taking her mouth hard and deep, muffling her cry when he penetrated her in a single slide home. She clutched his shoulders, wrapped her legs around his flanks and urged him deeper. Harder. He withdrew and slammed into her again. His mind blurred with the tight, slick, friction.

Holy shit, it was good… Was there anything better on God's green earth than immersing himself to the balls in this woman?

And it only seemed to get better as they increased the intensity. She ground up into him with soft, sensuous sounds, meeting him eagerly, and matching his furious rhythm. Wade pounded into her, ruthlessly and relentlessly, every thrust ratcheting him higher and closer to the peak. Though his balls ached for release, Wade held himself in check, gritting his teeth and easing himself back from the edge of oblivion. But three more hard thrusts sent her into the abyss.

She threw her head back with a scream, her channel convulsing in pleasure, her inner walls squeezing him in milking spasms. Holy hell, he'd never made a woman come so fast.

She gazed up at him with a dazed smile of repletion. "I think you've kept up your end of the bargain."

"Been awhile?" he asked.

"Yeah, too long."

"That so? Was that how you like it, Nikki? Hard and fast?"

Her mouth curved in the corner. "Hard, fast, slow, deep, I think I'd like *you* any which way." Her brow wrinkled. "Do you know, I think you're the first man who's ever asked me what I like?"

He gave her a crooked grin. "Just aiming to please."

She flicked her gaze southward and ran her tongue over her lips. "Then it seems only fair that I reciprocate."

"All in good time, darlin'. First, I want to make you do *that* all over again."

Chapter 11

NIKKI OPENED HER EYES TO WADE'S WARM BODY cloaking hers, his steady breath heating her neck. He mumbled in his sleep, dragging her closer, scraping a bristled jaw over her nape. She was afraid to move, almost afraid to breathe, for fear of breaking the spell. Had it all been just a wild erotic fantasy? But the air was still scented with sex. If that wasn't already enough to jar her memory of last night, her mental DVR began playing back the preceding hours in vivid and breath-catching clips.

She'd never experienced anything even close to being wrapped in him, filled by him. He'd made her come apart so many times she thought she'd lose her mind. They'd had hard, fast, mind-blowing sex—and she'd fallen just as hard and fast. Now she was struggling to deal with the emotional upshot. It wasn't just great chemistry; he was everything she'd ever dreamed of—big, strong, intelligent, compassionate, sexy, and with a great sense of humor. She couldn't suppress the tiny hope that that just *maybe* he'd felt something more too.

He stirred again. His erection pressed up against her ass. She wriggled into it with a moan. "I want you again, Wade."

"We can't," he murmured hotly against her neck. "I don't have any more protection, but here's a little re-minder until I *can* be inside you again."

His mouth came down at the junction of her neck and shoulder. He slipped his hand between her thighs, stroking and circling, making her crazy while biting softly, and sucking on her neck. She basked once more in his unselfishness, and even more in the mastery of his hands and mouth—until the sound of thunder shook the door and rattled the windows.

Startled, Nikki cried out. Wade jolted upright, scrambling blindly for his clothes.

More thunder sounded and then the door flew open, slamming against the wall with a thud. It was Dirk. A big, bad, glowering intruder casting his long shadow from the doorway.

His face hardened as he took in the scene. "Just fucking great, Wade. You told me you were going to bring down the strays. Instead, I come all the way up here to find you two knocking boots!"

Wade yanked on his jeans and tossed Nikki his shirt before stepping toward the door, effectively blocking her from Dirk's view. "What the hell are you doing up here anyway? I told you we'd bring them down and we will."

"I'm playing the messenger boy for Allison Evans, that's what. Seems she has a new offer on the table and *needs* you, Wade. She won't go into it with anyone else."

Nikki looked from one brother to the other with a sickening churning deep in her gut. "What's he talking about, Wade? Who's Allison Evans?"

"He hasn't a friggin' clue what he's blabbering about," Wade replied. "Allison is my partner's daughter. She's the ranch broker I've been working with. This is business, Nikki. Plain and simple."

"'Plain and simple'?" Dirk laughed outright. "Yeah, you just tell yourself that, little bro. Hell, it seems to me with such a fierce competition for that dick of yours, we should pin a blue ribbon on it."

"Shut the hell up, Dirk!" Wade snapped and glanced back at Nikki. "And get out!"

"You done fucking then?"

It was Wade's turn to glower. "One more word and my fist is going to get mighty familiar with your face."

Dirk's eyes darkened, his body stiffened for a moment, but then he turned and stalked out.

"Look, Nikki," Wade began as soon as the door closed. "This is nothing like it appears."

You're an idiot, Nikki Powell. You knew how this would turn out and you did it anyway. You deserve what you get for your stupidity.

"You don't need to explain anything," she said tightly. "I already knew this was a huge mistake even before it happened." She shook her head. "No, make that a *colossal* mistake."

She climbed out of the sleeping bag and snatched at her own discarded clothes.

"Sweetheart." Wade wrapped his arms around her. "I've got only one reply to that. If you think last night was a mistake, I'd better try again until I get it right."

She averted her face. "Last night was last night. Now it's done. Over. It's not going to happen again. There's no point in continuing what never should have started to begin with."

He gave an exasperated groan. "Please, listen to me. I know you must be feeling pretty raw after that asshole barged in on us, but don't be getting wrong ideas about me and Allie."

"Let it be, Wade. I meant what I said. Let me be."

"I'm sorry, but I can't accept that."

"Why's that? Because *I'm* the one ending it? Is that a novelty for you?"

He cocked his head. "Damn straight it is, and I don't like it. Not a bit."

"Guess you'll have to get used to it."

She took off his shirt and threw it at him. He caught it in one hand. "You'd better go now. Dirk and the cattle are waiting." She jerked her head toward the door. "You go ahead and I'll catch up with you later. I'd like to get cleaned up before I see anyone else."

"You can take your time. We'll be driving them back down this way anyhow. You can join us then."

He pulled his shirt on, grabbed his hat and jacket, stomped into his boots, and then headed for the door. He only made it three strides before turning back. "We'll talk more about this when I get back."

She shrugged indifferently. "It doesn't matter. I'm leaving in a few days."

He hesitated, a muscle twitching in his jaw. "Maybe. Maybe not. You've still got a number of legal matters to attend to." He opened the door, and threw over his shoulder, "In any case, we're not done. Not by a long shot."

When the door closed, she whispered, "Yes, cowboy. We're done."

———⁓⁓⁓———

Nikki shivered at the blast of icy spring water on her face. Though she'd mixed it with what little hot remained on the stove, it still wasn't enough to take the chill out. After quickly dressing, she struggled to saddle up Redman. It took three grunting heaves before she finally managed to hoist the saddle high enough to get it on his back.

The horse truly had the patience of Job, standing quietly while she ranted and cursed. She also hoped he had the wilderness instincts of Davy Crockett. She was counting on it anyway. Nikki figured if she just turned him in the correct general direction, the old ranch horse would have no trouble finding his way back. It was chancy perhaps, and no doubt stupid as hell, but her only thought was to get away from the *cowboy*.

They passed the next three hours picking their way carefully down the mountain and into the valley, where thank God, she spotted the Knowlton homestead. Nikki thought dryly that while her instincts about men still sucked, at least her judgment about the horse had proven correct.

Redman's pace picked up the nearer they got, until he was close enough to nicker to his buddies who stood in the corrals contentedly munching alfalfa. Nikki's ass ached and her legs felt like jelly when she dismounted, though Redman was far less to blame for that than Wade. The man had impressive stamina. She supposed he needed it to keep up with his collection of women.

As heavy as the saddle was, and as weak as she felt, she knew she'd never be able to untack the horse without help, but there appeared to be no one around. It hadn't struck her until now that she hadn't encountered any hired hands. A place this size would surely need a number of able bodies to run it, but she'd only seen Dirk, Wade, and their parents.

Nikki tethered the horse, but just as she wondered if she'd have to go to the house for help, the back door opened. Wade's father appeared, followed by Donna and a tall, gorgeous blonde who could only be Allison Evans. One look at her incinerated any lingering hope that Wade's interest in Nikki had ever been real.

What an idiot she'd been! What was she thinking to fall into such a fantasy that someone like *him* would ever want someone like *her*—other than for just a good time between the sheets? A giant knot formed in the pit of her stomach. If she could only rewind the last forty-eight hours she swore she would play them out so differently.

Fate was such a bitch.

She wished she could disappear, just slip away unnoticed, but Wade's mother spotted her and beckoned with that big-as-Texas smile. The blonde followed suit with her own blinding white flash of perfect teeth. Realizing she had no escape from the happy threesome, Nikki waved back and forced her stiff-feeling lips to curve upward in return.

Justin Knowlton approached with a bowlegged swagger. "Need some help there, young lady?" He jerked his head to Redman.

"Actually, yes. The darned saddle weighs a ton. I doubt I can even lift it off his back."

He grinned. "Stick around long enough and we'll make a real cowhand out of you yet."

Nikki snorted. "There's little chance of either, I'm afraid."

"Is that so?" His weathered face split into a grin. "I

get the feeling Wade might try to persuade you otherwise." He patted the horse's rump and proceeded to loosen the cinch. "Speaking of which, where the dickens are my boys?"

"Still gathering cattle, I imagine."

His mouth hardened. "You don't mean you rode down that mountain *all by yourself*?"

Nikki fidgeted with the bridle. "Yeah, I did. Well, Redman really brought me."

Donna's crystal blue gaze flickered in disbelief. "Wade let you ride *alone*?"

Nikki squirmed. "Well, he didn't exactly know I was leaving. He thinks I'm still at the cabin."

"The cabin?" Allison asked. "What cabin?"

"The hunting camp up on the mountain," Nikki explained. "We went to up there to gather some strays yesterday afternoon, but then it got dark and we had to stay."

"*We?*" The blonde's blue gaze turned to ice. "*You.* And Wade?" Her smile suddenly became brittle. Slightly hostile. Definitely territorial. The message wasn't lost on Nikki.

"Yeah. Me and Wade."

Donna's gaze darted between the two women. "I'm sorry, sugar. I've not introduced—"

"Allison Evans." The blonde extended her hand.

Although the smile never left her face, she eyed Nikki with a look that hinted at contempt. Small wonder. Allison looked like a cover model, while Nikki resembled something the cat dragged in. Nevertheless, she burned under the obvious scrutiny.

"Nicole Powell," Nikki replied tightly. "I'm up from Atlanta."

"Really? What brings a girl like you so far above the Mason-Dixon Line?"

A girl like you? What the hell did that mean?

"I have some personal business to settle here," Nikki replied, purposefully vague.

Wade had told her that Allison was just a business associate, but Allison's manner indicated a much more personal relationship than he'd claimed—the lying sonofabitch. Only hours ago, she'd awakened beside him in a blissful lust-induced daze. He'd made her feel like the only woman in the world—in his world anyway. What a gullible idiot she was.

Allison's brows rose. "Business? Really? And I suppose Wade's taking care of this business for you out *here* on his family ranch?"

Nikki bristled. "As a matter of fact, he is, or will be soon enough."

"Sweet tea anyone?" Donna Knowlton chimed in.

"I'd love some," Nikki replied, desperate for any excuse to get away from Allison.

"None for me thanks," Allison said. "I'll just stay out here and visit with my little Sunshine."

Nikki was about to follow Donna inside but stopped in her tracks. "*Your* Sunshine? The palomino mare is yours?"

"Well, not quite," Allison said. "I've been wanting to buy her for a good while, but Dirk wouldn't part with her. But once the ranch deal is done, it's just a matter of negotiation. Dirk won't have any reason to keep her then. I don't know why he's held on to her all this time anyway, unless it's just to torture poor Wade."

"Torture poor Wade?" Nikki shook her head in

growing puzzlement. "What do you mean by that? Why would keeping a horse bother him?"

Allison cocked her head with a smug smile. "I guess Wade hasn't told you about Rachel?"

"Rachel?" Nikki asked.

"Please, Allie. We don't need to go there," Donna interjected with a tight smile. "Let's just let sleeping dogs lie, all right?" She hooked her arm through Nikki's, steering her toward the house. "How about that tea now, sugar? We can wait for the boys inside."

The last thing Nikki wanted was to see Wade and Allison together. She already abused herself with that mental image...and it hurt like hell. The longer she'd studied Allison, the more her insecurities had bloomed. She cursed herself as ten kinds of fool for thinking Wade was interested, and refused to make things worse by hanging around like a dog who'd just lost its bone.

"Donna," she asked, "is there any possibility I could get a ride back into Sheridan?"

"Don't you think you should wait for Wade? I expect he and Dirk will be back before too long—"

"I'm so sorry to be such trouble, but it's really quite urgent. I really have a lot to do and need an Internet connection," Nikki insisted.

Given the opportunity to leave now, rather than waiting for Wade to return, she'd beg a ride or even hitchhike if necessary. At this point she'd do just about *anything* to avoid further contact with him or incur any greater obligation. She only hoped the balance on the prepaid Visa card would be sufficient to cover a couple of nights lodging at a cheap motel until she got her ID and credit cards back.

"If you can't," Allison interjected, "I'm sure I could run her into town."

Hell no! Nikki wanted to scream. Instead, she forced a smile. "How kind of you to offer. Are you sure you don't mind?"

Donna looked from one woman to the other. The tension had to be impossible to miss. To Nikki's relief, she volunteered. "No need to trouble yourself, Allie. I'll drive her into town. I have to pick up a few things at Walter's IGA anyway."

A few minutes later, after gathering up her things, Nikki hopped back into the old white truck with Wade's mother behind the wheel.

"I'm sorry to see you go so soon," Donna said. "I hope Allie didn't chase you off. She might bare her claws, but don't worry, sugar. She's got nothing on you."

Nikki felt a flush invading her cheeks. "What do you mean?"

"Though she'd have you think otherwise, Wade's never really taken to her. She might be a glamour girl and even comes from big money, but truth is, she was just there when he was at rock bottom and vulnerable."

"Vulnerable?" Nikki couldn't picture *that* at all.

Donna continued on, as if she hadn't heard the implied question. "Don't let his smooth exterior fool you. Wade's a real soft touch and he's been burned for it, too. Badly. It's taken him a long time to get over it—if he even is over it."

Nikki recalled the brief exchange with Iris that Wade had squelched. She now wondered if that's what Donna referred to. "What happened, Donna?" she asked.

"What's the root of all the hostility between Wade and Dirk? It's more than just the ranch, isn't it?"

"Yes. It's much more than just the ranch."

"I thought so," Nikki replied. "I don't understand what Allison was saying about the horse torturing Wade. What did she mean?"

Donna's face contorted with emotion. A moment of silence followed. She looked like she wouldn't respond, but then drew a deep breath. "Has Wade told you anything about him and Dirk? How it was between them growing up?"

"A little. I gather they had a strong sibling rivalry."

"That's an understatement," Donna said. "When they were young boys Wade idolized Dirk, but things changed as they grew older. By high school Wade was determined not to be overshadowed by his brother. It all came to a head when they both fell for the same girl."

"Let me guess," Nikki said, "she was a pert blonde cheerleader and homecoming queen all rolled into one."

Donna gave a dry laugh. "Named Rachel Carson."

"And being the typical girl, she went for the bad boy?"

Donna nodded. "Yeah. Dirk was involved in rodeo back then and had a wild streak a country mile wide. What girl can resist that?"

"Only the ones who have their heads screwed on straight and aren't bent on self-destruction—unfortunately I speak from experience of the second kind. So what has their old rivalry to do with the present rift?"

"It didn't end with high school. Dirk and Rachel were a steady item all through college, but when they graduated, Dirk wasn't ready to settle down. Rachel had expectations, but out of the blue, Dirk up and enlisted in the Marines. When he left her without a ring or any promises, Rachel turned to Wade. One thing led to another."

"So this fierce antagonism is all because Wade stole Dirk's high school sweetheart?"

Another silence followed. "It's a bit more than that but it's not my place to say more." Donna shook her head with a look of profound regret. "It all ended very badly, and my boys have never been the same since." She sighed. "I don't think things will ever be straight between Wade and Dirk until they each find the right woman. Unfortunately, neither of them has been the least inclined to put himself out to look. Wade's a good man, Nikki. He's been through a lot and deserves a good woman." She eyed Nikki meaningfully. "A nice Southern girl might suit him real well."

"It could never work," Nikki said.

"Why not?"

"Because I'm not right for him at all. He needs someone more like—"

"Allison?" Donna supplied and shook her head. "No, sugar. She's not the one for Wade. I said he deserves a *good* woman."

"You don't care for her?" Nikki asked, still trying to wrap her mind around what she'd just heard.

Donna rolled her eyes. "I didn't raise my sons to fall for such a shallow and self-serving type. She might have designs on Wade, but if you ask me, she's just become a habit with him. It's never been serious. Now, *you* on the other hand, are another case altogether. He really *likes* you."

"Why would you think that?" Nikki protested. "He doesn't even *know* me."

Donna gave her a sly grin. "He must know you well enough to think his mama would approve. Else he wouldn't have brought you out here."

"It's not like that at all! You're reading way too much into this. I lost my ID. I had nowhere to go. He just took pity on me."

"Pity? You think that's all it is, do you?"

"Yes, I do. Besides, what makes you think *I'm* interested in your son? No offense, but he's simply not my type at all!"

Donna laughed outright. "You just keep telling yourself that, sugar—especially when he comes hightailin' it to Sheridan in a few hours looking for you."

———

Wade and Dirk arrived back at the ranch—dirty, dog-tired, and empty-handed, although they'd at least come to a truce of sorts after finding the animals—or at least the animal carcasses. The carnage, presumably by wolves, would have to be reported to Wildlife Services, and the BLM would need to be notified about the band of mustangs they'd discovered, but he'd leave all that for Dirk to deal with. Right now, Wade only had only one thing on his mind—Nikki.

He'd pushed the hell out of Skoal in haste to get back to the cabin and was still furious that she had ridden off alone. Only Redman's presence in the corral gave him any sense of relief. Thank God she'd found her way back safe and sound.

"Wade!" Allie rushed out to greet him the minute he'd dismounted. "So glad you're back. We have to talk. I have big news."

"It'll have to wait," he said, struggling to keep the scowl from his face and the apprehension out of his voice. "Where's Nikki?"

"Nikki?" Allie blinked. "Oh, she went back to Sheridan."

"Sheridan?" he repeated. She was gone again? "How? She doesn't have a car...or even a license for that matter."

"Your mother drove her." Allie gave a dismissive wave. "She said she needed to take care of some urgent business. Speaking of which, we have a new offer. The buyer's come up another two hundred thousand!"

"The Broncos player?" Dirk asked.

"Yes," she replied. "He's really hot to have the place as a hunting retreat and even says he doesn't care anything about the livestock. You're free to sell it off and keep *all* the money!"

"How generous considering it's my fucking stock," Dirk scoffed. "Tell him no deal."

Allie's jaw dropped. "What? Why?"

Dirk shrugged. "I don't like the Broncos."

"You are joking, right?" She cast a pleading look to Wade. "Please tell me he's jerking my chain."

Wade shrugged. "No can do. He probably means it."

Allie recoiled. "But there are two others who have a say in this. Right, Wade? You'll accept the deal, won't you?" She added in a frosty undertone. "I busted my ass to put this back together. You *won't* get another shot at this. I can promise you that!"

"Then you'll just have to work on my father until I get back."

"Get back?" Allie repeated dumbly. "What are you saying?"

"That I don't have time to discuss this right now."

"Look, Wade. I flew all the way from Denver for this!" she hissed.

"I'm sorry for your trouble, but the world doesn't turn on your command, Allie. I've got personal business to see to. We'll talk about this when I return."

Wade handed his horse off to his brother. "Take care of Skoal, will you?"

Dirk's scowl transformed to a smirk. "Sure thing, li'l bro. It's no skin off my nose if you're back to thinking with your prick."

Chapter 12

NIKKI CHECKED INTO THE MORIAH MOTEL, A TWELVE-room lodge on Main Street in Sheridan. The motel had wireless Internet and cable TV, and was only half a mile from the funeral home—a double blessing, given her lack of transportation. Although she'd have to deal with Wade eventually, the more distance she could keep between them in the meantime, the better.

After unpacking a few things, Nikki's stomach sounded a loud protest against two days of neglect. She'd only seen one restaurant when they drove through town, but it too was within walking distance. Hating to eat alone, and even worse, to become a subject of local speculation, Nikki called the Prospector Café to place a takeout order—a large burger with the works, beer-battered onion rings, a shake, and a slab of chocolate cake. Only a humongous caloric overload could even begin to soothe her hurt.

After hanging up the phone, she undressed for a much needed shower. She was in her bra and panties and had just turned on the tap when a knock sounded on the door. She froze with her heart in her throat. Wade? It was what she most wanted and most dreaded all at the same time.

Don't be ridiculous, Nikki. Regardless of what his mother had said, he'd never come to Sheridan with Allie waiting for him at the ranch. Still, she peered through the peephole. *Shit!* It *was* him, leaning on the door-jamb, hat pulled down over his eyes, and looking like sin incarnate.

"Open the door, Nikki," he said in a low voice. "We need to talk."

Leaving the chain on, she flipped the dead bolt and opened only a crack. "Go away, Wade. There's nothing to say."

"The hell there isn't!" he growled. "You left with some harebrained notions. We need to settle this. Now. C'mon. Open the door... Please." He sounded angry and frustrated, but it was his pleading look that did her in.

"All right," she sighed. "Just give me a minute, I'm not dressed."

"Don't go to any trouble on my behalf."

She closed the door on a snort and pulled out the least provocative thing she owned—an oversized Georgia Bulldogs T-shirt. The frown on his face when she opened the door almost made her laugh. It also told her she'd made the right choice.

"Your ugly alma mater wasn't quite what I'd hoped for."

"Speak your piece, Wade. My shower and dinner are waiting."

He doffed his hat and raked his hair. "Why'd you leave me like that?"

"Like what?" she asked, feigning indifference.

"Just slinking off like you did. I told you when I left with Dirk that we needed to talk about some things."

"Things? What things? We spent a night together. It was a mistake, but it's done. I just want to move past it now."

"Damn it! If you're put off because of Allie, I told you—it's just business."

"So you keep saying, but I got quite another impression."

"All right," he groaned. "I won't say there was *never* anything between us, because there was. *Past tense*. But it wasn't serious and it pretty much ended on this last trip of mine to Denver. If she insinuated anything different, she was just blowing smoke up your pretty ass."

"Look, Wade, I appreciate your desire to set things straight, but it truly doesn't matter to me. I came here to say good-bye to my dead father. That's it. As soon as I settle things, I'm gone. I don't want or need any complications."

He took a step toward her. "I wasn't looking for this either, sweetheart, but it's too late to turn back now. There's already something between us. I don't know what it is, or where it's going any more than you do, but I sure as hell want to ride it out and see."

"That's the difference between us. I don't. I told you it was a mistake, Wade. Why can't you get it through your thick skull? I don't want to continue this. Please just go now. If there's anything else we need to discuss, I'll make an appointment at your office on Monday."

"Appointment, my ass! I'm not done with *you* by half, and setting the record straight, darlin', you haven't had your fill of me either."

Nikki snorted. "There you go again with all that big talk. Is your ego really that inflated? Do you really think you're so irresistible?"

He advanced another step with a dangerous look.

"You're wasting your breath if you think to convince me you don't feel it too."

"That's where you're wrong." Another bold-faced lie. Last night was *all* she'd been able to think about, but that didn't mean she was fool enough to repeat it.

He laughed. "You're a piss-poor liar, Nikki Powell. And if you even draw another breath to protest, I swear I'll bury my face in that pretty little *nectarine* of yours until your mind is empty of any thought beyond how fast I can get my prick inside you."

Her breathing hitched as her mind filled with visions of his dirty promises.

As if reading her thoughts, his mouth came down on hers—deep, hot, and devouring, tangling her reason and emotion in knots and sending a ripple of raw lust ripping through her.

Wade held nothing back. His mouth was everywhere, on her mouth, her neck, nibbling her lobes, breathing nasty words in her ear, and purging her mind of every thought but what he'd just threatened to do. *Damn him!*

Powerless to resist, Nikki tumbled headlong into his arms, and into his kiss. Her brain cried out *insanity*, but he drove her to the brink of it every time he touched her. Her mouth and hands were equally hungry, growing more fevered and frenzied with every searing stroke of his tongue. Breaking apart for breath, Nikki gazed up at him, licking her kiss-swollen lips. "M-my shower is still running."

"Is it? Then maybe we should catch it together."

His slow, sexy smile sent a gush of liquid heat straight to her core.

Before she could utter a word of protest, he'd slid his

hands under her legs, and lifted her clean off the ground. Taking his cue, Nikki wrapped her legs tightly around him, panting and moaning between deep drugging kisses, as he carried her through the narrow doorway into the bathroom. They devoured one another until they were both gasping for air.

When Wade set her down, they rapidly shed clothing. Frantic to feel his hot skin under her hands, Nikki went to work on his buttons, ripping his shirt away to map her hands over his strong pecs and sculpted abs. While she fumbled with his belt, he balanced on one foot, toeing off his boots. Then his hands joined hers, tugging frantically at his zipper until he sprang out, big and hard. He kicked out of his jeans and then tore off her bulldog shirt and bra. Her panties followed.

With his hands firmly anchored on her hips, his hot gazed raked her from head to toe. Nikki shifted under his hungry stare, feeling self-conscious to be completely exposed in broad daylight. In the cabin, they'd made love in near darkness, with only the flickering light of the fire.

"Hot damn." A wolfish grin stretched his mouth. "I don't know that I've ever seen a prettier sight." He kissed her again, long and deep, releasing her only long enough to grab some soap before joining her in the shower.

Stripped of his clothes, Wade followed her into the steamy shower, kissing her again, long, lush, and deep. She was already achingly aroused, but just like last night, Wade seemed to be totally in control.

She wondered what it would take to make him come unglued.

"There's something I want, Wade." She was determined to send *him* over the edge with the same mindless want he so effortlessly wrested from her.

"Anything darlin.' Just name it."

In response, she pressed her palms against his chest, sending him backward under the shower head, forcing him to shut his eyes against the blast of streaming water. Hands shaking, she took up the bar of soap to begin an eager tactile exploration of his beautiful body. Wasn't it only a couple of days ago that she'd fantasized about this very thing? All six-feet-plus of his wet, male magnificence? But Wade naked, wet, and highly aroused was so much more than her imagination could ever have conjured.

Sliding her hands up and over his broad, muscular shoulders, she worked her way over his chest and torso slowly devouring every rock solid inch of him, until she was lost in lust. With her mouth, she worked her way down his body, noting the tightening in his jaw and compression of his lips as she traced the dark trail of hair leading to his erection. The sight of it, big, hard, and ready, made her insides clench with desire.

His eyes jerked open wide when she cupped his sac, gently fondling it, loving the weight of him in her hand. He drew a harsh breath when she wrapped her hand around his length, stroking, teasing, and squeezing until the urge to take him into her mouth overwhelmed her.

—⁓—

Wade sucked in a gasp when she gripped his thighs and sank to her knees. *Holy shit!* He hadn't expected *that* move. His hips bucked involuntarily at the sensation of her hot hungry mouth engulfing him to the root. Adding slick, sliding, strokes of her velvety tongue, she fondled his balls with soft, skillful, soap-slicked hands, while working him in and out with long, lush pulls and the sweet, hot suction of her mouth. With a reeling head and weak knees, Wade plastered one hand on the wall behind him and cupped the back of her head with the other. She responded by clutching his ass tighter and taking him deeper.

Sweet Jesus it was good. So damned good.

Oh, he'd had plenty of women go down on him, but mostly in reciprocation, or in Allie's case, as a means of coercion to get something she wanted. He'd never had a lover suck him off so eagerly. Wade gazed down at her just as she stole a look up at him, heedless of the water streaming down her face. Their gazes locked then his leveled on the beautiful, generous mouth that was driving him out of his mind.

His chest grew tight, his balls contracted. His knees threatened to give way. *Shit, if she doesn't stop soon… like now…* He drew a deep, wrenching breath, grinding his teeth against the urge to shoot his load into her mouth. It was almost more than he could bear but it wasn't how he'd wanted this to play out. Reaching down, he stroked his thumb over her lips, withdrawing himself with a groan and then pulling her back up to her feet. She'd blown more than his cock; she'd blown his effing mind.

"I didn't expect *that*, Nikki."

"I know." She smiled. "But it was what I wanted. We didn't have to stop, you know."

"Yes. We did."

He kissed her slow and deep, then took her hands in his, lathering them up, and then bringing them to her breasts. "My turn now," he said darkly.

"Your turn?"

"Yeah. I want you to wash yourself. Touch yourself."

With their joined hands, he guided her, soaping, caressing, fondling, and squeezing her breasts. "Don't stop." He released her hands, tonguing her ear and sucking her neck. "It turns me on to no end, Nikki. It's sexy as hell." Her gaze locked with his, He released her hands to make a more thorough exploration of her body.

She froze. "Is that really what you want?"

"Oh, yeah, sweetheart."

Her gaze narrowed. "Does this voyeuristic inclination extend to other things?"

"Like what?" he asked.

"Like watching me with someone else?"

"Fuck no!" he retorted. "If one man's not enough for you, I'm sorry. I'm just not into that shit. I don't share."

She returned a meaningful look. "Neither do I."

"Glad we got that straight up front." He kissed her hands one at a time and brought them back to her own body, sliding them slowly over her hips and belly. "Do this for me, darlin', and I'm all yours…anything you want."

"I'll hold you to that, Wade," she replied low and husky.

Nikki leaned against the shower wall, closing her eyes, and dropping her head back with a sigh. Letting water stream over her, she glided her hands over her breasts, molding and squeezing them together, offering him a visual banquet.

While she teased her nipples with one hand, she held the bar of soap in the other, guiding it downward over her belly, pausing to circle her navel and then stealing a daring look at him through her wet lashes before her hand continued its descent, plunging at last into her sexy hairless slit. "Is this what you wanted?" Her voice was breathless, her nipples pebbled as she slowly, tauntingly undulated against herself.

Holy hell. The erotic vision was suddenly too much.

With a guttural sound, Wade pinned her to the wall, shoving his thigh between hers, dipping his head and feasting on her breasts—licking, biting, sucking. She rode his leg as they clung together, writhing and grinding, cranking their need until he thought he would explode. She reached for his shaft and he clasped her wrist. He wanted her like hell, but he wouldn't last if she began pumping his cock.

"No you don't," he said. "I'm not done with you yet."

He released her wrist to grip her shoulders, spinning her before she could protest and then placing her hands on the shower wall above her head. Last night they'd fumbled in the dark. Now he was gonna take his damn sweet time.

"Spread your legs, sweetheart." He urged her thighs apart. "I want to feel that pretty ass of yours squeezing my dick."

Wade resumed his earlier slick and soapy survey of her body, concentrating now on her delicious ass. He loved her curvy womanly ass. He ran his hands over the smooth cheeks, eliciting a needy whimper from her when he took himself in hand, rubbing the soapy head of his cock along her ass crack. Stepping closer, he positioned his shaft between her cheeks.

Sweet Jesus.

The sight of his cock nestled inside her slick globes made him want to bend her over in the worst way, but he held himself back. Prolonging the mutual torment, he slid himself slowly up and down her cleft. She squirmed against him, urging in no uncertain terms.

"All in good time, darlin'," he growled in her ear, determined not to rush.

Still holding himself with one hand, he slid the other down her belly, over her baby-smooth mound and into her soap-slickened slit. Still stroking his cock up and down, Wade circled her clit with his thumb, coaxing her ever closer to climax. His hips rocked. His tempo increased. "Give it to me now, sweetheart," he urged, low and husky. "Come for me."

"I can't... I need... Please..." she begged between broken breaths.

"I live to please you, sweetheart." Wade plied his mouth to her shoulder, biting down softly as he plunged two fingers into her, pumping in and out even as he worked her clit. Her head fell back against his chest with a cry as her body squeezed his fingers and then let loose long spastic shudders that left her limp and dazed in his arms.

Wade held her upright until she came back down and then turned around with another long lingering kiss. He then cut off the water, long past ready to move onto new games in new places—like the bed.

Grabbing the towels, they dried each other between

more fevered kisses, and somehow managed to stumble into the bedroom. They toppled together onto the bed, where he rolled her on top and cupped her delectable ass.

Nikki was eager for more, rubbing her bare mons on the head of his prick, and purring like a cat about to get cream. He was primed, but when she raised her hips to impale herself on him, he gripped her hips and shook his head. "Not yet."

"But—" Her brows furrowed.

"Turnabout is fair play."

But he *wasn't* playing fair. He knew he was driving her insane with anticipation...with raw need. Hell, he was killing himself, too, but he had something to prove. This kind of chemistry didn't come along every day and he was gonna make damn sure she knew it.

He shifted his hands under her ass, urging her up his body, until she was straddling his face. Nikki gazed down at him wide-eyed, looking shy and uncertain. As his own gaze swept slowly, hungrily over her, he was overcome with the powerful urge to touch and taste every inch of her. Her heady, musky, mouthwatering scent wafted over him, engulfing and overpowering him with the urge to bury his face in her pretty little snatch.

He felt her resistance, but refused to be denied. He kissed her inner thigh and then the other, wet his lips, and then lowered her hips toward his questing mouth.

"No Wade," she gasped and tried to buck away. "You can't. Not like *this*."

"Wrong again. I intend to explore every luscious bit of you."

"B-but it's too...too...intimate."

His mouth twitched. "And what you did to me wasn't? Tit for tat, sweetheart."

"That was different."

"How? Because *you* were in control? Is that what this is really about? Are you afraid of giving it up?"

"No, that's not it at all." Her gaze wavered, belying her denial.

"Let me do this, Nikki," he coaxed. "I want to. I want to tongue you, taste you, drown myself in you. I want to look up at your face when you fall apart."

"But—"

"Shh." He placed his index finger over her mouth. "No more talk. Just shut your eyes now, empty your mind, let go and enjoy the ride." He slid her hands over her hips to cup her ass. She tensed under his hands, but he pulled her closer. Close enough to touch, to taste. He began gently, with soft and teasing flicks of his tongue, increasing to long deep lashes when she started rhythmically rocking her hips. Letting her set the cadence, he probing deeper, licking, swirling, and sucking, growing drunk on her tangy essence. He stole another gaze upward. Her lids were squeezed tight, her cheeks flushed, her lips softly parted. Her breaths came shorter, sharper.

His hands wandered over her sweet ass as he made love to her with his mouth, stroking, caressing, and then probing her passage in time with her undulating hips. She gripped the sides of his head, her fingers threading through his hair, clutching and clutching spastically as she careened toward climax. With one hand on her hips, he honed in on her clitoris, single-mindedly circling and sucking. Faster, harder, his sex-slickened fingers plunged and thrust, in and out, until her body seized and convulsed in the first waves of her orgasm.

She cried out, throwing her head back on a scream as she came against his mouth. Releasing her while she still quivered with the aftershocks, Wade flipped her onto her back and then gloved himself. Coming over her with elbows braced on either side, he watched her lids flutter shut as he sank into her depths with his own shudder of raw, unadulterated pleasure.

He stilled, buried to the root, basking in the sensation of being sheathed in her hot little snatch. Stealing a breath, he withdrew and drove into her again, alternating with short stabs and long drags until she came back to life beneath him. Clutching his ass, she met him stroke for stroke, panting squeezing, spurring him on. Wade ground his teeth, thrusting deeper, harder, finally giving her everything he'd been holding back.

Unaware of anything but the glistening sheen of sweat that coated them, the slick friction, and sultry slap of flesh on flesh, Wade increased his tempo, pounding ruthlessly into her until her legs trembled and her passage milked him with rhythmic contractions of another climax. His chest tightened. His balls drew up. Several more hammering thrusts sent his orgasm crashing over him, in long, shuddering, mind-melting spasms. He withdrew, collapsing beside her and pulling her into his arms even as he fought for breath. Nikki gazed into his eyes with a soft laugh. He looked down at her with a feigned scowl. "You thought that was *funny*?"

"No." She chuckled again. "Not funny. I think I'm delirious."

"As in deliriously happy? As in 'You're hands down the best I've ever had, Wade'?"

Her smile faded. "Without a doubt."

Her words humbled him. He couldn't begin to fathom what Nikki did to him. Maybe it was that she was so damned responsive…so warm…so real after two women who'd only used him; Rachel to get to Dirk, and Allie, purely for recreation. Whatever it was, he couldn't get enough of this Nikki.

"You think so?" He nuzzled her. "Just give me a little time to recover, sweetheart, 'cause we're only getting started." Everything about *this*, about them, together, felt so damn good.

And *that* thought jarred him to the core.

Chapter 13

WADE DOZED WITH LIPS PARTED ON A HALF SMILE—
an expression of supreme contentment that made
Nikki's heart surge. Wade was so considerate, so atten-
tive. Everything about him drove her wild. He was everything she never even dared to hope for—intelligent,
charming, and, sweet heaven, the man knew how to use
his mouth and hands.

But while her body was sated, her mind was restless, overwhelming her with doubts and fears. It was
so good with him, it nearly scared the hell out of
her. How long would they continue burning hot and
bright—in a frenzied fever of lust—before their shooting star crashed to earth? How soon before he lost
interest and sought greener pastures? Men like him
always did.

*Why are you torturing yourself like this? It was beau-
tiful. It was incredible, but you already know it can't go
anywhere. Just let it be, Nikki.*

She shifted, her thigh inadvertently brushing his
shaft. It stirred instantly back to life. Wade opened his
eyes on a lazy smile. "Time for round three already?"

Nikki's stomach answered with a loud and embar-
rassing growl.

He gave her a mock frown. "Hungry for something
besides me then?"

"Well, yeah," she confessed. "I ordered food hours

ago. After all this exercise, I think I'm in real danger
of perishing."

He whipped the sheets away and sat her up. "Get
dressed and I'll make it up to you."

Nikki took another quick shower and dressed while
Wade went to the Prospector to pay for the food she'd
never picked up. He said he'd also make a detour to
the drugstore to replace the condoms they'd used. She
hadn't brought much for clothing, given the airline baggage restrictions and the brevity of her planned stay,
but had at least packed a simple slim black dress for
the funeral. She decided to wear it now along with a
pair of black pumps and thigh highs. By the time Wade
returned, she'd pinned her hair up and applied a bit
of makeup.

His whistle of appreciation made her glad she'd ex-
pended the effort.

"Looks like we're headed out of Sheridan."

"What do you mean?"

"I'm not about to take you to the Prospector or the
Wagon Wheel looking like that."

"Then, where are we going?" she asked.

"I've got a place in mind," he replied cryptically.

They headed back toward Twin Bridges, driving the
ten miles in companionable silence with Wade's left
hand guiding the wheel of the Lexus and his right resting
on her thigh. It was a casual gesture, but the implied pos-
sessiveness incited a fluttery feeling in Nikki's stomach.

The vibe between them had relaxed in the past few
hours, morphing into something that felt comfortable
but with an underlying excitement. There was an edge of
sexual tension between them that hadn't even begun to

abate. Even after several bouts of lovemaking, Nikki still thought she'd combust with a look or touch from him.

They pulled up in front of an old brick building on Main Street. "It's rustic, but The Old Hotel is one of the better places around here. The cuisine choices are slim pickin's once you leave greater Bozeman, but there are a few well-kept secrets around these parts."

They entered a small but cozy dining room with knotty pine flooring, floral valances over mullioned windows, and fewer than a dozen oak tables, with mismatched chairs and calico cushions.

"It reminds me of MeeMaw's kitchen, and not much bigger either," Nikki remarked in bemusement.

"Yeah," he agreed. "But I promise it's not your *MeeMaw's* home cookin'. The owners moved here from Hawaii and have brought quite an international flair to our little neck of the woods."

"Hello, Wade!" the hostess greeted them. "Just the two of you?"

He nodded. "Paula, this is Nicole, up from Atlanta. I wanted to show her that Twin Bridges isn't completely without sophistication. I'm glad you had something available tonight without a reservation."

"Things slow down this time of year," Paula said and led them to a table in the corner. "A month ago would have been another story."

Nikki waited for Wade to pull out her chair, meeting his grin with a smile. She sat and looked for a menu.

"They don't print one," Wade explained, reading her mind. "The dishes change weekly based on availability of local meat and produce."

"And the chef's whim," Paula added. She handed

Wade the beer and wine list. "Would you care for a cocktail or some wine? Or do you want to hear the specials first?"

"Beck's nonalcoholic for me. Wine, Nikki?" Wade asked. "They have a good selection here."

"Nonalcoholic?" Nikki regarded him with a wrinkled brow.

"Yeah, I don't drink...anymore."

"But the other night?" She recalled the frosty mugs of brew he'd drunk, and then realized she'd never seen the bottles. "Do you mean to say you were drinking unleaded while you were tanking me up?"

He flashed a guilty grin.

"How underhanded." Her head reeled from Wade's interesting little revelation, but this wasn't the moment to press him. She opted to file it for later.

"You needed it. I didn't." He shrugged. "As to wine, I'd recommend a red to accompany the cowboy sushi."

"*Cowboy sushi?*"

"It's the house specialty," Paula said. "We had to get creative due to the lack of sushi-grade fish in Montana."

"What do you use instead of fish?" Nikki asked.

"Barbecue beef."

"Barbecue sushi? You're kidding, right?"

"Not at all." Paula laughed. "My husband came up with the idea. We think of it as our unique fusion of East and West. It's a nigiri roll with rice, vegetables, and the barbecue beef that we serve with red chili aioli in place of wasabi and soy sauce."

"All right," Nikki said. "I'm game for this gastronomic adventure."

Paula then rattled off the choice of appetizers:

mushroom and brie tarts with balsamic syrup or blue-crab cakes with lemon parmesan aioli. She followed with the entrées, several featuring home-raised Montana beef and lamb. "We also serve American Kobe beef upon request."

"American Kobe?" Nikki looked to Wade. "Isn't that what your brother is raising?"

"Yes," Paula said. "The Flying K is our supplier."

"And how is my brother's experiment working out?" Wade asked.

"Surprisingly, we're finding many people prefer the taste of it over domestic beef."

"Really? That is surprising."

"Wade, why don't you choose for both of us," Nikki suggested.

"Sure thing." He ordered several dishes to sample and a bottle of Australian Shiraz.

"Shiraz?" Nikki asked when Paula departed.

He leaned back in his chair with a slow sexy smile. "Of all the things every man should know—a woman's hot spots and a few good wines are foremost."

Nikki chuckled. "I wouldn't dare dispute your expertise on the first, so I suppose I'll just have to trust you on the second."

"You *should* trust me more often," he said, suddenly serious.

"What's that supposed to mean?"

"It means I want to know why you're so guarded."

"Experience," she replied, running a finger over the rim of her glass. "It's been a tough teacher. I haven't always exercised the best judgment where relationships with men are concerned."

"You can't let one asshole ruin your life."

"One? Try six."

"Six, eh?"

"Yeah. Sad, isn't it?"

"Maybe seven's your lucky number."

She licked her lips, studying his expression with uncertainty. "Are you suggesting *this* is the start of something?"

"The start?" He made a scoffing sound. "Sweetheart, I think we're well past the starting gate, don't you?"

"Most men don't like to think in those kinda terms."

"I told you I'm not most men." Wade caught her hand in his. "C'mon, Nikki, tell me about it. Tell me why you think you can't trust men. Why you don't want to trust me. I wanna understand."

"I really don't want to. I don't see the point in digging up the past."

"Sometimes it helps to unload the baggage."

Nikki felt suddenly maudlin. "What does it matter? Why do you want to invest the effort when I'm leaving in a few days?"

His blue gaze caught and held hers. "You're here with me now, aren't you?"

"Yeah," she said softly. "I'm here."

She licked her dry lips and then took another sip of wine, wishing this time with him could go on forever, but knowing it couldn't.

"You're already thinking about leaving," he accused. "I can see it in your eyes."

"Because it's reality, Wade. I have a job to return to. A life."

"Tell me about it," he said.

"Tell you what?"

"Your life…*you*."

"Me?" She gave a dry laugh. "There's not much to say."

"Sure there is. And I'm interested in hearing it. You're different from other women. I wanna understand what makes you tick."

"You and me both," she snorted.

"I'm serious, sweetheart. I want to get to know you better."

"I'd rather talk about you," she replied.

He leaned back in his chair with an air of nonchalance. "What do you want to know? Ask away."

"All right, Wade, I propose a question for a question. I'll answer yours if you answer mine."

He nodded. "Fair enough."

"Then I'll let you start. What do you want to know?"

"Anything." He shrugged. "Everything."

"Care to narrow it down a little?"

He pursed his mouth and then took a thoughtful sip of his beer. "Tell me why you despise cowboys."

"I don't really," Nikki finally confessed. "Truth is, men in hats and boots have always been a fatal attraction."

His gaze narrowed. "Fatal? Care to elaborate?"

"Not particularly," she said. "I already told you I've made a lot of stupid mistakes."

"But you promised to answer my questions."

She sucked in a big breath and blew it out on a resign sigh. "You really wanna hear this?"

"I do. I want to know what I'm dealing with."

"All right. The first one was named Donnie. He was a hotshot bronc rider I met at the Toccoa Rodeo. I was seventeen and moonstruck. He got me drunk and took my virginity in the back of his horse trailer. Not five minutes later, he asked me to blow his best friend while he watched. I refused and he dumped me for a more willing buckle-bunny."

"Ah," he said. "I guess that explains your earlier concern about voyeurism."

"Yeah. I'm a bit gun-shy about stuff like that."

"And after Donnie?" he prompted her.

"Unfortunately, my cowboy addiction didn't end with him. After I left home, me and my girlfriends got into line dancing and started hitting the honky-tonks. We went to Wild Bill's in Duluth every Friday night and the Electric Cowboy on Saturdays. 'Course you can guess the kinda guys I met at those places—a long string of drinkers, liars, cheaters—all of them wearing tight Wranglers, boots, and hats. The last one was the worst though—the one I thought I was going to marry."

"What happened?"

"I caught him in bed with my roommate. I should have seen it coming, but I didn't want to. I kicked them both out and they married six months later. The worst part of it wasn't the boyfriend but losing my best friend since grade school. We'd always dreamed of being each other's maids of honor one day. Needless to say, I didn't get an invitation to their wedding—not that I would have gone," she added dryly. "That was the last cowboy I dated."

"I'm sorry… Well, about the best friend, not about the fiancé," he confessed.

"Me too. It's hard to get over a betrayal like that. So you see why I've sworn off cowboys?"

Wade shook his head with a snort. "Hate to burst your bubble, sweetheart, but a Stetson and a pair of Tony Lamas doesn't make a man a cowboy."

"I think maybe I'm starting to know the difference," she said.

"I'm glad to hear that."

"My turn now," she said.

Wade shrugged. "I'm an open book."

"So you claim, but somehow I doubt that."

"Try me, sweetheart."

"All right. There are several things I'd like to know."

"Oh yeah?" He poured her a second glass of wine.

"For starters, is there a particular reason why you don't drink?"

His hand froze. His expression hardened. "Yeah… there's a reason."

"Does it have anything to do with your brother?" She wanted to know him so badly, to understand him, but judging by his hardening expression, this was dangerous territory.

His gaze narrowed. "Why would you ask that?"

Nikki tried to affect an offhand manner. "Just something your mother said."

Wade stared up at the ceiling. "There's a helluva lot of history behind our antagonism."

"Care to elaborate?"

"Not *particularly*," he echoed her earlier reply.

"You've already broken the rules. I just answered half a dozen of your questions. You can't expect me to lay out my history for your inspection without reciprocation. Doesn't seem fair, Wade."

He inhaled and then released it with an exasperated

sound. "Look, it's nothing personal, Nikki. I'll talk about anything else, but I'd rather forget that entire chapter of my life."

"And you think I enjoyed dredging up mine?" She looked away, picked up her glass, and drained it.

They finished the meal in a strained silence. The dinner was excellent, much better than Nikki had expected. The Kobe beef accompanied by the Shiraz had been a particular delight to her taste buds, but now she could hardly taste it. She stared at her plate, idly pushing the food around.

Leaning in close, Wade covered her hand with his. He said nothing for a moment, as if he waited to see if she'd snatch it away. When she didn't, he brought her palm to his lips and kissed it.

"I'm sorry, Nikki. Please understand I'm not trying to be secretive. I just didn't expect any of this to come up tonight. Something happened four years ago that part of me is still dealing with, and I'm not ready to talk about it yet. Can you please *try* to understand that?"

The pain in his eyes was unmistakable.

Her resentment evaporated. "Yes," she answered softly. "I can understand. There's a number of things I'm trying to work out too. It's part of the reason I came here—to figure things out."

"I promise you I'm trying real hard to work through it all."

"I'm sorry I pressed you."

"There's nothing for you to be sorry about. I'm the one who said I'd answer your questions and then reneged."

"Let's just agree to let it go. I'm OK with that. Really," she insisted.

Wade moved to pour her another glass of wine.

"I think I've had enough already."

"It's a shame to waste a good wine."

"What? Are you thinking to have your wicked way with me?"

"I was more hoping you'd want to have yours with me." His answering look made her mouth go dry. "You devastate me, Nikki. Do you know that?"

"Me?" She gave an incredulous laugh.

"Yes. *You*. I haven't wanted anyone this bad in a very long time. Hell…" He raked his hair with a self-deprecating laugh. "I don't know that I've *ever* wanted anyone this bad." His gaze slid down to her mouth while a half smile hovered over his. "I'm sitting here looking at you with my mind bursting with all the things I still want to do to you."

"Even after this afternoon?" She was growing flushed and it definitely wasn't the wine.

"This afternoon only whetted my appetite for more. Hell, if this table had a decent cover on it, I'd slide my hand up those sleek, smooth thighs of yours right here and now."

Nikki stifled a gasp and squeezed her thighs against the sudden warm gush.

His mouth curved into a slow, knowing smile. "Am I making you wet? So easily, Nikki?"

"Yes, damn you!" she hissed.

He chuckled. "Then, darlin', I'm making it my personal goal to have you squirming in your panties before the check comes."

"Oh really?" She arched a brow. "What if I'm not wearing any?"

She noted his heavy swallow with a surge of satisfaction. "Are you sure you want to go there, Wade? I thought I'd already demonstrated that two can play these games."

"I'm up for it all right." His grin stretched wide and sexy. "Bring it on, darlin'…gimme all you got."

Paula arrived a moment later with the check. Wade reached for his wallet, but Nikki stalled him. "You know, on second thought, I think I'd like some dessert."

"Anything in particular?" Paula asked.

"Yes. I have a sudden craving for some fresh fruit. Do you have any peaches or nectarines perhaps? With cream." She slanted Wade a sultry look. "I love nice, juicy peaches drowning in cream, don't you, Wade?"

His pupils flared. He wet his lips.

"I'm so sorry," Paula said, "but we don't have peaches. Could I tempt you with something else? We have a luscious triple chocolate terrine or crème brûlée. We also have a mascarpone, dark chocolate, and hazelnut cannoli."

"Cannoli?" Nikki's gaze darted to Wade. "You mean those wonderful Italian pastries that you eat with your fingers?"

"Yes. These are excellent."

"Perfect." Nikki smiled deviously.

"Coffee with that?"

"No, thank you. Just the cannoli."

"Oh no you don't," Wade murmured in warning the moment Paula departed.

"Oh yes, Wade. I love cannoli. Especially if they're big and long and so filled to bursting that they explode in your mouth."

His jaw twitched. "Stop. Just stop now or I'll make you *so* sorry."

"No, I'm going to savor the hell out of my dessert. I'm going to lick and nibble all the chocolate off the outside, and then swish my tongue on the inside. And after that, I'll suck out all the filling…and you're going to watch me."

"The hell I will!" Leaping out of his chair, Wade threw a wad of bills on the table. He then jerked Nikki to her feet, hauling her out the front door before dessert ever arrived.

They'd barely made it to the car before he pinned her up against the passenger door. He dipped his head and groaned, "I told you I'd make you sorry."

She licked her lips with a shiver of excitement. "How?"

"I'm going to make you whimper and beg, Nikki. I'm going to reduce you to a puddle of moist, hot mayhem." His hand was already sliding up her dress and gliding over her thighs.

"You can't! We're in the parking lot." She protested on a gasp at the paradoxical softness of his calloused hands.

He nuzzled her neck, lightly abrading her skin with his deliciously bristled jaw, his breath a heated caress against her skin. "It's dark enough…and I'm blocking you from view. Hmm. I *like* these, Nikki. A lot." He traced the lace band at the top of her stockings with his fingers. "Now I'm wondering…"

She knew what he was thinking. Her remark about her

lack of panties was meant to drive him wild. She hissed
when he probed higher and dipped into her wetness with
a grunt of deep satisfaction. But he didn't stop there. He
slid deeper, his fingers exploring her passage, his thumb
slowly circling, swirling the wetness around her clit.

He took her ear lobe between his teeth. "You're going
to sob for mercy, Nicole."

Dear God, we're in a freaking parking lot!

But he wasn't about to let her off the hook. *No indeed-y.* Not after how brazenly she'd teased him. Her
heart raced. His fingers plunged, working in and out of
her sheath. Her breath came in short pants. Her legs felt
like jelly. She clutched his shoulders for balance as her
climax formed low in her belly, like a storm gaining
momentum by the minute.

"Please, Wade," she whispered.

"That wasn't good enough, Nikki." He swirled his
hot tongue in her ear. "How about 'pretty please with
sugar on top'?"

"Yes. Yes. With sugar on top," she whimpered. He
settled into a ruthless rhythm that was making her mind
melt. "You *have* to stop this now."

"You want me to *stop*, darlin'? Maybe I wasn't
clear. I want you to beg me to make you come. *Here
and now*. Then you're going to straddle my lap and ride
me cowgirl-style until we fog every damned window in
that SUV."

His words were all it took to send her toppling over
the edge. She buried her face in his chest until the ripples ceased. She watched on wobbly legs, growing more
breathless at the dark glitter in his blue eyes as Wade
prepared to make as good on his second promise as he

had on the first. Opening the passenger door, he adjusted the seat all the way back. Then, instead of handing her up, he climbed inside and pulled her onto his lap.

"Wouldn't the backseat be easier?" she asked.

"Not how I want you," he growled, yanking her shoes off and throwing them over his shoulder. "I gave you yours, sweetheart. This one's all mine. Turn around. Straddle me," he commanded, his manner brusque, his actions almost rough as he guided her into the position he wanted—facing away from him.

She heard the metallic slide of his zipper and then felt his hips rise and shift as he shoved his jeans down. She felt the release of his hard hot flesh as it sprang free, slapping her ass. She reached behind, eager to feel it in her hands, but he stopped her.

"Hands on the dashboard, sweetheart. You're gonna need it."

He reached under her dress, pushing it up over her hips and held it there, his big hands holding her firmly at the waist. He thrust into her. Hard. Deep. Giving her no time to catch her breath. The next seconds unfurled in a frantic and feral frenzy. Squeezing her waist and jerking her hips, Wade pounded mercilessly into her from behind, the slap of flesh filling the air even as Nikki's gasps painted clouds all over the windshield. He climaxed fast and hard, his lungs emptying with a primal roar. She immediately followed, pulsing around him as he came in searing surges until they both slumped into the seat, still joined, but sedated and spent.

It was raw, animalistic, and probably the hottest sex she'd ever known.

Chapter 14

AFTER RECOVERING SUFFICIENTLY FROM THEIR MUTUAL post-climactic coma, they drove back to Sheridan. Nikki's hand was on *his* thigh this time. His arm was curled around her shoulders and her head rested against his chest while a Josh Turner ballad played on the radio.

Nikki shut her eyes, basking in his warmth, his generosity, and his strength. She still marveled at how Wade had been there for her ever since she'd arrived in Montana. She wasn't used to having anyone stand up for her. But as a total stranger, he had come to her rescue when she desperately needed someone. In three short days, he'd managed to turn her world inside out and upside down; more than any man she'd ever known.

She slanted him a sidelong look and found him gazing back at her, a soft smile stretching his mouth — a smile that enveloped her in its warm cocoon. He pulled her tighter against him. She nuzzled her face into his shirt just to breathe in his heady musky male scent. God, how she wished again that this could last forever — but she was leaving in a matter of days. The thought jarred her, shattering her serenity as effectively as his voice broke the silence.

"There's something weighing on me, Nikki. Something I think you deserve to know."

Shit! Damn it all to hell! She should have known he

was too damned good to be true. Part of her had been waiting for just this moment. Her pulse roared in her ears as she waited for the other shoe to drop. "There's someone else?"

"No." He shook his head. "It's nothing like that, but there's something that's had me real messed up for a long time. I told you at dinner that I wasn't ready to talk about it, but maybe it's time to unload my own baggage. I don't want to screw up again. It's too important to me. *You* are too important to me."

His words made her heart skip. She waited in silence for him to continue.

"I've been stuck in the past for almost four years, but I really want to get over it now. I *want* to move on and put it all behind me. You've made me want to do that, Nikki. Can you understand?"

"I'm not sure I do." Her gaze searched his face. "You wanna explain?"

"There's a lot more to the story I told you about my brother and me. There's a shitload more." He drew a breath, and then exhaled. "Damn, this is hard."

"Is it about Rachel? Your mother told me how she came between you and Dirk, but I still don't understand how your rivalry over a high school sweetheart could destroy your relationship."

He hesitated again, his mouth firming. "She wasn't just a girlfriend, Nikki. Rachel was my wife."

Nikki's head reeled as if she'd been struck by a two-by-four. His confession just didn't fit. It distorted everything she thought she knew about him. "Your wife?" she repeated once she found her voice again. "You were married?"

"Yup. For three and a half years. I took up with her right after Dirk left for the Marines. We got engaged six months before he was scheduled to come home. I think I was afraid she'd dump me as soon as he returned so I married her." He gave a bitter laugh. "I made the biggest goddamn mistake of my life at twenty-four years old—and we all three paid for it."

Nikki studied the planes of his face, grown harsh in the shadows. As hard as it was for her to hear all this it was much harder on him. "Did you love her?" she asked softly.

"Thought I did, but it was really a mixed bag of infatuation and ego."

She was almost afraid to ask but still had to know. "What about her?"

"She wanted *him*."

"So she only used you to get back at your brother?"

"Damn right she did. She was hurt and resentful and wanted to hurt him back. I should have known better, maybe deep down I did, but dumb-ass that I was…I married her anyway."

"But if he left without any promises, did he really want her? Did he love her?" Nikki asked.

He shook his head with a dry laugh. "That's the million-dollar question."

"He didn't try to stop it, did he?"

"Nope." He shook his head. "Not a word. I think that's what Rae was secretly hoping for—that he'd show up and put an end to her and me, but he didn't."

"So he didn't come home for your wedding?"

"No. When he heard the news he re-upped for another three years." Wade stared straight ahead at the road. "And then got half his leg blown off in Afghanistan."

"I begin to understand the rift," she said. "But it was his decision, Wade."

"But would it have happened if I hadn't done what I did?"

"You can't know either way and it's not worth torturing yourself over. So what happened after you and Rachel married?"

"We lived in Denver for a couple of years until after I passed the bar. I was still clerking for Evans then—that's Allie's father," he explained. "After that, I got a good job offer back East. I probably would have accepted it if the economy hadn't taken a major nosedive. That was in 2008 when everything went to shit and the ranch had to turn most of the help loose. Dirk was still in Iraq and the ol' man was on the verge of losing everything, so I came back home to do what I could. The marriage was already shaky before I started doing double duty, trying to get established in Bozeman while still helping at the ranch on the weekends. Maybe it could have worked out between us had we gone away, but family loyalty rooted me here."

"It obviously made a difference," she said. "You still have the ranch."

"Yeah. The ranch," he said bitterly. "It's always been all about the ranch. I saved the place and I resent the hell out of the price I paid. Between the practice and the ranch, I didn't have any time at all for Rachel. She'd set her sights on finding a PR job in the city. Had we gone east, she probably could have found something to make her feel more fulfilled, but there was nothing for her back here.

"She was bored and lonely, and started pressing me

to start a family. I wasn't ready for that. I already carried such a load and I resented her for pressuring me. When my hours in Bozeman got even longer I suggested she spend more time at the ranch. It kept her busy and seemed like a good solution…until Dirk came home, a situation that had trouble written all over it."

"Yeah. I can see why."

"Dirk was a real train wreck. Pushed us all away and spent a lot of time alone in that little shack up on the mountain. Maybe I thought his injuries and pissy attitude would put her off, but the harder Dirk pushed Rae away, the more I think she wanted him. I should have seen it coming."

Nikki *felt* his pain. "They betrayed you?"

"I've got no proof," he replied. "And Dirk still denies it, but Rachel wanted out of the marriage within a couple months of his coming back. What was I to make of that?"

"But you said she was already unhappy before. Maybe you're jumping to conclusions. She and Dirk aren't together, right? So what happened? Where is she now?"

"She's gone," he answered woodenly.

"Gone? She left you both?"

"You might say that… She's dead."

A cold shiver ran up Nikki's spine. "Dead?"

"It was an accident."

Nikki suddenly remembered Iris's reference to an accident and the warning look Wade had given her. "How?" Nikki asked. "She didn't…"

"I don't think it was suicide…but we'll never know for certain. She showed up at my office late one afternoon. Said she wanted a divorce. There was an ugly scene. I didn't go home that night, but neither did she. Next morning the cops knocked on my door saying they pulled her car out of the river."

"Dear God, I can't even imagine what that must have been like for you."

"Hell, I barely even remember it now. That's how hard and fast I hit the bottle. But the worst part was getting the autopsy report a week later showing elevated levels of HCG."

Nikki lips suddenly went dry. "HCG? She was pregnant?"

"Yeah…she hadn't told me that part. It was early enough that maybe she didn't even know. To this day I don't know if it was mine or not. We hadn't had much of a love life for months, but I couldn't bring myself to ask for a DNA test. The whole thing—Dirk's leg, her death, and the baby… It was all too much. The guilt hit me. Hard. I didn't know how to deal with any of it. I went on an eighteen-month bender that nearly killed me."

"How could you blame yourself? It wasn't your fault!"

"Wasn't it? Deep down, I always knew she was still his and being honest, that's probably why I wanted her so bad. And Dirk probably wouldn't have reenlisted— wouldn't have lost his leg, if I hadn't married her. I might not carry all the blame, but a good chunk of it sits rightfully on my shoulders."

They pulled into the motel parking lot. Wade cut the engine. They sat in silence.

"How did you quit drinking?" she finally asked. "Family intervention?"

"Intervention?" Wade laughed outright. "Yeah, I

guess you could call it that since Dirk's fist intervened with my body—multiple times. He laid me out flat for a week with three cracked ribs, a punctured lung, and a busted-up face."

"*That* was why he broke your nose?"

Her question seemed to break the tension.

Wade rubbed the hump with a laugh. "Yeah. It's a bad idea to piss off a Marine, even one missing a leg. On the bright side, the time I spent in the hospital dried me out. Shortly after that incident, my father had his heart attack. My brother and I have had a tenuous truce ever since."

"It doesn't *look* much like a truce."

"No," he agreed. "Not lately. The problems started up again when I decided to try and unload the ranch. I don't want it and the folks can't handle it anymore, but Dirk, stubborn ass that he is, won't give in. That's why Allie came today, Nikki. She has an offer—a very respectable offer. It was also the reason I was in Denver a few days ago, but it all came apart at the last minute. Allie blamed me and we had a major falling out over it."

"So you *were* romantically involved with Allie?"

"Romantically? No. There was nothing remotely 'romantic' about our relationship. Ever. We were always business associates first and occasional bedmates second. That's how it was. Always. It was convenient, but it was never more than sex."

"Maybe that's how it was for you, but I think it's more than that where *she's* concerned."

"Regardless of what she may have insinuated, it's exactly how I told you it is, Nikki. I was OK with that for a long time—emotionally detached sex. Maybe it was what I needed at the time, or maybe I just didn't know any better. But now I do. And *now* you have the *whole* ugly truth."

Nikki sat there stunned, barely able to digest all he'd told her. His story—the pain and guilt he carried, placing his own desires second to his family's needs. She couldn't believe how wrong she'd been about him, about everything.

"I'm so sorry," she whispered. "I had no idea about any of this."

"How could you? But I'm not looking for your pity, Nicole. I just thought you needed to know." He paused. "No. Let me rephrase that, I *needed you* to know."

"Why?"

"Why? Because we're damn good together."

Her chest tightened until it was hard to breathe. But then she mentally corrected him by filling in the two words he'd obviously left out—In. Bed.

In her heart she wanted to believe this was really turning into something special, but how could it be anything more than infatuation? He was smart, successful, responsible, and self-sacrificing to a fault. His love and affection for his family were obvious and genuine, and his charm and sex appeal were off the meter. Wade was so far out of her league that she couldn't even fathom what he saw in her—which also meant it couldn't possibly work.

Moments later he walked her to the door with a long and lingering goodnight kiss, a kiss that promised more that she'd ever dreamed, but she reminded herself it was *only* a dream. As wonderful as this felt right now, she knew not to trust it. They'd only know each other a few days. How many times had she thrown herself into a relationship only to live with regret later? Besides that, they lived two thousand miles apart. Nikki swore not to torture herself with impossible hopes, and to accept this thing with Wade for the short-term fling that it inevitably was.

———⁓———

With reluctance, Wade left Nikki alone at the motel. It was damned hard not to coerce her back into bed when he'd walked her to the door. Maybe if he'd brought a change of clothes he would have stayed, but they both needed sleep, and he sure as hell needed some perspective.

He'd already lost his head over her. He didn't know what had possessed him to walk out on Allie when she'd brought a multimillion dollar deal with her. He'd never done anything so irresponsible—at least not since he'd sobered up. But for the first time in years he'd shoved his responsibilities and worries aside in single-minded pursuit of what *he* wanted.

He'd been so wrapped up in Nikki that he'd forgotten everything else, but now he worried about the repercussions as he drove back to the ranch. He hoped to hell Allie was still waiting there. Maybe he'd pissed her off so bad she'd gone back to Denver. Any other woman probably would have after the way he'd left her standing there, but then again this was Allie, and Allie was all about business. It was the biggest reason he'd never entertained the thought of marriage with her.

If he ever did remarry—not that he'd given any thought to ever taking that step again—he wanted a

soul mate, not a business partner, a woman to complement, rather than compete with him. He wanted the
yin to his yang, someone spontaneous and genuine,
someone like Nikki, who warmed his insides as well
as his bed.

Nikki seemed his match in almost every way that
mattered. She was smart and sexy as hell but most im-
portantly, she made him laugh. Made him forget. He
loved her smile and her Southern sass. Not that he could
ever forget her sweet womanly ass or the way she gazed
up at him with her beautiful passion-filled eyes, with
her silky brown hair splayed out on the pillow as he
drove into her. He wanted to go to bed with her and
wake up and make love to her all the hours in between.
Hell, he was getting hard again just thinking about her.
He didn't recall any other woman who'd ever affected
him this way.

When he drove into the yard, he saw Allie's Escalade.
He was filled with relief that the deal was still on the
table but dreaded having to smooth her ruffled feathers
after walking out on her. Not wanting to wake anyone,
Wade pulled off his boots at the door and crept up the
stairs to his room, scowling at the crack of light shining
under his door. *She wouldn't.* He turned the knob and
pushed the door open. *Hell yeah, she would.* Allie was
in his bed.

She threw down her copy of *Cosmo* and cocked a
brow. "Fun night?"

"What the hell are you doing here?"

"You said we'd talk when you got back." She flashed
an overbright smile. "Well, now you're back."

"It's one a.m."

"You walked out on me today. I didn't appreciate that, Wade. Are you just eager to score a new piece of ass or is all this just payback because I was pissed and wouldn't let you stay the other night? Either way, you didn't have to take it that far. All you really had to do was ask me nicely."

"I shouldn't have to beg for favors like a lap-dog, Allie."

"All right, maybe I took a few things for granted," she conceded. "But now that we've cleared the air, let's just put all this behind us. Come to bed now, baby." She patted the space beside her. "I'm willing to kiss and make up now. And make-up sex is always the best kind."

"I don't think so."

"What do you mean?" Her eyes flickered with disbelief.

"C'mon, Allie. You and I both know this is going nowhere and that's no good for either of us."

"What do you mean going nowhere? We have an ideal alliance, Wade. Daddy's retiring soon and—"

"If I ever marry again, it'll be for a *wife*, not an *alliance*, and if I take over the firm, it'll be by merit not nepotism."

She licked her lips with a nervous laugh. "But what is marriage if not the ultimate partnership?"

Wade shook his head. "Look, Allie, you're a beautiful woman. I respect your intelligence and your drive, but those aren't the qualities I want in a long-term relationship."

She rose naked from the bed, approaching him with a sway of her lithe hips. "You never complained about our kind of relationship before. You're not thinking clearly, Wade. You have your future to consider. Once you've unloaded this money-sucking ranch and move back to Denver—"

"But that's just it, Allie. I *am* thinking about my future now. For the first time in a long while I'm thinking about what I want from life."

"And you'll have it all. In Denver. With me."

"I'm not sure that's what I want."

"But it's all we've talked about for years," she insisted.

"No," he said. "It's all *you've* talked about. I was always ambivalent about the idea at best."

"But Wade. Baby," she was *almost* pleading. "It only makes *sense* for us to be together. Imagine what you could achieve with Daddy's connections. A few years in Denver and you could even pursue the political career you've talked about."

Shit. How he hated this. Although she had her faults, Allie had been a friend when friends were scarce. He took her gently by the shoulders. "Allie, I'm sorry. It was never my intent to hurt you—"

Her green eyes flashed. "Then don't!"

"—but we both just need to move on now." Even as he apologized, he knew it was only stung pride. She didn't love him any more than he loved her.

"You'll regret this big-time once she's gone and you aren't thinking with your prick anymore."

"This goes much deeper than just Nikki and you know it."

"I don't think so," she said. "Everything was fine before. C'mon, Wade, I've accepted your punitive damages with grace." She came closer, wrapping her arms around his neck. "Can't we just start over?"

He gently uncoiled her arms. "No, Allie. We're going in different directions. We don't want the same things."

"What things? Success? Financial freedom? Tell me who *doesn't* want those things? Especially these days?"

"How about love…affection…family?"

Her gaze wavered. For the first time in their acquaintance she looked unsure of herself.

"Family? You mean *kids*? Is that what this is about? That I don't want kids?" She gave a sigh of capitulation. "If I'd known that was a deal-breaker for you—"

"Deal-breaker? You just don't get it at all."

"Oh, I get it all right." She retreated a step, hugging herself. "I just thought you were more intelligent. Three days ago Little Miss Peaches comes along and suddenly you have visions of the stay-at-home wife and one-point-five kids? I had no idea you clung to such ridiculous fantasies of domestic bliss—especially given how things worked out for you the *first* time."

"You *don't* want to go there," he growled. "Please just accept that we're done, Allie."

"Fine," she answered tightly. "Have it your way." She snatched up her robe from the foot of the bed, jerked her arms into it, and then stood with her back to him for several minutes. Thank God, no false tears materialized. After a protracted silence she asked, "What about the deal?"

Wade shook his head. This was Allie after all. The woman was hard as nails. "I think we should take the deal and run," he said. "I don't expect Dirk will change his mind, but I'll talk to the ol' man in the morning."

"Good." She made her exit with a tight smile. "I'm glad to know you're still *capable* of thinking with your *brain*."

Chapter 15

NIKKI AWOKE TO A SHARP THUMP ON THE DOOR. SHE rolled over to look at the clock and groaned. *Nine a.m.?* She never slept that late! *Damn.* She should have been up hours ago. FedEx might even have delivered her license by now. She hauled herself out of bed and peered through the peep hole. There was Wade holding two steaming cups of coffee and balancing on one leg as he prepared to thump the door with his boot again.

She raked her hands through her hair, knowing it was a futile effort. At least he'd already seen her at her worst. She pulled the chain, flipped the dead bolt, and opened the door.

"Did I wake you? Sorry about that," he said with a sheepish look. "My hands were full." He handed her a coffee and stared disparagingly at her Bulldogs T-shirt. "Sweetheart, that ugly-ass bulldog's gotta go."

"Doesn't do it for you?" She gave him a coy look. "Should I just take it off?"

"Not if you want to get anything done today." He set the coffee down to nuzzle her neck.

"Why's that?" she asked already growing breathless with lust. "You'd hold me hostage here?"

"Something like that." He smirked. "I have rope in the truck."

Her brows pulled together. "Rope?"

His grin broadened. "Yeah. It comes in handy from time to time. There's all kinds of interesting things I can do with rope, but I guess it'll have to wait till another time. I've got some business to take care of today, and so do you."

"Lemme just shower. I'll be quick," she said, and slipped into the bathroom. She opened the door again, just wide enough to toss the T-shirt at him.

He caught it with one hand. "I'll probably burn this, you know."

"Then what will I sleep in?"

"Nothing's fine with me, but if that doesn't suit I'll get you anything you like from Victoria's Secret. I'll take you when we go back to Bozeman."

Toothbrush in mouth, she stuck her head out again. "While I appreciate your generosity, when I return to Bozeman, it'll more than likely be to the airport, not to the mall."

"Speaking of that…" He suddenly stood in the doorway, she caught his gaze in the mirror as it slid down to linger on her ass with a wistful look, before sliding back up to meet her face in the mirror. "Are you sure you want to be in such a hurry to go back to Georgia?"

She stole another look at him and their gazes caught in the mirror. She swallowed hard, almost choking on toothpaste when he flashed that heart-stopping grin. Wade's smile warmed her to the core. His laugh sent ripples to her belly. *Dear God, the things he did with his mouth*. It was all she could do to keep herself in check every time he looked at her.

I've got it bad.

This was infatuation of the worst possible kind—the

SLOW HAND   193

kind that could be so easily mistaken for something deeper, the kind that had the power to devastate her.

He cupped her ass and applied a lingering kiss to her bare shoulder. His warm lips sent a ripple of pleasure through her followed by something more—something that made her chest feel tight. She turned and planted her palms on his chest, pushing him toward the door. "I—I need to get dressed now."

———

Iris handed Nikki an express package from the Georgia Department of Driver's Services the moment she entered Wade's office. She received it with mixed feelings. Now that she had her license she could finally attend to the matter that brought her to Montana to begin with. With Wade's help she should be able to get everything taken care of and be on a plane by the weekend. As much as it hurt to think about leaving, the sooner she returned to Atlanta, the better. Every hour spent with Wade only made leaving him harder. Shaking off these thoughts, she tore the envelope open and scowled at the horrible mug shot.

"You see. It's me, Nicole Marie Powell." She waved her license under Wade's nose. "Am I now *authenticated* to your satisfaction? Can I *finally* take care of what brought me here?"

"It'll do." He gave her a grim nod. Nikki noted the shift in demeanor that occurred the moment they'd walked into his office. He continued with no sign of the teasing glint she'd become so accustomed to. "The first order of business is obtaining a death certificate so you can properly dispose of your father's remains. Iris should be able to help expedite that process."

"Sure, Wade," his assistant answered. "I'll be glad to help."

"Thanks." He turned back to Nikki. "I've got a number of things to take care of at the courthouse and then I'll be back to read you the will."

"So formal all of a sudden, *Counselor*?" she teased. "Is this because you've exchanged your cowboy hat for your lawyer hat?"

"Something like that," he replied "Since I'm now working for you, *Miz Powell*, there is indeed a protocol to follow. I'll be back in an hour or two."

Puzzled by this abrupt about-face, Nikki watched his departure with a hollow feeling in her chest. Iris pursed her lips with a knowing head shake.

"He knows you're leaving soon and doesn't like it. Not one bit. He hasn't taken any real interest in anyone since—"

"Rachel?" Nikki volunteered.

"So he told you about that, did he?" She didn't look too surprised. "He doesn't like to talk about her, you know."

"I can't imagine he does, given the circumstances."

"It says a lot that he told *you*." She gave Nikki a conspiratorial smile.

Nikki wondered once more if there really could be more to his feelings than she was willing to let herself believe. If only she had more time to find out. But two thousand miles distance was impossible to ignore.

"Iris, do you think we can see about that death certificate now?"

"Sure thing," Iris replied. "Usually the process takes several days, but Wade has influence with a number of people in Helena. The man has more charm than should be legal. But I guess you know that." She winked. "If I fax a request with his signature, we should get an official copy for the mortuary in a day or two."

———⟨⟩⟨⟩⟨⟩———

Wade left his office in a black mood. What the hell was wrong with him to be in such a funk over a woman he'd known for all of four days? Truth is, he hadn't even realized how empty his life was until she'd come along and burrowed into that hollow spot he didn't know existed. She'd be leaving in a matter of days, and suddenly, how to deal with that was his biggest dilemma.

For the longest time he'd thought much like Allie— that professional and financial success would bring contentment—but it never had. There was always a bigger case or a more lucrative deal to chase. If he let ambition and avarice take hold in his life he'd never have enough. Material possessions and professional achievements offered little more than empty promises of happiness. He had his parents to thank for that bit of clarity. They'd ridden the trail together for almost forty years in a strong and happy marriage. Deep down he wanted the same thing, but had given up hope of ever having it after making such a fuckup of his marriage with Rachel. But they'd never really stood a chance with a relationship built on lies. She'd said her vows to one man while secretly pining for another. A lasting relationship had to be built on truth, honesty, and trust.

Trust. That thought brought him back to Nikki. He'd done his damnedest to earn hers, but sensed she still held back. He understood her guardedness but still wished he could pound the shit out of every one of the assholes who'd made her so wary of men.

"Where's Nikki?" Wade asked Iris when he returned to his office. He felt a surge of irrational panic in discovering her gone. "I told her I'd be reviewing the will with her when I got back."

"She went over to Wells Fargo," Iris replied. "Now that she has her ID, she said she was going to get some cash to pay you back, and then see about replacing her credit cards so she can rent a car."

"There's no need for her to do all that when I'm happy to drive her."

For some strange reason the idea rankled him. Maybe he'd just gotten used to being needed, or maybe it was the novelty of it after three years of Allie, but he liked taking care of Nikki.

"I don't think she likes depending on you so much, Wade. She strikes me as an independent kinda gal, one used to taking care of herself."

"Maybe more than she should have to," Wade remarked almost to himself.

Thinking it better to handle the will outside of the office, he grabbed the documents and a couple of sets of keys, jammed everything in his coat pockets, and made a beeline for the bank.

"Hey, Jane!" He greeted the branch manager with a smile. His mood instantly lightened at the sight of Nikki. "Did you get everything taken care of for Miz Powell?"

"I think so," Jane replied.

"They've been wonderful," Nikki gushed. "I've got the cash I need to repay you and a replacement debit card. I don't think I'll need anything else until I get home. Thanks again, Jane," Nikki finished. She stood and gathered up her things.

"If you do need anything else, all you have to do is ask," Wade said.

"I appreciate that." Nikki gave him a rueful look. "But I've taken advantage of you far too much already."

"It's not like that, sweetheart. I haven't done anything for you I didn't *want* to do."

"No matter how you want to wrap it, I've still been an imposition on you."

He grabbed her arm and turned her to face him. "You are not hearing me, Nikki. Your so-called imposition has been the best thing that's happened to me in years."

"You can't mean that," she said.

"Yeah." He grinned. "I do. All work and no play makes Wade a dull boy."

"Are you finished at your office now?" she asked.

"For a while. I didn't have anything pressing. I also had Iris move a few appointments to next week so I can help you settle your father's estate."

"Estate?" She laughed. "Is that what they call a pickup truck and travel trailer in Montana? The last I heard that was the sum of his worldly possessions."

"That so? Well, there may be a bit more than you think," he answered vaguely.

"What do you mean?"

"While I wish I could, I can't put this off any longer." He pressed his hand to the small of her back. "C'mon. Let's take a drive. There's something you need to see."

As they drove north on Highway 287 toward Sheridan, Nikki lost herself again in the majesty of the snowcapped mountains and endless acres of grassy pastures where cattle and horses contentedly grazed. She wondered what it would be like to make a life in such a rugged place. Could she be happy in a place like this? Alone, probably not. But with Wade? That was another question completely.

He'd implied that he'd like her to stay, but how could she even consider ditching her life? Not that there was so very much worth returning to but it was the principle of the thing. They barely knew each other. Maybe it was something the young and stupid Nikki would have done, but she was older and wiser now, right? She tasted the salty tang of blood on her tongue and realized she'd chewed through her lip.

"Are you completely surrounded by mountains here?" she asked, more to distract herself than anything else.

"Yeah," he replied, "but the winters are surprisingly mild. The Ruby Valley is insulated by seven ranges. That's the Tobacco Root range." He pointed to the craggy white peaks to the east.

"Where are we going?" she asked when he turned off the main highway and onto what appeared to be a service road.

"You'll see soon enough. We're almost there," he answered cryptically. "That's the Ruby River, known for some of the best angling in the country."

"Angling?"

"Fly fishing," he explained. "People come to this part of the country from all over the world for our prize sport fishing. The Ruby produces rainbows, cutthroats, and graylings in abundance because access is so limited."

"Limited? Why's that?"

"Most of this section of river is privately owned. Like this prime piece right here."

They continued driving almost parallel to the river, then lost it for a few miles until the road abruptly ended. Wade turned into a private drive, came to a stop, and then killed the engine. He gestured toward the river and mountains. "This tract stretches north for two miles, along the riverbank, then extends just as far in that direction."

Nikki gazed over the wide expanse of treeless landscape covered with grass that stretched for miles. The beauty touched her. "Is this someone's farm?" She noted the log cabin and old pickup truck parked out front. "There's no cattle here. Is it abandoned?"

"You might say that. This place used to be a fishing and hunting retreat, but no one's using it anymore."

"Is it yours?" she asked, wondering why they were here and where this was going.

"No. It's not mine."

"Then why are we here? Who owns it?"

"You do."

Chapter 16

"ME?" NIKKI GASPED. "HOW? I DON'T UNDERSTAND."

Wade turned to face her, his eyes sober, his expression stern. "Pursuant to the execution of Raymond Powell's will, you, Nicole Marie Powell, are the sole owner of over twelve hundred prime acres in Madison County, Montana."

"This was my father's place?" Nikki was at first stunned, then fury set in. "Damn you, Wade! You knew all this time and said nothing?"

"No." He shook his head. "I didn't know *all* of it until this morning when I reviewed the will. The property is yours free and clear, by the way. I pulled all the real estate records and checked for liens."

"You've let me fret and worry for days!" she accused. "Why didn't you tell me any of this before?"

"I couldn't. I swear my hands were tied. Legally, you had no claim to any of it until you could prove your identity, and now you have."

Nikki was still shaking her head in disbelief when Wade came around to open her door. She hopped down from the SUV and Wade followed, retrieving a thick envelope from his breast pocket. He pulled out a bundle of documents from inside. "According to the plat, there's two full sections here."

"Sections? What's a section?"

"In farming communities land is generally parceled in sections and quarter sections. A section is a square mile."

Nikki stared dumbfounded over the river, the grass-land, and the mountains. "You're saying I own *two square miles* of this? How on earth did my father come by all this land? He was a heavy equipment mechanic, for goodness' sake! You are really telling me that he owned this cabin and *twelve hundred acres*?"

"Yup. According to Evans, who closed the deals, your father fell in love with the fishing here twenty years ago and bought the first quarter section when land was still cheap as dirt. He added to the property over time when his investments started to pay off."

"What's the place worth?" she asked.

Wade pursed his mouth and dug his boot heel into the dirt. "Can't really say."

"Surely you have *some* idea," she insisted.

"Real estate's taken a nosedive in the past few years, but my best guess would be about fifteen hundred per acre for the grasslands, plus the cabin."

Nikki's performed mental calculations that made her heart race. "That's got be close to two million dollars!"

"More than that, sweetheart. The waterfront is worth a lot more than the grazing lands. Allie could tell you more precisely about the entire value. She specializes in large acreage and high-end ranch properties. There's something else," he said. "Your father also left behind a substantial sum in bonds and annuities."

"Wh-what do you mean substantial?"

"Close to a quarter million. Your father was either an incredibly savvy investor, or a damned lucky bastard. He bought several thousand dollars of cheap tech stocks in the late eighties—including shares in Dell Computer and Microsoft—that paid off big-time."

"Oh. My. God." Nikki's legs gave way beneath her. She sank to the ground, gaping up at Wade. "I can't believe all this. It's all too much to process."

He squatted down with a grin. "Kinda puts matters in a different light, don't you think? Now you can tell your be-atch of a boss to kiss your sweet, rosy-red ass."

Nikki stared at the cabin shaking her head in disbelief. "This is really all mine?"

"Yes, Nikki." Wade pulled her back to her feet and then produced a key. "I have his will in my hands. We still need to go through the formalities. Do you want to step inside for that?"

"I don't know," she murmured. "It doesn't seem right somehow."

"You shouldn't feel that way," Wade said.

When he unlocked the door and Nikki stepped over the threshold, she wished she had taken some time to prepare herself. The cabin was a distinctly a male domain with a bearskin rug in front of the big stone fireplace that dominated the great room. A number of mounted animal heads—elk, mountain sheep, and even a bison hung on the walls. She noted the hunting rifles and fishing poles and the copies of fishing and hunting magazines scattered about the room. Her gaze lit on a pair of reading glasses sitting beside a half pack of Marlboro red cigarettes, on the side table by an overstuffed leather recliner. "I remember so little about him. I feel like an intruder." She stroked her fingers over the glasses, suddenly struck by the loss of the daddy she never knew.

"You're his daughter. Just because you didn't see each other for a long time, doesn't mean he forgot that fact. Wanna sit down now, Nikki? I need to go through the legalities of your inheritance. It'll only take a few minutes." He handed her a copy.

"All right. But I'm not very fluent in legalese. No doubt you'll need to interpret it all for me."

"I doubt that. It's a very simple will." Wade opened the enveloped he'd carried inside, reading aloud, "I, Raymond Albert Powell, of Twin Bridges, Montana, revoke all former wills and codicils and declare this to be my Last Will and Testament. I am not currently married. The name of my only child is Nicole Marie Powell. All references in this Will to my 'children' are references to the above-named child. I direct that all my debts and funeral expenses be paid from my estate. I direct that my residuary estate be distributed to Nicole Marie Powell of Decatur, Georgia…"

Nikki stood abruptly, blinking against the burning sensation in her eyes. "He tried to make things right between us, but I wouldn't let him."

Wade stopped reading. "It's not your fault, Nikki. You were only a child."

"Not when I got the letter," she argued. "I told you he sent me one. It arrived eighteen months ago but I never read it…well, not until it was too late. I shoved it in a desk drawer and ignored it. I didn't want to read it, but I couldn't bring myself to destroy it either. Then when I got the phone call from the hospital telling me Daddy had died, I finally opened it."

"What did he say?"

"That he was sorry and that he'd always loved me. He said he couldn't have raised me because he was on the road all the time. He admitted he drank too much and thought I was better off with my mom. He swore he sent me letters and cards for years, but they all came back as return to sender. I never knew anything about them."

She swallowed down the lump in her throat and covertly wiped her leaky eyes on her sleeve. "My mother had no right to do that to me—to let me believe a lie. My father and I were estranged for twenty years because of it. I always thought he was a no-account loser like all the rest of them, but that wasn't exactly true. Maybe he wasn't the best man in the world, and he certainly wasn't the ideal father, but he was the only one I had. I feel cheated, Wade. The whole damned thing just makes me feel so sad and angry…and empty."

"So it was his letter that brought you up here?"

"Yeah. I came hoping to find a way to deal with it all. I thought maybe I could lay all the hurt to rest along with him."

"It hardly seems that he blamed you, given he left everything he owned to you. Shall I continue?"

She nodded.

"I nominate Nicole Marie Powell, of Decatur, Georgia, as the executor without bond or security. My executor shall have the right to administer my estate without unnecessary intervention by the probate court…"

As Wade read through the articles of the will, Nikki wandered the rest of the great room. The television was the old tube-style. Beside it was a rack of VHS tapes. She couldn't remember the last time she'd even seen a VCR and tapes. She squatted down to the case wondering what he liked to watch. *Deliverance* and *A River Runs Through It* held places of honor on the top shelf.

Beside these were a number of John Wayne and Clint Eastwood movies and then there was another well-worn case—*They Call Me Trinity*.

She pulled that one loose and almost choked on the vivid memory of eating Jiffy Pop and watching old spaghetti Westerns with him. He'd loved both. So had she. "I didn't even know him," Nikki interrupted. "How can this all be mine? Somehow, it just doesn't seem right."

"You don't have to accept the bequest if you don't want it," Wade said. "You could always donate it to some worthy charity—maybe even start one of your own." One corner of his mouth kicked up. "How about a foundation to save the pronghorn antelope?"

"Are they endangered?" She gave him a dubious look.

"No. Not yet, but you could be proactive."

His levity did the trick. Nikki couldn't help grinning back. He always seemed to know just what she needed. She loved that about him—how easily he read and understood her. "I admit I feel guilty about the inheritance," she said. "But I'm not crazy. Of course I want it. I just have to get used to the whole idea."

"Yeah, you do have a lot to think about. Let me finish up the rest of this with you."

"How much more is there?" she asked.

"Only another two pages," he said. "Mostly legal jargon that protects you from liability."

"Go ahead." She nodded, only half listening until he got to the end.

"I, Raymond Albert Powell, the Testator, sign my name to this instrument this 5th day of June 2008, and do thereby execute it as my free and voluntary act for the purposes expressed in this Will, and that I am of sound mind and under no constraint or undue influence." Wade looked up. "It was witnessed and filed by Jack Evans. Everything's in perfect order, Nikki. Will you be changing your travel plans now?"

"Is this my *lawyer* asking?"

"No." He came behind, wrapping his big arms around her. "I checked *that* hat at the door."

She closed her eyes and inhaled him. God, it felt so damned good to be wrapped in Wade. She let her head drop back against the warm and solid wall of his chest. She wished the feeling could last forever, but knew it couldn't. His life was here and hers was two thousand miles away. It was just getting so damn hard to remember that. *If wishes were horses, Nikki…*

At length, she pulled herself out of his arms. "How long will it take to settle everything?"

"Guess you want the lawyer now instead?" He released her with a sigh. "Although Montana probate law is pretty simple, there's still a time-sensitive process you need to follow. It begins with posting a death notice in the paper that has to run for three weeks to flush out creditors. Then you have insurance policies to deal with, financial documents to transfer, as well as locating all of his account statements. This includes insurance, bank, brokerage, social security, unpaid bills, and his prior tax returns. You'll need to find the title to the truck and the deed to the house in order to get those titles transferred. This all has to be done before you can dispose of any assets. There's a shitload of paperwork."

"So, how long?" she repeated.

"Given the size of the inheritance, it'll be several weeks at least, more likely a few months."

"Months?" She stepped back with a frown. "I can't do that. I only have until the end of the week. My flight is Friday. I can maybe stay one more day, but if I'm not home by Sunday, my job is at risk."

"You're still planning to leave? You really need to rethink that plan. Settling your father's estate is going to take some time."

"Can't I hire you to take care of things for me? That's what you do, isn't it?"

"Yes. It's what I do—at a considerable cost. I could help you dispose of assets and close out the estate, if that's what you want, but my time is expensive, Nikki. I'd have to bill you for simple things that you could do yourself for free. I don't have a choice in that. It's not my practice."

"How much are we talking about?"

"The legal fees in settling an estate often run into thousands. So, you see? In the long run, it would be worth it for you to stick around."

"But I have a job—"

"That you hate."

"A family—"

"That you hardly speak to."

"How do you know that?" she asked defensively.

"You've been stranded here, for all intents and purposes, and you haven't called any of them."

"No. I haven't," she confessed. "I have a half sister I'm somewhat close to, but she's a major screwup, and my mother—well, don't even get me started there."

"Got a house or do you rent?" he asked.

"I rent."

"Got a dog?"

"Nope."

"A cat?"

She shook her head.

"How about a goldfish?"

She laughed outright this time.

"Then what's keeping you there?" he asked.

"What are you suggesting? That I just stay here in Montana?"

He shrugged. "It's not so bad. I think it might even grow on you if you give it a chance, though Bozeman might be a better fit for you since you're a city girl."

"But what would I even do with myself? What is there for me here?"

"Do you really need to ask?" He bent his head and plied a warm kiss to her neck. "I'd sure like to think I could make it worth your while to stay."

She shook her head, tamping down the shiver of lust. She wondered what it would be like to spend every night with him. To spend her life with him. His suggestion both thrilled and scared her witless. "I can't believe you're even saying this. We've only known each other a few days."

"Long enough for me to know I don't want you to go yet."

Yet. Nikki latched onto that word and held it tight as she pulled once more out of his arms. "Why try to turn this into something that could never work out? Your life is here and mine is a couple thousand miles away. For all that, it might as well be in the next galaxy."

"It's not so complicated, Nikki. You've just said so yourself. People do it all the time. Move to new places. Start over. Just look at Bill and Paula."

"The couple from the restaurant?"

"Yeah. They had a life in Hawaii. Now they have a new one in Montana. Doesn't sound like there's much to hold you in Georgia, is there?"

"How can you expect me to just walk away from my entire life?"

"Why can't you trust in this, Nikki? Why can't you trust *me*?"

Trust. How many times had she made that mistake before—trusted pretty words and promises? Though she wanted to believe Wade, she couldn't suppress the doubts. Nikki clenched her teeth, her protective instincts kicking in full force. Why would he want her when no one else ever had?

"Maybe because it's too good to be true. Damsel in distress is rescued by a charming cowboy in his not-so-gleaming white pickup and they live happily ever after?"

"Why not?" he said.

"Because it's a fairy tale, Wade. I don't believe in fairy tales."

"Bullshit," he hissed and spun her around. "Don't try to feed me that line. You think whatever this is comes along every day? I've sure as hell not experienced it. You can't just ignore it and *hope* it goes away, 'cause I won't let you, and it won't anyway. We fit. Can't you see that?"

Hope it goes away? In time she hoped it would, but right now the ache in her chest was excruciating. "You say all these things *now*. Maybe you even mean them *now*, but it will all change. I already know it can't last. Feelings always fade with time."

"Why do you want to believe that? Why are you fighting me when all I want to do is *prove* this is real?

That I *want* you?" He made an exasperated sound. "Damn it, Nicole! Do I look like a man who doesn't know his own mind?"

"But it can't work," she insisted. "I have no family here, no friends, and no connections. I'd only have you and I don't like the idea of being totally dependent on one person."

"Because it requires trust?" he said. "How can you be so cynical? Hell, if anyone has cause for cynicism it's me. Yet, here I stand with open arms."

He spread them wide and her heart slammed in her chest. It was all she could do *not* to throw herself into his arms, but this whole idea was crazy. Common sense held her back.

"Please," she pleaded. "Let's not ruin this with pointless arguments. I'm going to take care of my father and then I'm going back home to Georgia."

"Are you sure that's what you really want?"

No. It wasn't what she really wanted, but she'd made far too many mistakes from emotional decisions. It would be so easy to let go…to let herself believe in him but she refused ever again to let her feelings overrule her good sense.

"How can I possibly know what I want?" she replied. "For the first time, I'm going to have the freedom to do whatever I like. Now I need time to figure out exactly what that is."

She ventured to the window to look out over the shimmering river. "I think I'll bring his ashes back here to the river. It's what drew him to Montana, after all. I can't help feeling it's what he would have wanted."

"He didn't state a preference so the choice is yours."

She turned back from the window and announced,

"I'm going to check out of the Moriah and stay here for a few days."

"Here?"

"Yes. I might as well. The electricity is still on, isn't it?"

"Nothing's been disconnected yet," Wade replied.

"Then it makes no sense for me to pay for a motel. It'll still be a couple of days before I get the death certificate so I'd like to use this opportunity to go through his personal effects. It's going to take some time and I only have a few days to do it. When the death certificate arrives, I'll go back to Sheridan and take care of the arrangements for his cremation."

"If you stay here, you won't get anything else done," he argued. "There's no Internet connection and the cellular signal is iffy at best."

"Then I'll sort through everything I find over the next day or two and bring it all back with me to your office."

"You don't have a car," he argued.

"What about my father's truck? I have my license now. Can't I have use of it?"

"Yeah. You can use it. The truck is fully insured." Wade retrieved a set of keys and wallet from his pocket and dropped them in her hand.

"Thank you, Wade."

"Please, Nikki. Come back to the ranch with me tonight and I'll help you with all of this tomorrow."

"With Allie there?" She snorted. "Yeah, right."

"I told you there's nothing—"

"I believe you, but it would still be awkward as hell."

"Then I'll stay here with you."

"No," she said softly. "I have a lot to do and so

do you. I've already monopolized far too much of your time. Besides, I need to be alone to think about everything."

"Are you *telling* me to leave? If that's what you really want, say the word."

She didn't answer straight away. "It's probably for the best."

"I'm not comfortable with you staying here by yourself, Nikki. It's too remote."

She bristled at that. "Since when did you become my keeper?"

"I'd say about the minute I laid eyes on you, sweetheart."

"Really?" She spun on him, hands on hips. "I've been taking care of myself just fine for the past decade— thank you very much."

"Do you really like it that way?"

"Yes," she spat. He held her gaze and probed deeply. "Well, not always," she finally confessed.

"Then why are you doing this?" he asked.

"Doing what?"

"Pushing me away when I only want to help you. I get the feeling you've been trying to sabotage this thing between us from the start, and I'll be damned if I can figure out why."

Was it true? Was she subconsciously trying to sabotage herself just to prove she was right and he was wrong? At a loss for reply, she opened her mouth, and then closed it again.

Wade walked out shaking his head and cursing under his breath, the door slamming behind him. Nikki shut her eyes to that vision, his expression of pain and frustration.

She stood with her back to the door, fighting the well of tears, listening for the car engine and the crunch of gravel beneath his wheels. Minutes later, she was surprised instead by the crash of splintering wood.

What the heck?

She cracked the blinds to find Wade standing beside a wood pile, shirtsleeves rolled up and ax in hand. Any other man she'd ever been involved with would have torn out of the drive in a cloud of burning rubber after such an argument, gotten drunk, and then looked for someone new to screw.

Wade wasn't any other man.

She tried to tear herself away, but her feet were nailed to the floor, and eyes glued to the window. After a few more stokes of the ax, he slammed it into the block to pull off his shirt. He threw it down and then yanked the ax head back out of the block. This was a side of him she'd not yet seen—the angry outdoorsman. Watching the play of his flexing muscles, Nikki's mouth went dry. God, he was one gorgeous man. Wade was everything she thought she could never have. What kind of fool was she to be inside feeling sorry for herself when he was still here and still hers…for three more days.

Wade had to leave the cabin before he exploded. The last thing he needed was to act like an asshole, make a big scene, and give her a legitimate reason to mistrust him. He'd then have about a snowball's chance in hell of getting her to stay. By the way she was pushing him away he knew he was already on shaky ground. It seemed all he'd done was piss her off by pushing her.

Why the hell was this happening? He'd just bared his damn soul to her. He'd *never* done that before, yet she seemed all too prepared to walk right out of his life. Now he felt like a real jackass, but he was desperate to buy more time with her. The thought of her leaving in three days nearly had him in a tailspin.

In retrospect, maybe he should have given her some time to sort out her feelings about her father before springing anything else one her. He should have waited instead of pressuring her for decisions she wasn't yet prepared to make. She didn't need the added stress of his emotions right now. He took in a ragged breath and exhaled on a curse. "Fucked that up good, didn't you, cowboy?"

He was frustrated as hell and even more pissed off at himself. Hell, what he really wanted was a stiff drink—a mighty dangerous thought after two-and-a-half agonizing years of sobriety.

He needed to blow off steam something fierce, but couldn't leave her here alone. Desperate for something, *anything* to occupy his mind and body, Wade paced the yard until spotting an ax lying against the wood shed. It'd been a helluva long time since he'd split a log, but under present circumstances, it seemed the ideal therapy.

Discarding his jacket, he rolled up his sleeves, and picked up the ax. His actions were thoughtless and methodical. Standing the log on end, he raised the ax, and then slammed it down with splintering force. Mechanically, he stacked the two pieces, then grabbed the next log. It was mindless work, but he threw himself into it with a vengeance, relishing each blow of the ax, until his muscles screamed and his lungs burned. He'd no doubt regret this like hell in the morning, but it felt damned good right now.

He didn't know how long he'd been at it before he noticed her leaning against the pickup, watching. Judging by the four-foot-high wood pile, it must have been at least an hour. Although the temperature probably wasn't much above fifty degrees, he'd long since shed his shirt. He paused to wipe the sweat from his brow. Their gazes met briefly, silently, before he focused back on the task. Slamming the ax down again with a crash, he threw two more logs onto the pile.

"I'm sorry," she said.

"For what?" He paused again, leaning on the ax handle. "I should be the one to apologize for making demands you're not ready for. I guess I'm just used to going after what I want."

"And also accustomed to getting it?" she supplied.

"Yeah," he confessed. "I'm ruthless when I want something, Nikki. And I want you. I don't like being thwarted." He took up the ax again.

"It wasn't fair, Wade. I have so much to think about. I'm feeling very overwhelmed. Why does it have to be all or nothing with you? We don't exactly live in the Stone Age, you know. There's cell phones, texting...and airplanes." He noticed she spoke the last word with a grimace.

"So what are you suggesting? Weekly Skype sex?" He drove the ax down again, planting the ax head solidly into the chopping block and then snatched up his shirt.

"That's exactly my point, Wade. How can you expect me to give up my life when I don't know if there's anything more between us than just great chemistry? Can't we just wait this out a bit and see?"

He went to her, pinning his arms on either side of her. "Do you intend for us to see other people?"

"No. Do you?"

"I'm not the one who's ambivalent."

"I just need some time to think."

"How long?" he demanded. He knew he was being an asshole. Again. But he was damned if he'd make it easy on her.

"I don't know."

"You complain that I want all or nothing, but you seem to want it *both ways*. You can't have your cake and eat it too, Nikki. I'm not interested in a protracted long-distance relationship."

A hurt look flared in her eyes. "So *you* want to see other people?"

"No. Damn it! That's not what I'm saying. I'm looking for your trust. I want you. Here."

"I want you too," she admitted softly. He recognized the flicker of lust. "*Want* isn't a problem for me. That part isn't an issue at all." Her gaze met his, and then tracked lower, sweeping slowly over his torso. An unmistakable look of hunger flared in her eyes. Her hands followed her gaze, sliding down his sweat-slickened chest and abs to toy with his belt buckle.

"That isn't how I meant it," he said.

She licked her lips then traced his fly with her fingers. "But I did. We still have three days together, Wade..."

He knew what she wanted and was resentful as hell that she'd initiate sex when they hadn't resolved anything. "Don't play with me, Nikki," he growled. "You're running hot and cold and I don't like it."

Her gaze flickered up at him with uncertainty. "So you don't want to?"

He was growing rock-hard despite himself, which only pissed him off even more. Yes, he wanted her. He didn't think he'd ever stop wanting her. As if reading his thoughts, she pulled his head down to kiss him greedily, drawing his tongue into her mouth. The contact sent a jolt of molten lust through him. His frustration suddenly found a new outlet.

He lifted her, guiding her legs around his waist. She clung to him with feverish kisses as he walked around to the back of the truck, removing one hand from her ass only long enough to drop the tailgate. The minute he set her down, they went to work on buttons and zippers. He pulled off her boots, tossing them on the ground, then kissed and licked down her belly as she wriggled out of her jeans. His mouth wandered over her thighs, before stopping to suck her through the thin fabric of her panties.

"Now who's playing?" She bucked her hips with a whimper. "I want you now, Wade."

"Do you?" He retrieved a condom from his pocket and quickly sheathed himself. "Seems this is the only part of me you really want. If that's the case…" He jerked her hips to the edge of the tailgate, then spread her wide, gritting his teeth as he thrust to the hilt. "Be careful what you wish for…" If she wanted a frenzied fuck on the truck bed, he wasn't about to deny her…or himself.

He drove into her, fast and punishing. She urged him on with whimpers and moans, squeezing his ass with both hands, meeting him with every grunting, panting, flesh-slapping thrust. Wade pounded into her, using raw sensation to dull his equally raw emotions. She squeezed harder, forcing him deeper. The moment her climax began, he pumped to his own, pulling out the moment he'd shot his load. Wordlessly, he disposed of the condom, helped her up, and then handed her the jeans and boots she'd discarded. No kisses, no tender touches, no endearments. It was manic, mindless, and ultimately empty and unfulfilling. For the first time he was left wanting more—and hoped she felt it too.

Her hurt expression as she wiggled back into her clothes told him she did. "You must know this isn't how I wanted it to be."

"I didn't perform up to your expectations this time? Sure sounded like you were enjoying yourself." He felt a slight pull of conscience at the lash of his words.

"Why are you doing this? I thought we'd agreed—"

"We agreed to nothing. I offered to stay and you told me to go. Your message was pretty damn clear. Have you changed your mind?"

"No." Her blue-green eyes met his. "I'm going to take care of my father and then I'm going back home."

"So I don't even factor into your equation?" He waited, needing an answer. "For the last time, Nikki, I'm asking you not to go."

"Why are you making this so difficult?"

"Because I want you to stay."

"I told you I can't just blindly leap into something when we've known each other less than a week. How can you even expect it?"

"You can't always play it safe, Nikki. Some things in life are worth a gamble."

She stared back at him, her eyes flickering with emotion. "That's easy for you to say, when you aren't the one giving up anything."

"But you don't have any real ties. I do. You know that. I have to stay here at least until the ranch is sold. After that maybe I'll want to make some changes too. I've got a life to live too, Nicole and I'd like you to be part of it."

"I told you I need to think. Why can't you understand that? Things have happened so fast my head is spinning."

"That's the difference between us. I don't have to think about 'us.' I'm willing to take the chance."

"Because you have nothing to lose!" she insisted.

"In reality you don't either," he insisted. He jerked his head toward the cabin. "Take a good look. This wasn't a bad haul for you, Miz Powell. You came to Montana without a red cent, and will leave shortly with a net worth in the millions."

Anger flashed in her eyes. "I can't believe you said that! You make me sound like some gold digger when you know damned well I had no knowledge of my father's estate. Please, just go, Wade. Let's not let this get any uglier than it already has."

Nikki spun on her heel, leaving him staring after her.

"Now it's over," he muttered with a shake of his head. Part of him ached to follow her inside but he was done making an ass of himself.

Chapter 17

DESPERATE TO FOCUS ON ANYTHING BUT WADE, NIKKI busied herself inside the house, opening drawers and cupboards, seeking clues about her father's life, hoping to learn something about him but discovering very little to reveal the true man. She didn't find any books, which led her to conclude that he didn't read anything beyond his outdoor magazines. But she pretty much knew that already. She was, however, surprised to learn that he didn't own a cell phone or a computer but perhaps shouldn't have been. The old VCR should have clued her into his lack of interest in electronics.

In the bedside nightstand she found a bundle of greeting cards and letters that made her eyes blur. There were over a dozen unopened cards postmarked between 1993 and 2005. All were sent in the month of July—her birth month—and all were stamped return to sender. Once more, she felt an overwhelming choking sensation. He hadn't lied.

She wanted to rant. She wanted to cry. More than anything she wanted a pair of strong arms around her and a broad shoulder to cry on—Wade's shoulder. Wade's arms.

Their last exchange was bitter. She told herself the rift was all for the best; it made parting easier. Another big fat lie. Nothing made leaving him easy. Although she'd been the one to push him away, she still couldn't believe he'd driven off.

What did you expect? It's what you told him you wanted.

Maybe Wade was right that she wanted to have her cake and eat it too, but she wanted him to be more patient, to wait for her. To prove he really cared. If he did care, he would wait, wouldn't he? But he'd made it clear he wasn't about to be left dangling in uncertainty. Why did it have to be all or nothing with him? The question made her chest ache.

Later that afternoon, Nikki drove into town, checked out of the motel, and then bought a few groceries. She filled the evening hours going through more personal effects, and boxing up clothing and other household items. It was an emotional process, but she needed the time alone to figure out her feelings. When she finally crawled into bed, she'd come to only one conclusion— she missed Wade.

The next morning she was sitting on the front porch, lost in her thoughts and sipping instant coffee when a brand-new Cadillac Escalade came up the gravel drive. Her brows pulled together in a frown when Allison Evans climbed out. She shaded her eyes against the bright morning sun to survey the vast grassland and then approached Nikki with a smile.

"Nice spread you have here."

"Thanks. It was my father's place and an unexpected bequest. To be honest, I was shocked. I had no idea about any of it."

"So I heard."

So he'd returned to the ranch after all. The knowledge

that he'd discussed her with his ex-lover galled Nikki to no end. She wondered what else they had talked about— and if they had done more than just talk. Had he already taken up with Allison again? The thought made her stomach knot. "I guess word spreads fast around here," Nikki replied dryly.

"Wade sent me out here," Allison explained. "He called last night to say you'd asked him about the property value."

Nikki breathed only slightly easier to hear he'd called Allison. At least they hadn't spent last night together. "So you came as a favor to Wade or just out of idle curiosity?" Nikki asked.

Allison laughed. "My curiosity is never *idle*. I thought I'd come out and take a look while I'm still in town in case you wanted to sell. Have you decided what you're going to do with it yet?"

Nikki hadn't known what to expect from Allie, but didn't sense any of the underlying antipathy she'd felt the first time they'd met. Once again, Wade was right. To Allie, Nikki represented a sizable commission and now she was all business.

"I suppose the wisest thing would be to sell. What else can I do? I don't have any use for a hunting re- treat." She feared committing herself, but by sending Wade away she already had. "Yeah, I guess I'm going to sell."

"If that's what you want, I'm your best bet. I can get you top dollar for the place," Allie replied with a confidence that made Nikki's heart sink. "I haven't had a chance to pull the plat yet, but I'll get it as soon as I re- turn to my office. It's over twelve hundred acres, right?"

"So I'm told." With a feeling of emptiness, Nikki gazed out at the vast expanse of green.

"The property goes all the way to the Ruby River here?"

"Yes. According to Wade I have a full mile of river frontage," Nikki answered.

"Really?" Allie's smile brightened to blazing proportions. "Forget the grazing lands, Nicole. I can call you that, can't I?"

Nikki nodded.

"The river is your gold mine," Allie continued. "There are people who fly in from as far as Asia for the fishing in those waters." Allie pulled an iPad from her purse and made some notes. "What would you say if I told you that with a few phone calls, I could probably get you more than double what the grassland land is worth for this quarter section alone?"

Nikki was astounded. "You're kidding, right?"

"Not at all. I have two people in mind. Both are Japanese angling enthusiasts—and highly competitive with one another, which will likely drive your price even higher."

"What about the grazing lands?" Nikki asked. "I can't believe all this native grass has been wasted. Surely it should be put to use for cattle."

"That market is really soft right now. Of course you can sell off some of the pasture separately if you like, but you're probably better off leasing it out until the market improves. You might also look at it as an opportunity to reduce your tax burden. Wade could advise you best on the tax benefits."

Although Nikki might not like her very much, she

had to confess a certain amount of respect and admiration for the woman. She knew her clients and her business, and would surely get Nikki the best price for the property. Nikki offered her hand, feeling much as if they'd reached a truce. "All right, Allie. I'm ready. The sooner I do this the better. Let's write up the listing contract."

The rest of the day passed in a blur while Nikki concluded the exhaustive and mind-numbing process of boxing up personal effects and slogging through all the bills, paperwork, and tax records that were needed to settle her father's estate. Though she'd tried to keep her mind busy, her thoughts kept returning to Wade. She already harbored deep regrets about yesterday, but what could she have done differently? At least a dozen times she paused and picked up her phone, only to set it down again. What was the point?

She'd wanted time alone to think, but he still invaded almost every waking thought. By Thursday morning, she was almost desperate to see him. Carting the load of documents to his office seemed the best excuse. Once she'd located the bulk of what she needed, Nikki drove to Virginia City. To her dismay, it was Iris not Wade who met her inside. She struggled to mask her disappointment.

"I have a bunch of records that Wade will need to file my father's taxes and close out the estate."

"I can take those," Iris said.

"Where is Wade?" Nikki tried to sound casual, but suspected she didn't fool Iris.

"Gone back to Bozeman," Iris said. "He said he had a number of important appointments to keep. To be honest, I was surprised he stayed around here this long. It isn't his habit, but then I suppose he had a personal reason." She gave Nikki a meaningful look.

"Do you expect him back soon?"

"Not until his next court day." Iris consulted her desk calendar. "That would be in two weeks."

Nikki's heart sank to the pit of her stomach. She couldn't believe that he'd left without even a word of farewell after he'd practically begged her to stay. She bit her quivering lip, willing back the anger and the hurt that threatened to burst from her. She didn't know what she'd expected when she came to his office. Part of her had hoped...she didn't even dare admit what she'd hoped...but this was certainly not the way she'd pictured it all ending.

She told herself his actions only proved she'd made the right decision. If he'd really cared about her, he would at least have said good-bye. Now, other than an occasional business-related phone conference, they were unlikely ever to cross paths again.

"Do you have everything you need from me now, Iris? Is there anything I need to sign before I go?"

"Actually I do," Iris replied. "Allison Evans faxed over some paperwork."

"Is that it?" Nikki asked after signing the listing contract.

"Yes. I think that's everything for now," Iris replied. "From this point we should be able to take care of all the rest by email, fax, or FedEx."

"How long should it take?"

"Probably three to four months, but Wade could tell you better."

"I don't believe I'll be seeing Wade again," Nikki said tightly.

"Then here's his card in case you have any other questions." Iris pressed it onto Nikki's palm. "Maybe you should go ahead and give him a call before you go?"

"I don't think there's anything that can't wait until I get home."

"That so?" Iris replied with a sad shake of her head. "More's the pity."

"What's that supposed to mean?"

"I thought maybe the two of you—"

"No," Nikki said. "There's no chance of that... not anymore."

After leaving Wade's office, Nikki drove into Sheridan to collect her father's ashes from the mortuary, and then returned to the cabin for the very last time. A huge "for sale" sign greeted her at the end of the drive. Allie certainly hadn't wasted any time. Although Nikki knew she'd never return to this place, her throat still tightened at the finality.

She didn't go inside this time but unloaded a box and headed straight to the river. On the bank she set down the box and unpacked the urn. Struggling for balance, she hopped from rock to rock until she reached a large boulder in the middle of the river. Although his will hadn't specified, Nikki knew intuitively that this was what he would have wanted.

She sat in a reflective silence before slowly sprinkling the ashes into the Ruby River.

"Good-bye, Daddy," she whispered, closing her

eyes in an effort to lose herself in the peaceful sounds of rushing water. But rather than finding comfort, she felt doubly bereft. It was as if she mourned not only the passing of a father she'd barely known, but a love that *might* have been.

She consoled herself that soon this entire episode of her life would all be a distant memory. By this time tomorrow, she'd be landing at Hartsfield-Jackson International. Given time, Wade's image would eventually fade from her mind, but his mark would remain branded on her heart.

Nikki's thoughts were still filled with Wade when she boarded the plane in Bozeman Friday morning. Although he'd made no effort to contact her again, a secret part of her fantasized that he'd show up at the airport at the last minute and sweep her into his arms like a scene from a sappy romantic movie.

When he failed to appear, reality stuck her hard—it was truly over. Once more, he'd had the last word. *Damn him to hell!*

She congratulated herself again for being strong, for saving herself inevitable heartbreak. But why was it so hard to breathe?

She arrived back in Atlanta late that afternoon, thankful that her return flight wasn't as traumatic as the one that had taken her to Montana. After an uneventful landing, Nikki collected her bags and boarded the MARTA for Decatur. Although bustling with people, it seemed so lifeless. Lost in her thoughts, she stared sightlessly out at the urban landscape; the towering skyscrapers, the graffiti-covered concrete walls, and the bumper-to-bumper commuter traffic. She realized she missed the mountains and two-lane highways, and came perilously close to missing her transfer station.

Arriving in Decatur, she walked four blocks, passing St. Agnes College, several quaint coffee shops, and the bohemian boutiques she'd frequented in the years since she'd left Toccoa. She'd always liked Decatur, but now she viewed everything with emotional detachment. It was quaint, affordable, and convenient, and she'd always felt at home in the college town, but she'd never thought she'd still be living in the same college apartment at almost twenty-nine. She'd assumed she'd be settled in a nice little house in one of the better burbs by now, maybe even with a couple of kids. Why hadn't she moved on? It seemed all her friends had.

She'd doggedly insisted her life was here, but what had she really returned to?

What kept her rooted to a job she hated under a boss she despised?

Was it fear of losing control as Wade suggested? Fear of dependency on another? Was this really why she'd walked away from Wade without giving it a real chance? When had she become such a coward? Her life had followed the same patterns for so long but change had come to her whether she'd wanted it or not.

She could hardly believe how radically her circumstances had altered almost overnight. Soon she'd have financial security she'd never dreamed of. Although she wouldn't have full access to the money until the estate closed, she was already able to draw enough to pay her bills. Before long she'd be able to replace her POS car, pay off all her credit cards, student loans—and even quit her job if she wanted to. Maybe she'd go back to school to get her MBA or look for a new job.

But then what? The question lingered in the back of her mind. She hadn't a clue.

Life was all about choices now. She could start over again. How many people ever got to do that? What did she really want? It wasn't the big house in Dunwoody and a shiny new SUV. Expensive jewelry and designer clothes wouldn't satisfy her. She'd never been the materialistic type. Travel to exotic places didn't interest her, probably because she hated to fly.

Although she maintained that she was a city girl, the happiest moments in her life were still the simplest ones—like the hours sipping sweet tea and playing cards in her MeeMaw's kitchen back in Lavonia. Although she'd dropped her drawl and eradicated the outward signs of her rural upbringing, she was still small town in her heart. Could she have found contentment in Montana?

Damn it, Nikki! You made your choice—the right one. It was great with Wade while it lasted, but it's done. Now accept it and move on.

She found herself staring at her own front door without even remembering how she got there. Dropping her bags, Nikki fished her keys from her purse only to discover the door unlocked.

What the hell?

She dug her cell out of her purse with trembling fingers, and was about to dial 911 when she noticed a familiar looking car in the parking lot—the only one in worse shape than hers—and one she suspected would be

repossessed at any time. The second thing she noted was
the TV blaring inside her apartment. She slapped the
phone shut, dropped it back into her purse, and pushed
the door open. Once inside she drew in a lungful of
air, letting it out with an exasperated cry, "Shelby Jane
Baker! What the *hell* are you doing in my apartment?"

Her younger sister never took her eyes off the TV.
"Watching Jerry Springer."

Nikki slammed her bags down and picked up the remote, furiously clicking off the television. "Why here?
Did they repo your TV, too?" She was about to give
Shelby another earful until her sister turned her platinum
head to face Nikki straight on. Her lip was split and her
left eye was mottled shades of green and purple, and
hideously swollen.

"Holy shit!" Nikki cried. "What did that bastard-son-
of-a-bitch-asshole do to you?"

"I keyed his new truck for screwing my neighbor.
He beat the bejesus out of me. Then I left," Shelby answered in classic, blunt Shelby style.

"And broke into my place?"

She shrugged. "Where else was I to go?"

"Did you call the police? You need to file a restrain-
ing order."

"Yeah, right." Shelby snorted. "As if I want *them* to
know where I am."

"What is it this time?" Nikki groaned.

"Don't be melodramatic. It was only a couple of
bad checks."

"Does Asshole know you're here?"

"Not yet. Probably won't know much of anything
even after he wakes up."

"Wakes up?" Nikki scowled. "What is that supposed to mean?"

"I slipped some valium into his bottle of Crown. How was your trip?"

Chapter 18

JOLTED AWAKE AFTER ANOTHER RESTLESS NIGHT, NIKKI slapped the snooze bar on her alarm clock, and then pulled a pillow over her head, dreading her return to work. Although she was tempted to blow it off altogether, wisdom told her not to act rashly—at least not until she had enough money in the bank to tell her boss to kiss her ass.

After dozing through two more alarm cycles, she finally dragged herself from bed and stumbled to the kitchen to start the coffee. On her way back to shower, she thumped loudly on Shelby's door.

"Go away," her sister groaned.

Nikki cracked the door open. "Don't you have someplace to be?"

"Like where?" Shelby mumbled, her head still buried under the covers.

"Like work," Nikki snapped. "Aren't you going?"

Shelby sat up with a guilty look. "About that. I meant to tell you that I'm kinda between gigs right now."

"Again? Did you get fired?"

"No. I quit." Shelby heaved a dramatic sigh. "Don't look at me like I'm some kind of vermin, Nikki! A lot of people are out of work right now."

"But you were only there a month!"

"Almost two, and I had good reason for leaving."

"Yeah and what was that?" Nikki couldn't hide her skepticism.

"You don't understand how it is, Nikki. You just sit there all day in cubieland. You've never had to deal with the kind of dickwads I have to face every day—like the ones demanding blow jobs. That asshole offered me an extra fifty bucks to blow him." Shelby rolled her eyes. "Fifty...as if I'd ever."

"You're shitting me."

"Wish I was. You'd be surprised how many clients think a 'happy ending' is included with a massage. Tantric costs extra. *Mucho extra*."

"Tantric?"

"You know, erotic massage."

"No. I don't know." Nikki shook her head. "And I think I don't *want* to know."

"Probably not," Shelby smirked.

"Are you at least *looking* for something else?"

"I was planning to," Shelby said. "But you can hardly expect me to show up for an interview looking like this."

She had a point. The bruising was hideous. "Look, Shel, you can stay here for a while, but I expect you to earn your keep."

Shelby scowled. "What does that mean?"

"I want you to help out. You can at least clean the place up while I'm gone. You know, dishes, vacuuming, windows..."

Shelby's eyes widened in incredulity. "You expect me to wash the freaking windows?"

"Yeah, I do."

She cursed under her breath.

"What's that?" Nikki asked.

"I'll comb the want ads today."

"That might be best." Nikki closed the door with a smile.

The rest of the morning followed her normal routine, sipping coffee from her travel mug while sitting in bumper-to-bumper traffic, jockeying for a decent parking space, and then rushing to punch the time clock. Her week spent in Montana was the first break she'd had in three years from a life of redundancy. Every day for Nikki was pretty much like the last, but predictability was safe, right? And security was what she craved most after a lifetime of revolving door relationships.

What Wade had offered her was neither safe nor secure. He was a gamble she wasn't ready to take. So why did she now feel so hollow? Why did every action feel dull and mechanical, as if she was now nothing but a walking automaton? As usual, she stopped by the break room to refill her coffee mug before proceeding to her cube where Jessica and Robert prairie-dogged from the other side to greet her.

"Morning, Nik," said Jess. "Welcome back."

"Have a good trip?" Robert asked.

"Not good, exactly. But definitely interesting. Thanks for asking."

Robert was a decent sort and she'd even dated him a few times in her effort at rehabilitation. But he had really sucked in bed the one time she'd gotten drunk enough to give him a shot. He'd been good-humored about it when she'd turned him down for another date after that. They both realized they were better as friends than lovers. She hoped he and Jess might eventually make a go of it. She was really cute in a geek-girl way. Maybe he'd take notice if she talked Jess into a makeover? Nikki decided to put it on her to-do list.

Nikki booted her computer and opened the bottom desk drawer to stash her purse, but then hesitated. She hadn't checked her phone messages since last night. She wondered if *he'd* tried to call. It had been almost five days since they'd spoken. Surely there was some news about the estate. She swiped her iPhone screen to the message menu. Nothing. No texts either. Maybe he'd sent her an email?

"You might want to watch your ass, Nikster," Robert warned, adding in his best Austin Powers voice, "Mini-Me's on the warpath." At least Robert kept things interesting. He had nicknames for just about everyone. The department head was Dr. Evil, and their four-foot-ten-inch supervisor was Mini-Me.

"Thanks." Nikki laughed and set the phone down, logging onto the Internet to check her webmail account. An email from Wade, even if it was only business, would at least reopen communication.

"Psst!" The hissed warning from Jess came too late. Mini-Me had materialized out of nowhere. *Shit!* Nikki's stomach dropped. Why couldn't she have had at least had five minutes before the be-atch came breathing down her neck?

Hoping to block the view of her monitor, Nikki spun around in her chair. Flashing a bright smile, she greeted her supervisor. "Good morning, Phyllis."

"So you finally made it back?" Phyllis replied. "Good thing too. You really put me on the spot, you know. I doubt I could have held your job any longer."

"I apologize for any trouble, but things got

complicated. I lost my wallet on the trip and couldn't do anything until I replaced my ID."

Phyllis stood on her tiptoes to squint over Nikki's shoulder. Her face screwed up. "Personal use of the Internet is prohibited. You're already treading on thin ice, Nicole. There are a lot of people looking for work, many of whom would show up as expected and follow the rules."

"I'm sorry, Phyllis." Nikki forced a look of contrition. "I'm expecting some important communication from the probate attorney."

"I don't care what you're expecting. You're on the clock now. Or do you think you're special? That corporate policy doesn't apply to you?"

God, how she despised working under a petty, nit-picky little tyrant.

"Of course not," Nikki replied. "It won't happen again."

Phyllis's lips got even thinner. "Is that your cell phone? Why isn't it stored in your locker? That makes two infractions."

Nikki couldn't hold back any longer. "Then I guess I've really made your day, haven't I?"

"Are you trying for insubordination now, Nicole? I'd be more than happy to write you up for that too."

"You know what, Phyllis? I think I'll save you the trouble."

Phyllis's gaze narrowed. "If you walk out of here, you'll lose all your remaining vacation pay as well as any chance of a reference."

Nikki smiled tightly remembering Wade's words. "All things considered, I think it's more than a fair trade. 'Cause I won't have to kiss your bony little ass anymore." Nikki stood and snatched up both her phone and her purse. Her body trembled, but she held her chin high, walking out to a universal standing ovation.

She'd never done anything so reckless and impulsive, but it felt damned good—so good she even decided to celebrate. On her second impulse of the day, she pulled into the new Organic Emporium, a high-end grocery where she'd previously only window shopped. Now with a wicker basket over her arm, she strolled the neatly stocked aisles of gourmet and exotic foods.

She paused at the meat counter where they displayed only certified grass-fed and hormone-free choices. In addition to the expected chicken, beef, pork, lamb, and veal, there was ostrich, rabbit, bison, elk, and even alligator.

Nikki couldn't help inquiring of the butcher, "Do you carry American Kobe beef?"

"*American* Kobe?" he asked with surprise.

"Yeah," she said. "I've heard a few ranchers out West are cross-breeding Japanese cows with American Angus."

The butcher scratched his chin. "I know of a few outfits out West supplying the upscale steak houses, but we don't carry it in the market yet. I could look into special ordering it for you if you like. Do you want me to ask our buyers?"

"No, thank you," Nikki replied. "I was just curious to know if it was catching on at all."

She wondered if Dirk had any chance of making a go of it or if Wade was right about cattle ranching being an altogether losing proposition. Then again, *someone* had to raise cattle for the high-end markets.

Nikki hesitated over a twenty-dollar bison steak, but decided that her vegan sister would probably gag at the sight of it. With a sigh, she opted for veggie burgers instead and then headed to the bakery for Shelby's gluten-free buns. Stopping midway to wander the wine aisle, Nikki lingered indecisively in the enormous selection of reds. She knew almost nothing about wine, as all her prior boyfriends had been beer drinkers. Her eyes lit on the Shiraz. She'd never tried it until the dinner with Wade. Thinking about it, she was stunned to realize just how closed to new things she'd been and how limited her world had become.

New things weren't safe. There was always a chance she wouldn't like them—but she'd liked the Shiraz very much. She'd like the beef too. And the mountains. Being truthful, she hadn't even minded the night in the cabin that much. It had felt like an adventure. Every day with Wade had brought something new and exciting. Yet, she'd played it safe, choosing to return to dull and predictable.

Was this who she really was? Who she wanted to be?

Nikki closed her eyes to the image of Wade sitting across the table from her and filling her glass that night at the Old Hotel. She'd tried many new things with him. The wine labels blurred before her burning eyes. Passing on the Shiraz, Nikki opted for a bottle of Biltmore Merlot instead.

After grabbing a bag of buns for the veggie burgers, she decided to quash her misery with something wickedly chocolate. She moved on to the pastry section where she nearly drooled over the mouthwatering selections—until her gaze lit on the cannoli. The remembrance of what had followed their last meal together incited a yearning that went bone deep.

Damn it! Am I so far gone that I can't even make a trip to the grocery store without thinking about him?

No matter how hard she tried to push them aside, her thoughts kept returning to Wade. She wandered the aisles, replaying almost every minute they'd spent together—from the first cocky wink at the Denver airport to the breath-stealing vision of his soap-slickened body. She mentally freeze-framed the last day together when he was shirtless, wielding the ax and gleaming with sweat.

Aching for him in the worst possible way, Nikki abandoned the bakery for the freezer section where she hoped to drown her misery in a tub of Mayfield Cookies 'n' Cream topped with a large jar of fudge sauce.

Nikki pulled into the parking lot of her apartment complex with an ominous feeling. She supposed the three police squad cars and crowd of gawkers had a great deal to do with that, and strongly suspected she'd find Shelby in the thick of it. Leaving her groceries in the car, she approached her building with jangling nerves. Judging by the demolition-derby condition of Shelby's car and the smashed apartment windows, her fears that Shelby's psycho ex would eventually show up had materialized. Given the evidence, his weapon of mass destruction must have been a sledgehammer. She pushed through the crowd to find the police questioning her sister who, thank goodness, looked unharmed.

Her landlord intercepted, confronting Nikki and shaking a fist. "I'm holding you liable for these damages, Miss Powell. The rental insurance doesn't cover willful destruction of property."

"Wait a minute," Nikki replied. "How can you blame me? I wasn't even here and don't have a clue what happened."

"Your sister was here," he accused. "Maybe she can tell us all what happened."

"Are you all right, Shelby?" Nikki asked.

"I am now."

"What happened?" Nikki asked.

"Dwight showed up...wanting money."

"Money?"

"Yeah. He heard you had some. Said he needed a loan. He didn't like the answer I gave."

"Which was?"

"I told him to piss off."

"You know the assailant?" one of the officers asked.

"Yeah. I know the dickhead," Shelby replied.

"Did he threaten you?" the officer asked.

Shelby rolled her eyes. "No. He brought me a damned posy of pink carnations. What the hell does it look like?"

"Look, miss..." The cop scowled. "I have a report to make and I'll need a little cooperation from you."

"You're going to arrest him, aren't you?" Nikki asked.

"We will if we have sufficient witnesses to identify him and if you and your sister decide to press charges. It's a felony offense."

"Really?" Shelby interrupted. "How much time will he do?"

"If convicted, up to five years."

"That so?" Shelby's eyes lit up. "Where do I sign?"

———ᴧᴧ———

Hours later, after filling out police reports, calling the insurance company, a tow truck for the wrecked car, and a glass company for the smashed windows, Nikki finally sat down with two spoons and an entire tub of somewhat soupy Cookies 'n' Cream.

"Helluva day, eh?" said Shelby, picking up a spoon. "I don't suppose you remembered to get chocolate sauce?"

Nikki gaped at her. "Is that all you have to say?"

"What do you expect? It isn't like I invited him over."

"So you're saying he just showed up out of the blue?"

"Guess he figured I'd come here."

Nikki dug her spoon into the tub, fishing around for the biggest hunk of Oreo but then paused, spoon midway to her mouth. "Wait a minute. You said Dwight wanted money, but how could he even know anything about my inheritance?"

Shelby looked guilty. "Maybe I...er...let it slip."

"Why would you even be talking to the asshole after what he did to you?"

"He has all my stuff. I wanted it back."

"What stuff?" Nikki asked.

"My clothes and things."

"You can buy new clothes, Shelby. There's nothing you own that's worth negotiating with that scumbag."

"Easy for you to say, Miss Moneybags. You can buy whatever you want now."

"I don't have any of it yet, Shelby, but even when I do, I don't plan to do anything stupid, and I still want to work."

"Speaking of work…" Shelby's brow wrinkled. "Why are you home so early?"

"Because I quit today."

"You quit?" Shelby laughed. "Good for you! I hope you went out with a bang. Did you wipe any computer drives? Paint graffiti on the bathroom wall with your nail polish?"

"I told Phyllis off."

Shelby's eyes glimmered. "Oh yeah? Whadya say to the old bag?"

"Told her I wasn't going to kiss her bony ass any more."

"And?"

"And what? I left."

Shelby looked crestfallen. "Hell, that'll be forgotten in a week. Tops. I need to give you some lessons on leavin'."

"Like your adventure in leaving Dwight?"

Shelby looked mildly chagrined. "All right, you have me there." She added defiantly, "I shoulda taken better advantage of his unconsciousness and castrated the bastard."

"Do you think he'll be back?" Nikki asked.

"Probably. He said something about bringing his forty-five next time."

"Holy shit! He threatened your life?"

Shelby shrugged. "It's not like it's the first time. You don't understand how it is with us. It's a complicated relationship."

"Why, Shel?" Nikki asked. "Why do you go for these assholes?"

Shelby glowered with her good eye. "Isn't that the

pot calling the kettle back? I've met some of your win-
ners, too, you know."

"They haven't *all* been bad, and *none* have been
homicidal maniacs."

"Oh yeah? If you're so great a picking 'em, name me
one that wasn't a lying, cheating asshole."

"Wade," Nikki blurted without a second thought.

"Wade?" Shelby scrunched her face. "I don't remember a Wade. Who was he?"

"The lawyer in Montana."

"A lawyer?" Shelby grinned a mile wide. "Wow,
Nik! You've graduated from bottom-feeding rednecks
to white-collar professionals? Whoo-hoo, look at you!
Big sister is moving up the food chain."

"Maybe not so much. He's also a cowboy. Well, a
rancher, to be precise."

"You shagged a *cowboy* lawyer?"

Nikki blushed. "Shagged? You make it sound cheap
and dirty. It was more than that."

"Really? Then what's the deal with you and him?"

"Deal? There isn't one. He's there and I'm here. End.
Of. Story."

"But you're going back there, right? You still have to
settle the estate and sell the place, don't you?"

"Yes, but I don't have to go back to do any of that.
He's going to handle it all for me—well, his legal assistant is anyway."

"Ah." Shelby pursed her pouty lips with a knowing
look. "That explains everything."

"Everything what?"

"Why you've been such a bitch…well, a worse one
than usual…since you got back. It's not hard to add one

and one, i.e., you and Wade. Or maybe I should have said you *minus* Wade." She balanced the bowl of the spoon on her nose. "So what are you going to do about it?"

"Nothing. I told you it's already over."

"Why's that? Did he lie about a wife and kids?"

"No."

"He cheated?"

"Don't be ridiculous. I wasn't there long enough."

"You're wrong there. Where there's a cheater there's a way. I speak from experience. The length of the relationship is irrelevant. So did he get drunk and slap you around?"

"No. He's a perfect gentleman and doesn't drink. Well, not anymore."

"Did he suck in bed?"

"God no! He was incredible. The best. Ever. No contest."

"All right, time to cut through the bullshit," Shelby said, blunt as ever. "What is your freaking problem, Nikki? Why the hell are you sitting here in Georgia completely miserable, when you could be happily boffing like bunnies with your hot Montana cowboy lawyer?"

Nikki gaped at Shelby as if she were Confucius incarnate. "You know, Shelby, that's a damned good question."

Chapter 19

WADE HAD LEFT NIKKI IN A RAGE, BUT HIS BOTTLED fury had faded to really pissed-off by the time he'd driven back to Bozeman. Now after weeks of aging, it had mellowed all the way down the scale to moderate resentment. Although he still hadn't spoken to her directly, he'd kept up with the smallest details regarding her estate. Wanting to avoid any awkwardness in their professional relationship, he'd limited his communication with her as much as possible, instructing Iris to field her questions and return calls on his behalf.

It was easier for them both this way. He missed her like hell, but didn't know what he could say to her that he hadn't already said. Well, there was one thing. It had even been on the tip of his tongue more than once, but repeating those three words without some assurance of reciprocation scared the shit out of him.

Since she left, he'd gone back to his old routine, filling all his days and more than half his nights with work. Defying his best efforts, she still invaded his thoughts every moment he let his mind stray. Wade vividly recalled every detail, from their first meeting at the airport to their bitter parting, and everything in between—especially what had come in between.

His mind lingered on those days and nights that now left him feeling sexually frustrated and confused. There were still so many things he'd wanted to do to her. Hell, he couldn't even look at a cannoli without getting a hard-on. He'd never experienced anything like it. He craved her voice, laugh, the feel of her beneath him, surrounding him, but it was much more than great sex. Everything about them together seemed to fit. It had seemed like some kind of karma the way they had come together. It had to be. She was so damned easy to be with. He loved that about her. There was no pretense about her. Nikki was the real thing. *They* were the real thing. Why couldn't she see it, too?

Wade toed off his boots and then shrugged out of his shirt. He was considering whether he should relieve his sexual frustration with a cold shower or just go ahead and jerk himself off, when the phone rang. His chest tightened when he recognized her number. For a moment he considered letting it go to voice mail, but on the fourth ring, he snatched up the phone.

"Hello, Nikki." He paused. "What can I do for you?"

"Hi, Wade." Silence. "Do you think we can talk?"

"Depends on what you want to talk about. Anything business related is billable time." He winced at his tone. He sounded like a real asshole.

"I know that," she replied. "But I need your advice."

"That so? Then I'm all ears, sweetheart."

"Allie called me with an offer on the riverfront piece today."

"Yeah, I heard about that. She worked some magic pulling that deal together. The buyer's the same guy who wanted the Flying K. When that deal fell through, she showed him your quarter section on the river. Turns out he's an avid angler and snapped at it like a trout to live bait."

"Lucky me," she said dryly.

"You don't sound too excited," he couldn't help remarking. "You're gonna accept the offer, aren't you? I understand it's a cash deal."

"So you think I should accept it?"

"Yeah. Take the money and run...wait," he couldn't help adding, "I guess you already did that second part."

"That was unfair."

"Never said I play fair."

Another silence. "Allie says there's also an offer on the pasturelands, but it's a lease. That's what I really needed to talk to you about."

"There are significant tax advantages to leasing it out, especially if you keep it agricultural. If you sell off everything at once, you're likely to lose your ass in taxes."

"That's what I thought, but I want to better understand the ins and outs of all this before I decided anything. So you think I should accept the lease deal as well?"

"Yes, as long as the price is fair."

"I don't know if you're going to feel the same about the offer when I tell you who's made it."

"Why would that matter? Who is it?"

"Your brother?"

"Dirk?" That news took him by surprise.

"Why would your brother want to lease pastureland from me?"

"I'm not involved," Wade replied curtly.

"I thought maybe you could explain his plans."

"You'll need to talk to Dirk directly," Wade said. "My brother's decided to expand his cattle operation, and I've pretty much washed my hands of it."

"So things between you and Dirk—"

"Haven't changed for the better."

"I'm sorry to hear that... I'm thinking I might come up there for the closings."

Wade's pulse quickened at the thought of seeing her again, but then he wondered at her motives. He couldn't see the point of her return when she already said she was selling everything. "It's not necessary," he said, "especially given how you hate to fly."

"I do, but it wouldn't be so bad with a companion."

"A companion?" He felt a violent surge of jealousy.

"Yes. I'm thinking about asking Shelby to come with me. I'd rather not leave her alone with her stalker ex-boyfriend still on the lam."

"Shelby? That would be your sister?"

"Yeah. I'm surprised you remembered that."

"I remember everything, sweetheart."

Silence.

"You do realize it's winter here, right?" Wade said. "Your thin Southern blood probably won't tolerate sub-zero temperatures very well."

"I can take it." Another pause. "Are you trying to talk me out of coming?"

"Just trying to save you expense, discomfort, and aggravation." More like *his* discomfort and aggravation. "You really don't have to be here for the closings, you know."

"I know, but I'll be there anyway. I'm flying up next Friday. We're gonna spend the weekend. Any suggestions on where we should stay?"

Yeah, in my bed. He had little doubt they'd end up in there anyway. But as much as he missed her, it would only be like a quick fix to a junkie. The high would be great, but the crash would be hell. And then what?

"You might enjoy Big Sky," he suggested, telling himself it was all for the best.

Another pause.

"Thanks," she said. "I'll book a reservation there. See you Friday?"

"Sure. Bye, Nikki." He disconnected on the lie. Evans would be handling the closings. He'd be long gone.

Nikki clicked the phone off with a hollow feeling. But then again, what did she expect after almost three months? Initially, the sound of his mellow baritone had sent a warm ripple through her, but then he'd become so painfully aloof. Their conversation hadn't played out at all as she'd thought…as she'd hoped. She'd taken a huge step to call him. Why couldn't he at least have met her halfway?

She wondered if it was really worth all the trouble to go up there. She hated to fly. It was early December, freezing cold, and Wade's reception on the phone had been anything but warm. Was there any chance he'd welcome her back? Was there even a glimmer of hope? It was impossible to know his true feelings when she couldn't see his face. Maybe the whole thing was a waste of time.

Shelby plopped onto the sofa beside her. "So what did he say?"

"Not much. He advised me to sell the river piece and lease the rest."

"Why lease any of it if you can sell? I'd take the money in a heartbeat," Shelby said.

"Yeah, you would," Nikki said dryly. "And you'd probably head straight to Vegas with it."

"Probably." Shelby grinned. "A girl's gotta have some fun, after all."

"He tried to talk me out of coming back."

"He told you not to come?"

"Not exactly but he was very discouraging."

"Cold shoulder, eh? It has been a long time, Nik. Do you think that maybe…"

"He's involved with someone else?" Nikki finished the thought she hadn't wanted to acknowledge aloud. She mentally kicked herself for her stupidity. Just because she'd been pining didn't mean he was doing the same. In all likelihood, he was involved with someone. The thought that she might have lost him for good made her stomach churn.

"You're probably right. I'm just going to make a giant ass of myself, aren't I?"

"Maybe so." Shelby's reply didn't make her feel any better. "But you're still planning to go, aren't you?"

"Yes. But my going really has nothing to do with him and me. The closing on the riverfront parcel is next Friday and I have a lease offer to consider on the remaining pasture lands. If I sell everything the taxes are going to kill me, so I might be better off to entertain the lease. If I do that, if I keep the land, I should at least learn a little about how it all works, don't you think? So I'm going up there to talk this deal over. It's all strictly business," Nikki insisted.

"You trying to convince me or yourself?"

Nikki frowned. "It's all true."

"C'mon, Nik," Shelby cajoled. "It's past time to come clean. I think there's a much more personal reason why you want to hold on to some of that land. It's your only tie to him. Once it's sold, you've got no connection at all to him, no reason ever to go back. Why is it so impossible for you to admit?"

"Because I'm scared!" Nikki cried. "He might be the best thing that ever happened to me and I was too afraid to even give it a chance. Now it's probably too late."

"Maybe it is and maybe it isn't," Shelby said. "There's only one way to find out."

"I know. That's why I'm going," Nikki said. "I'm probably setting myself up for a horrible fall, but I have to know if it's really over. Seeing him face-to-face is the only way I'm ever going to know for certain."

"And then what?" Shelby asked. "What happens if he *does* want to pick it back up again?"

"I'm going to cross that bridge when I come to it. I don't want to get my hopes up when he might not even want me anymore."

"If he doesn't, he's a dumb-ass."

"No. I was. You don't know how I treated him." *Damned fool that I was, I let him go.* No, that wasn't true either. Wade had accused her of pushing him away and he was right. She had actually *pushed him away*— the only decent man who'd ever wanted her. She had many regrets and wondered if she could ever make it up to him. She hoped she'd get the chance.

"Why don't you come with me, Shelby? I don't like the idea of leaving you alone with that psycho Dwight still on the loose."

"Really?"

"Yeah. Consider it an early Christmas present."

"Can we stay at one of those plush ski resorts?" Shelby asked.

"You don't know *how* to ski."

"Then I'll snowboard. How hard can that be? Besides, that's what lessons are for—preferably with a really hot instructor."

"It isn't a vacation, Shel."

"Why not make it one? I don't get you at all, Nikki. You've got all this money now. Why don't you enjoy some of it? Have some fun for a change?"

"Your idea of fun usually ends with a tattoo or a jail cell."

Shelby made a face. "Not *all* the time. C'mon, Nik, just a couple of days. I've always wanted to go skiing."

"All right. You win," Nikki conceded. "We'll spend the weekend at Big Sky."

—◊◊◊—

"Are you really sure about this move, Wade?" Allie leaned against the doorjamb as he taped up his last box. "You've worked so hard to build this practice. I can't believe you're just walking away from it."

"I'm not walking, Allie," Wade answered dryly, "I'm running. Now that Dirk has scored that organic foods contract, I don't feel chained to the ranch anymore. If he wants to buy me out, I'm happy to let him."

"But why give up this practice too?"

"Because I need a change. I've needed one for a long time. I feel like I'm suffocating here."

"But Helena of all places? There's nothing in Helena."

"There's a job with the DOJ in Helena."

"At what…a third of your present salary? You really need to think this through, Wade. Even though things didn't work between us, Daddy still thinks you're one of the best associates he has. Given a few more years, the Denver practice could still be yours."

"It's not all about money, Allie. Maybe once I thought that's all I wanted—a lucrative private practice and a loaded bank account—but a lot of things have changed." He hated to admit it, but Nikki was no small part of that.

She stood up and wiped her hands. "All the more reason to come to Denver."

Wade shook his head. "Maybe I'm not obligated to the ranch anymore, but that doesn't mean I want to abandon my family altogether."

"But you're wasted here in Montana," Allie insisted. "There's so much more opportunity for a man of your talents in Colorado."

He propped a hip on his empty desk in his empty office—empty of all but the neatly stacked boxes. "Maybe not the kind of opportunity I'm looking for. This job with the DOJ will allow me to make the contacts I need so I can do what I really want to do."

"And what's that?"

"I want to make a difference to the people here. We're one of the poorest states in the country, but have some of the most abundant natural resources. I'm sick and tired of all the bureaucrats dictating how we manage those lands and resources at the expense of the people like my family whose roots stretch back four and five generations. It's not right, damn it!" He slammed a fist on the desk. "It's high time we reclaimed what's ours so we can have a shot at a better future. That's what I really want."

Allie stared at him incredulously, and then clapped her hands. "Sign me up as the campaign manager. That was quite a speech, Wade."

"Just tellin' it like it is. It's about time someone spoke up."

She arched a brow. "So this lousy paying job you've taken is really just a stepping stone into politics?"

"Maybe." Wade grinned. If anyone could cut to the chase, it was Allie.

She stood in front of him and reached out to straighten his tie. "You know Wade, if you change your mind and want to make a political career in Denver, I'd make an ideal politician's wife."

"Undoubtedly, but we've been down this road before."

"Yeah, well things change...people change." Her gaze sought his. "Are you seeing anyone else?"

"Nope." He shook his head, avoiding the eye contact she desired. "Not for a while now."

"Going on three months, isn't it?"

"Yeah, I guess that's about right." He shrugged. It was ten weeks to be precise since Nikki had left. He hadn't had sex with anyone else, but he wasn't about to admit that.

"I thought we were pretty good together. Was it really that much better with her?"

Dangerous question, Wade. Tread carefully.

He took a deep breath. "It was completely different, Allie. Nikki and I had a connection that I can't explain. I only hope you also experience it with someone one day."

"Yeah well, you know I prefer to keep things simple. I'm not like other women. I don't want or need emotional entanglements. They only make women needy."

"It isn't weakness to need somebody, Allie. Hell, we *all* need somebody sometimes."

"So they say," she remarked blithely. "But I don't get it. Maybe I'm just wired differently. I don't need a husband and children to make me feel 'fulfilled.'"

"Maybe that'll change when you meet the right man."

She snorted. "I don't think so. I'm perfectly happy as I am." She stroked her fingers down the length of his silk tie. "You sure you don't want to blow off some steam? I'm experiencing a dry spell myself. You can consider it a going-away present."

"Thanks, Allie. That's mighty generous, but I don't think it's a good idea to start anything up again."

She offered up her palms. "No strings attached."

Allie was more than willing to pick things back up. She'd probably let him take her right here on the desk if he'd wanted to. Although he felt the strain of celibacy, he had no desire for a casual hook up. He shook his head. "Thanks again but I'm still gonna pass."

"Damn." Allie's mouth turned down in disappointment. "I didn't expect that." She stepped back with a smile that looked forced. "Can't blame a gal for trying."

Wade took her hand in both of his and held it. "I'm sorry, Allie, but it wouldn't be right—you and me. We'd only be cheating ourselves. We both deserve more."

"More?" She laughed dryly. "What else is there?"

"I don't know," he answered. "But I think I was damned close to finding out."

The experience with Nikki had opened his eyes, but she'd gone before he ever had a chance to know if it could work.

Only a few weeks ago he would have been on the next plane to Atlanta if he'd thought there was any chance of persuading her to give it a go, but she'd made herself crystal clear. There was no point in pursuit when she'd expressed no intention of *ever* coming back.

"When do you leave?" Allie asked.

"Tomorrow."

Given Dirk's good fortune, the opportunity had finally come for Wade to break loose from the ranch. After almost two months of waiting and hoping Nikki might come around, he was finally ready to move on. He was making some big changes in his life. Her phone call had come too late. He was moving on— to Helena.

Nikki got off the plane at Bozeman Yellowstone Airport and inhaled the frosty air with a strange feeling of welcome. It was suddenly as if she belonged, as if she'd come home.

"It's freaking c-cold!" Shelby pulled the collar of her fuchsia faux fur jacket, the one she'd bought to offset the new pink highlights in her platinum hair, up around her ears. "You didn't warn me about that." Shelby glowered.

"Some snow bunny you make." Nikki laughed. "Generally speaking, Shelby, where there is snow there is also cold."

"Then all I can say is Big Sky better have some really *hawt* snowboarding instructors to make up for the lack of temperature."

"Have you ever seen mountains like this? Just look at them!" Nikki exclaimed.

"How can I not see them? They're everywhere. And that seems to be *all* there is. You didn't warn me about that either."

"But they're gorgeous. I haven't seen them like this before—all covered in snow."

"That's just flippin' great if you're into this kind of scenery, but I'm starting to think I prefer palm trees."

"Don't be such a crybaby, Shelby. Look, we don't have time to check into the hotel before my appointment with the attorney. Do you mind coming along with me?"

"If I do, can I use your credit card later?"

"For what?"

"Shopping of course. I'll need warmer clothes. Do you think they even *have* malls here?"

—―∽∾∿―—

Half an hour later, Nikki pulled up to the Bozeman offices of Evans and Knowlton with a heightening sense of anticipation. She'd taken pains with her hair and makeup that morning but now wished she'd flown in a day earlier just so she'd look her best. She approached the reception desk with butterflies in her stomach. The receptionist smiled and introduced herself as Stella.

"Allie and Mr. Evans are already in the big conference room if you'd like to head in there, Miss Powell. We're just waiting for the buyer. He called a moment ago to say his flight was late but expects to be here any minute."

"Mr. Evans?" Nikki repeated, barely hearing the rest. "What about Wa—Mr. Knowlton? I thought he was handling everything related to the estate."

"Mr. Knowlton? Didn't he tell you? He's no longer with the practice."

"What?" Nikki suppressed a gasp. "Since when? I just spoke to him last week."

"Last Friday was his last day. He's taken a job in Helena."

"Helena?" Nikki repeated dumbly. *Wade was gone?* This couldn't be happening.

"Yes. It's the state capital, about an hour and a half north."

"I know where...but why?"

"He accepted a position with the State Attorney's office. I hear he has his eye on the legislature."

"But he never mentioned anything about it."

Even as she voiced the words, she realized that wasn't quite true. He *had* hinted at it. She'd seen glimpses of his passion, his desire to effect change. *Maybe I want to leave a legacy besides my blood, sweat, and tears.* He probably would have shared much more of his hopes and desires if she hadn't been so totally self-absorbed.

Stella interrupted her thoughts. "It's a good thing for Montana if he does. He's well-known and respected around these parts. I think he'll do us all a lot of good."

"Yes, I imagine so," Nikki responded automatically, fighting the sudden tightness in her throat. She'd come with a secret hope of mending fences with Wade. On the entire flight she'd played out various scenarios in her head, most of them ending in a steamy reunion, but he'd obviously had other thoughts.

"Mr. Evans, the senior partner, flew in from Denver last night specifically to take care of you. I promise you're in good hands."

"I'm sure. I'm just surprised by the news," Nikki said.

"I'll walk you back there if you are ready."

"Do you mind waiting here, Shel? This shouldn't take too long."

Shelby's attention was riveted on the door. Her jaw dropped, "Oh. My. God," she whispered. "Is that who I think it is?"

"Who?" Nikki spun around to look.

"Brett Simmons!" Shelby hissed. "You know, the quarterback? I swear that's him. The freakin' TV does *not* do him justice."

"Close your mouth, Shel," Nikki urged in an undertone. "You're going to drool all over yourself."

Stella came around the desk to greet the two men. "Good afternoon, Mr. Simmons and Mr. Reed. This is Miss Powell and...

Shelby stood and extended her hand to Brett Simmons with a blazing smile. "Shelby Baker, huge Bronco fan."

"Are you now?" Brett turned to his agent. "Reed, when we're done, do you think we could produce a pair of tickets for such a big fan?"

"Sure, Brett." The manager raked Shelby over with an assessing look.

"Do you live here in Bozeman?" Brett asked Shelby.

"No. Atlanta. Just came up for the snowboarding. I don't suppose you snowboard, too?" she asked.

"I've been known to from time to time, though my manager discourages it. Is it a favorite pastime of yours, Miss Baker?"

"Matter of fact, I love snowboarding almost as much as I love football," Shelby replied.

"Oh yeah?" he asked. "Where are you staying?"

"Big Sky Resort."

"Big Sky? Me too. Why don't you leave your information with the office here and Reed'll see about those *box* tickets." Brett winked. "Maybe I'll see you around this weekend?"

"Maybe so." Shelby returned a coy smile.

"Right, then," Stella interrupted. "It looks like we're all here now. If you'll just follow me, Mr. Evans and Miss Evans are all ready for you."

"A huge fan?" Nikki whispered. "Since when? You hate football."

Shelby smirked. "Since *that* hot hunk of flesh walked through the door." Her gaze tracked Brett's departing ass. "You know, maybe I was wrong about the landscape up here. The view is looking better all the time."

———

"You said on the phone that you also have a lease offer from Dirk Knowlton on the pasturelands?" Nikki asked Allie half an hour later after Simmons and Reed left. Given it was a cash deal, the closing had taken less than fifteen minutes.

"Yes." Allie pulled another bundle of papers from her briefcase. "Things have taken an unexpected turn for the Flying K."

"What do you mean? Wade said his brother was expanding, but how can he do that if the ranch is struggling?"

"About two months ago, Dirk scored a big contract with a gourmet grocery chain. It seems they want to add American Kobe to their offering of high-end meats. He needs more grazing lands to increase his herd. It's a fair offer," Allie said.

Mr. Evans added, "I'm sure Wade advised you of the tax benefits in putting the land to agricultural use."

"But how does Dirk have the money? Especially if he's expanding his herd?"

"He's probably going to take out a loan to expand the cattle operation," Evans replied.

"Won't that put him in a tough spot financially?"

"Yes and no. There's a bit of a catch-22 in ranching. Dirk has to expand or he'll lose the deal, and he has to borrow to expand. It's how most ranches operate. They borrow large sums with the hope of profit when they sell their stock."

A crazy thought sprang to Nikki's mind. "Do you know if Dirk has considered investors rather than loans?"

"I doubt it," Allie said. "You've met the man. I don't think he plays well with others."

"You're probably right about that." Nikki laughed. "But he knows his business, and the deal he's made could be pretty lucrative."

"Do you mind if I ask where you're going with this?" Evans inquired.

"Well, this whole thing has me thinking. I've just come into a good deal of money and I'd really like to make an investment in an enterprise that I could maybe play some small part in."

Evans frowned over his glasses. "Let me make sure I understand. Are you saying you want to *invest* in the Flying K?"

"I'd like to talk to Dirk and learn more about it first, but it really does sound like a solid opportunity. If I were to offer use of the pasturelands, he'd have more capital available for livestock expansion, wouldn't he?"

"I suppose so." Evans pursed his lips with a nod. "It's

not a bad proposition for Dirk, but your return could be negligible."

"But I'm risking very little and gaining a tax break in the process. I'd at least like to explore the possibilities. Would you be willing to call Dirk on my behalf and explain what I have in mind?"

Evans stood. "I'll make the call. Maybe we can put something together while you're still in town."

"Thank you Mr. Evans. I appreciate your help."

Allie waited until her father departed and then asked, "Have you considered how Wade might feel about this?"

"It's a simple business proposition. Our personal history has nothing to do with it."

"While *I* agree with you wholeheartedly, he may feel differently. Wade doesn't like the risk Dirk is taking and says he's washing his hands of the ranch. That's no doubt part of his motivation for moving to Helena."

Nikki shrugged. "I don't see why he should care what I do. I haven't heard from him in weeks. In fact, I wondered if you and he might have…"

"Picked back up?" Allie finished for her. "No. There's nothing like that between us now. It's all ancient history. Besides, he's moved on…at least geographically."

"What are you saying?"

Allie arched a brow. "He hasn't seen anyone since you left."

Nikki's pulse sped at the news.

Allie continued, "Perhaps you have some unanswered questions pertaining to the estate? Questions that require meeting with your *former* legal counsel?"

"But he's gone," Nikki said.

"Are you going to give up that easily after you came all the way up here?"

"I came for the closing," Nikki argued.

"Which you surely could have handled through email and overnight express. Fess up, Nicole. You wanted to see him, didn't you?"

"Yes. I did," Nikki sighed her confession. "But apparently he feels differently. He left for Helena the minute I said I was coming, didn't he?"

"Pretty much."

"Then I guess there's nothing more to say. Actions speak louder than words, don't they?"

"What would you expect? The man has his pride."

"I don't get you at all, Allie. When I was here last time, you clearly tried to stake your claim, and now you're encouraging me to stake mine?"

"Wade's decision to pursue his future here has put an end to any designs I might have had on him. If I thought there was any possibility that he'd move back to Denver, we wouldn't be having this conversation, but he's taken a different road. Although Montana's a great place to visit, I have no desire to live here. So Wade Knowlton is now free game." Allie packed up her files and briefcase. "I'll be in touch as soon as Dad talks to Dirk. If he seems amenable do you want me to set something up? Would you be willing to travel out to the ranch for that?"

"Sure, as long as he's free this weekend. Otherwise it'll have to be a teleconference since I'm leaving Sunday."

"Unless Wade changes your mind."

"I'm not holding my breath," Nikki said. "He's given

no indication that he wants to see me, and I haven't decided if I'm even going to try."

"You'd be a fool not to. He's a damned good man and I don't just mean in bed." Allie took up a pen and scratched on the back of a card. "Here's his new address. Just don't tell him where you got it, OK?"

Nikki accepted the card. "You really think he's still interested?"

Allie cocked her head. "Let's just say, I think he's still *persuadable*, but that will depend on you."

Chapter 20

<small>AFTER LEAVING THE LEGAL OFFICE, NIKKI</small> DROVE THE hour south to Big Sky where she and Shelby checked into the luxurious Summit Resort. To Shelby's delight, an envelope awaited her at the check-in desk. Her eyes widened to discover two box tickets to the next Broncos game...and a card with a telephone number scrawled on it."

"Holy cow!" Nikki exclaimed. "Box seats for a play-off game? I can't believe how you finagled that."

Shelby regarded the tickets with a calculating look. "They aren't playing Atlanta by any chance, are they?"

"No. I think it's a Texas team. I can't recall which one. Why? Don't tell me you're going to put them on eBay."

"Depends on what they're worth," Shelby said.

"I would guess at least a grand."

Shelby's eyes lit up. "Then definitely Craigslist would be the place."

"What if Brett finds out?"

"How's he ever going to know? It isn't likely I'll ever run into him again, is it?"

"You might since he's staying here."

"Then I'll hold on to the tickets until we get home."

"That's his number, isn't it? Are you going to call him for some *après-ski*?"

"I might," Shelby replied and tapped the tickets

against her teeth. "But I'm not going to make it easy for him. The tickets cost him nothing. If he wants me, he's gonna have to work for it."

"You might want to reconsider since you're going to be on your own tonight."

"What do you mean?" Shelby looked puzzled. "You're here."

"I won't be for long," Nikki said. "I'm driving up to Helena."

"What, tonight?"

"Wade and I have to talk and I'm not wasting any more time. If he gives me the boot I'll check into a motel up there and drive back in the morning."

"You mean I'm going to have this place all to myself?" Shelby beamed.

"Yeah. Maybe you'll want to see if your quarterback has dinner plans, or I suppose you could always order room service and boil yourself alive in the hot tub."

"Alone? Not on your life. Hot tubs are made to be shared."

"Knock yourself out, Shel." Their accommodations were spacious, luxurious, and had a fantastic ski-in location complete with Jacuzzi. But Nikki had no plans to enjoy any of it.

Rather than face her, Wade had taken the easy route and split. She wasn't about to let him have the last word. Again. The more Nikki thought about it the madder she got. He could try to avoid her all he liked, but there was one thing Wade hadn't counted on—and that was a fight. Nikki was heading to Helena with her guns blazing. Wade Knowlton would never know what hit him.

The drive to Helena was a grueling two and a half hours on slushy roads. It also meant Nikki arrived well after dark. Thanks to the GPS on her mobile phone, she was able to locate Wade's address, a high-end condo in the historic district of Last Chance Gulch. After parking in the basement garage, she dialed his number, praying she'd have a strong enough signal to overcome her subterranean location.

The phone rang four times, her heart beating a little harder with each ring. He *had* to know it was her. Perhaps he wasn't going to answer? She really hadn't considered a contingency plan. On the fifth ring she closed her eyes in dismay. She was about to disconnect when his voice abruptly sounded on the other end.

"Nikki?"

"Hi, Wade. I s'pose you already know I arrived in Montana this morning." She tried to sound nonchalant.

"Yeah. I knew you were coming."

"Why didn't you tell me you wouldn't be there?"

"I didn't see the point when Evans was there to take care of everything. Is there a problem?"

"Yes. Well sort of." She walked across the garage and pressed the call button on the elevator. "There are a number of things that are still unsettled."

"Like what?"

"First of all, you and me, and the way we left things."

"*You left*, Nikki."

"And we never even said a proper good-bye."

"Maybe it wasn't *proper*, but I vividly recall the fare-well fuck."

Heat inflamed her face at the reminder of their encounter on the tailgate. "Is that all it was to you?"

"It seemed all you wanted," he replied. "And if that's
what you want from me now, I'm sorry I can't oblige
you—" The phone went dead.

She stared at the display trying to figure out if he'd
hung up on her, or if the call had dropped because the elevator door closed. Either way, he'd still had the last word.

"Not this time, cowboy," she muttered and then
jammed the button for the penthouse floor.

Wade was furious that she'd called him. He'd left
Bozeman thinking he was done with her, but the moment she spoke he was filled with the need to see her,
which pissed him off even more. Then she'd gone and
hung up! Shit! He didn't need this. He wasn't about to
let her tromp on his heart again. His doorbell buzzed.

He turned away from the door, intending to ignore
it and go shower, but the bell sounded again in rapid
succession. His uninvited caller was damned persistent.
Ready to unload on whoever disturbed his peace, he
padded barefoot and shirtless to the door and flung it
open to find Nikki standing there.

"You?" He glowered in disbelief.

"Yeah. Me. Can I come in?"

He hesitated, arms across his chest. "Why'd you
come here? Looking for another good-bye fuck? Is that
what you want from me?"

"No, Wade." Her eyes flickered at his confrontational
demeanor but her tone remained even. "Please, we really need to talk."

"There's nothing left to say. I'm not interested in picking this back up, Nikki. I told you I don't believe in long-distance relationships."

He'd made his feelings for her clear once and she'd walked away. Although he'd known the minute he laid eyes on her again that he wasn't over her yet—not by a long shot—he still couldn't put himself through that agony again.

"That's not why I'm here."

His gaze narrowed. "Then what *are* you here for?"

"I want to discuss a *business* proposition."

"What kind of business?" he demanded.

"Your brother wants to lease my pastureland, but I came to see if I can negotiate a different kind of deal with the Flying K."

"Shouldn't you be talking to Dirk about this?"

"Evans is already presenting my proposal to Dirk, but you're still involved in the business side of the ranch, aren't you?"

"I s'pose, but only until Dirk buys me out."

"Then you are part of this too. Can I come in?"

He stepped aside with an exasperated sigh, arm outstretched in reluctant invitation. She followed him inside, shrugged out of her coat, and handed it to him. Apparently this was not going to be the brief conversation he'd hoped for.

Involuntarily, his gaze tracked over her, lingering on her curves. *Shit*. She was wearing the black dress again. Had she worn it just to torture him? If so, it was working. It pissed him off royally that she'd wear that same dress, and even more that he was responding to it.

Preferring to avoid temptation, he didn't join her on

the sofa, but sprawled in an overstuffed chair opposite her. The dress was damned distracting. He wondered if she wore the thigh-highs. His mind wandered back to the last time she'd worn that dress and how she'd looked at him when he got her off in the parking lot, then how she'd ridden him in the SUV. He was getting hard just thinking about it.

Her skirt rose when she sat down, but not enough that he could tell what was underneath. Then she crossed her legs, giving him a better view. Yup. Sure as hell, she was wearing the damned thigh-highs.

"What kind of deal?" he asked, carefully modulating his voice. This was business. She was just another client. He'd treat her with strict professional courtesy, nothing more, no matter how hard she made his dick.

"Cattle, Wade."

"Cattle?" he repeated blankly.

"Yes, I came to talk about ranching."

"You *drove* to Helena to ask me questions about cattle ranching?"

"Yes, you advised me to make some investments and your brother's looking to expand."

"—against my advice."

"Why would you be against a perfectly good business opportunity?"

"Because it means taking on more debt. He could lose everything." He shook his head. "I'm done. If he falls on his face I'm not bailing him out."

"He wouldn't have to go into debt if he had an investor."

"Who'd be fool enough—"

"Me."

"You?" He stared at her as if she'd sprouted a second head. "Don't you recall *anything* I told you about ranching?"

"I remember *everything*, Wade. Look, I have a business degree that I worked six long years for, but haven't put to any real use. I also own a thousand prime acres in Montana. Why shouldn't I invest in cattle? It makes perfect sense—"

"It doesn't make a lick of sense! You don't know shit about cattle."

She jutted her chin. "You don't know anything about what I do or don't know about cows! As I recall, you didn't think I knew the backside of a horse either. Besides, I can learn, can't I?"

"You're out of your ever-lovin' mind if you wish to pursue this."

"But it was you who introduced me to the meat, after all. Do you remember that night, Wade?" How could he ever forget? He shifted in his chair. "It was tender and succulent." She ran her tongue over her lips.

His attention riveted to her mouth. He recalled the feel of her lips on him, surrounding him, and wanted like hell to feel them again.

"What I sampled with you was the best I ever had, Wade, and I haven't wanted any other since. Problem is," she continued, "I haven't found anything like it in Georgia, so who's going to satisfy my craving, Wade? It seems I have little choice now but to satisfy myself."

Was he imagining the sexual innuendo? Either way, he was getting as hard as a fucking post.

"You have no idea what you're getting into," he argued. "You don't have a clue about the economics of it.

It's not like you just throw some cows on the pasture, watch them eat grass, and count the days until they're fat enough to take to market."

"Then enlighten me."

"All right." He gave an exasperated groan. "In the most basic operation your first expense is the herd. At minimum, you need a bull and two or three dozen cows and heifers. Thirty is about the max a single bull can handle, unless you opt for artificial insemination."

"That seems unfair to the poor cows."

He gaped, feeling completely derailed. "What do you mean?"

"Depriving them of the bull. Don't you think they enjoy it too, Wade? It appears the bulls do, anyway. I've watched some YouTube videos. They mount, thrust frantically, ejaculate, and then move on to the next cow. Bulls are very well endowed, aren't they? Do you think they satisfy their cows?"

"I doubt they care very much either way."

"We're also a lot more versatile in our techniques, aren't we? I mean bulls and cows, stallions and mares, canines and felines, they all do it doggie-style, don't they? I guess that's the biggest difference between animals and humans, isn't it? Animals are so mechanical about it while we copulate for pleasure. You and I explored quite a few different ways, didn't we, Wade? I want happy cows. I could never deprive them of a good...*bull*. What's a decent one cost?"

The sudden invasion of erotic imagery had him struggling for coherency. "Cost? Probably five to ten grand, depending on the breed."

"Well, I'd want to make sure I got the best one. How

can you tell? By the size of his"—her gaze slowly passed over him—"apparatus? Does it matter, Wade? Does it help in breeding if they fit together real snug and tight?"

The question sent another surge of blood to his groin. She'd been so hot, wet, and tight it had blown his mind. He shook off those thoughts with an exasperated sound. "This is a ridiculous conversation!"

"No, it's not," she protested. "I want strong, virile bulls that will satisfy my cows. I'm sure bulls like that are real hard to find. I don't want frustrated cows, Wade. It's miserable not to be satisfied, do you know that?"

He could hardly think at all now…beyond dragging her into his bed and fucking some sense into her. "I can't believe you're seriously thinking about this."

"I am. I haven't stopped thinking about *it* since I got here." She held his gaze as if she read his thoughts.

"At startup you're already in to the tune of fifty grand and you still have to feed the animals."

"But I have a thousand acres of prime grassland."

"Which is covered with snow for five to six months. On top of feed, you still have the cost of ranch hands, vet visits, and general farm expenses. You see, Nikki? You're in belly-deep and will have negligible profit for years. Do you understand now? Ranching sucks—as a lifestyle and an investment."

"Well, speaking of what sucks, Wade…it sucked to be in a job I hated… I told you I wanted to be in control of my life…but it sucked to be alone…it seems I've become an expert at things that suck. I'd rather suck you, Wade."

He drew in a breath. Holy hell, it was agony to sit there after that remark and pretend he didn't feel anything. "Let me be sure I understand this," he replied slowly, deliberately. "You wouldn't stay here when I asked you to, but now you'd come back just because you suddenly have a harebrained notion to raise cattle? I'm not buying it."

He was slouched in the chair wearing only his faded jeans and a deepening frown. He'd never looked sexier, but he'd also never looked so distant. She was desperate to get a rise out of him but he'd hardly blinked when she'd blurted a crude offer of a blow job.

Had she just made a fool of herself? Had she come all this way for nothing?

"You're not really here to talk about ranching."

"No, Wade."

"Then why are you really here?" he demanded. "What do you want?

"There are some things I need to say to you."

"I'm listening."

"I've been thinking a lot about everything you said—about not trusting you. About pushing you away. You were right. You were right about a lot of things. When you asked me before I left what I wanted, I told you I didn't know. That wasn't exactly true. I already knew what I wanted but I didn't believe I could have it."

"And what's that?" he asked.

She took a deep breath. "You." She watched for any flicker of emotion, but he remained impassive, unreadable. She'd waltzed in with such bravado but now felt so uncertain, so vulnerable. "Am I too late? Are you already involved with someone else?"

"Not at present." His crystal gaze held hers.

"I want a joint venture with you, Wade. What's it gonna cost me?"

"I don't know," he replied slowly, hauling himself out of the chair. "You still talkin' ranching?"

"No," she answered, tension coiling in her belly as he came toward her. "Ranching just seemed like a good excuse to come."

"I can give you a much better reason to *come*," he said. "In fact I'd like to give you a whole mouthful. And for the record, I'd like you to suck me too. C'mere, Nikki."

The minute she was on her feet his arms came around her. She locked hers around his neck, shutting her eyes on a sound that was halfway between a sob and a sigh. She clung to him tightly as they moved, almost as if they were two-stepping across a dance floor as Wade backed her toward his bedroom. God, it was so damn good to be back in his arms. He was big and warm, smelled like heaven, and felt like it too.

"Did you really have any doubt about me?" His voice rumbled in her ear. "You must have been pretty damn sure of yourself to have put on that dress."

"Not at all. The dress was my secret weapon."

He cocked a brow. "A secret weapon?"

"Yes." She was growing breathless with lust but he still held back. "I came prepared to wage war."

Once through the bedroom door, he closed it with his foot, then spun her against it. His lips came down hungrily on hers, his kiss growing deeper, more intense, as he slid his hands with slow deliberation up her thighs, setting every inch of her skin on fire. His mouth broke from hers to glide up her neck, tracking her pulse with his hot tongue, and then tracing her ear.

"You must have known I was a goner the minute you walked in here." His hot words tickled in her ear, sending ripples low into her belly and a pool of moisture between her thighs.

"I only hoped," she murmured back, urging his hands higher. Her heart fluttered at his flaring pupils when he discovered nothing underneath but the thigh highs. "I was ready to pull out all the stops."

"Were you now?" The low rumble of his laugh warmed her insides. "And you thought to begin by talking about *cows*?"

"I had to infiltrate your camp," she explained. "I hoped we'd eventually move on to other things."

"Like what?"

"Like maybe how much you missed me?" She tilted her head and parted her lips, inviting his kiss, but he held back, cupping her face and stroking her mouth with the pad of his thumb.

"I've missed you all right. A day hasn't gone by that I haven't ached for you."

"Me too," she whispered and brought his hand to her heart, covering it with her own. "Right here. But you still haven't said you want me back."

He tangled his fingers in her hair and crushed his mouth to hers, kissing her as if he wished to devour her. Until she melted into him breathless and mindless.

"That answer good enough?" he asked. "Or do you still need more convincing?"

"Oh yeah, cowboy." She grinned. "Lots and lots more convincing."

He took her at her word, sliding to his knees and inching her skirt up, his lips following his hands. His hot mouth and questing tongue blazed a scorching trail from her knees to the tops of her stockings. He licked the lace edge and then nuzzled his bristled face between her thighs. Her knees buckled at the first hot, wet swipes of his tongue. She whimpered and clutched his shoulders for balance.

"So wet. So sweet. *So mine*," he groaned into her flesh.

She braced herself against the door as his masterful fingers plunged in and out in synchrony with the slick swirls of his hot tongue, her blood thrumming though her veins as he teased and tormented her. She plastered herself to him, grinding her hips against his mouth with every wrenching ripple of pleasure. "Please, Wade," she panted, her body aching for him. "I can't stand this anymore. I want… I need… Please…"

He looked up at her with a wicked smile. "You need what, sweetheart? This?"

He curled his fingers inside her, massaging that magical place while flicking his tongue over her bud. Her insides clenched. Her body quivered with mounting tension.

"God yes. Don't stop!"

His chuckle vibrated through her like a tuning fork. "Or maybe more like this?"

He latched onto her clit and sucked, launching her into a screaming climax.

Wade licked her juices from his lips and stood. Her face was flushed, swollen lips parted, and blue-green eyes glazed over with spent passion when he caught her against him. He swallowed her soft sobs, kissing her deeply and tenderly until she came back to earth. He'd never tire of making her come apart, and damned sure wasn't finished yet.

With his hands under her ass and her legs wrapped around his hips, he carried her to his bed, where he unzipped her dress, and peeled it slowly off. She wore only the black stockings. Her skin was flushed, her eyes were heavy-lidded, and her hair fanned out in loose waves on the pillow. He stepped back to admire the view he'd missed while he shucked his jeans.

God, she's a gorgeous sight.

He came over her, taking one tempting nipple into his mouth, suckling until she whimpered. He released it with a pop before moving to the other. She parted her thighs and reached for him. "Now. *Please*."

He pulled back. "Sorry, darlin', but I'm not finished yet."

"Is this some kind of punishment?"

"You might look at it that way. You made me wait a long time for you, Nikki. Didn't you once say payback's a bitch? Now roll over. Onto your stomach."

He stuffed a pillow under her hips, then knelt at the foot of the bed where he began anew, peeling off her stockings one at a time, nibbling at her ankles, stroking his fingers over the backs of her calves, scraping his teeth up the back of her legs. He licked and sucked the erogenous spot behind her knees until she quivered again with want.

He moved up her body to her delectable ass where his lust grew hotter and his attention more aggressive.

Molding and squeezing her buttocks, he added sting-
ing bites that made her buck, only to soothe her tender
flesh with hot open mouth kisses and long lashes of his
tongue. After savoring every luscious inch of her ass, he
worked his way up her spine licking, biting, and kissing
one vertebrae at a time until his chest hugged her back
and his cock lay nestled in the groove of her ass. He
began a rhythmic rocking of his hips. It was so damned
good just to feel her body beneath his again.

"Do you like that?" he breathed into her ear, then bit
down on her lobe.

She moaned her reply, squirming against him, urging
him inside her.

Beyond ready, Wade positioned her hips, and then
froze. *Shit!* He'd forgotten a goddamn condom. And he
was damned if he even knew where they were.

"What's wrong?" she asked.

"I don't have protection. Do you?"

"God no," she replied in dismay. "I didn't even think
of it."

"How long has it been for you?" he asked.

"Not since we were last together. What about you?"

"There's been no one else, Nikki."

"So we're exclusive?"

"Yeah. We are as far as I'm concerned."

"Then we don't need anything."

"Thank you, Jesus," he moaned, dipping into her
wetness, and sliding his bulbous head through her sex-
slickened folds. Having already tortured himself to the
brink of insanity, he closed his eyes, withdrew slightly,
and plunged deep, losing himself in the mind-melting
sensation of Nikki.

Determined to make up for lost time, they never left the apartment the entire weekend, and barely emerged from the bed. They made love until exhaustion set in, dozed for stretches, only to wake up and begin again. Between bouts of lovemaking, they laughed, talked, and even ate in bed, only to fall back into each other's arms. Their weekend together was like nothing Nikki had ever known. It was different now. The blossoming bud of trust as they rediscovered one another and explored new desires, made each time better than the last.

When Monday morning came, Nikki awoke cradled snugly by Wade's body. She lay there with her eyes closed, not daring to stir, only wanting to linger in his warmth, his scent, in the feel of him wrapped around her. Unable to resist, she wriggled against him and he responded with a guttural sound that vibrated through her back. Only half awake, he slid his hand from its position on her breast to the space between her thighs, pushing his fingers into her wetness.

Without even opening his eyes, he positioned himself at her entrance. She loved how he felt inside her, how completely he filled her, so big and hard and hot, and how he always ensured her pleasure. It began lazy and languid as they settled into a slow, steady, rocking rhythm while his bristly cheek nuzzled her neck.

Wade kissed his way to the junction of her shoulder and gently bit down, as he drove deeper, increasing the force of his thrusts while his finessing fingers traced slow, teasing circles around her clit. Wade was languid and tender, entering her deliciously deep, slow, and sweet, maintaining a steady cadence with her breathless sounds until she spiraled once more into shuddering bliss. It seemed as if Wade wanted to convince her with his body what words could never convey. For the first time in her life she felt safe and secure. Cherished. Loved.

Moments later, as she lay spent in his arms, she looked up to find him studying her, his eyes sober and his brows pulled together. "What is it?" she asked.

"You haven't changed your mind, have you? You're not going to hie on back to Georgia and never come back, are you?"

"No, Wade. It's different now. I'm different."

"How?"

"I went back the first time because I'd convinced myself we were doomed to fail before even giving it a chance. I was afraid of heartbreak."

"Why?"

"Because it seemed too good to be real. You were too good to be true. I was insecure and afraid to trust that you really cared for me beyond this."

"And now?" he asked.

"I'm still scared," she admitted.

"I told you a long time ago I'd never hurt you, Nikki." He kissed her softly. "I meant it."

"I know you did and I'm sorry that I was the one to hurt us both, but I'm ready now. I truly want us to make this work."

"I'm damn glad to hear that." He grinned. "Any more *convincing* at this juncture would surely kill me."

She laughed. "I doubt that, but you'll have time to rest up while I'm gone."

"How long before you come back?" he asked.

"Not long. I only need a few weeks to take care of things. I think I'll just let Shelby have the apartment until my lease is up. I doubt I can get everything done before Christmas, but I should be back in time for us to celebrate New Year's together."

"I can't think of a better way to begin it," he said.

She traced a random pattern on his chest. "Wade?"

"What, darlin'?"

She looked up into his face. "Promise me it'll always be like this with us."

He claimed her lips with an all-consuming kiss, the kind she'd never get enough of for as long as she lived.

He released her slowly, murmuring hotly against her mouth. "It always will be with us, sweetheart… As good as it gets."

Epilogue

A CRASH SOUNDED OUTSIDE HER APARTMENT, SENDING Nikki racing to the front door. She flung it open to find Shelby dragging a gargantuan fir tree up the steps.

"What the heck are you doing, Shel?"

Shelby looked up, her Santa hat askew. "What does it look like? The trees were on clearance at the Home Depot, so I thought I'd buy one and spread some Christmas cheer."

Nikki scrunched her face. "Don't you think it's a bit too big for the apartment? That thing must be seven feet tall!"

Shelby shrugged. "I wanted the best one. Though I think it's going to look more like a Charlie Brown tree by the time I get it in the door."

On closer examination, the tree was pretty dried up and its needles formed a trail of green all the way from the apartment steps to the parking lot.

"How on earth did you even get it home?" Nikki asked.

"Got a ride from the guy working in the garden department. I also have a date now for New Year's Eve." Shelby winked. "It was kind of a trade."

"Glad to know *one* of us will be having a good time."

"So, you still can't get a flight out?"

"No," Nikki sighed. "And I miss Wade horribly. We were supposed to spend New Year's Eve together, but the airlines are completely booked until the weekend *after* the holiday. I've called every day and put myself on all the waiting lists. I had no idea Montana is such a popular Christmas destination."

"You could always drive there," Shelby suggested.

Nikki shook her head. "Not on your life. I've never driven in snow before, let alone snow- and ice-covered mountains. The idea of it terrifies me even more than flying. Besides, I was going to leave you my car since you still don't have one."

"That old piece of—"

Nikki silenced her with a look. "It's still better than the one you *don't have*, isn't it?" she retorted, hands on her hips. "A little appreciation might not be out of order."

"Quit acting like my mother."

"Then don't be such an ungrateful little brat."

Shelby dropped the tree and threw her hands in the air. "Fine! I'm outta here!"

"C'mon, Shel," Nikki cajoled. "Let's not get into it again. It's Christmas Eve. I'd rather have eggnog than arguments."

Shelby's scowl softened. "You're right. And I could go for a drink. You got anything good to spike it with? Or do I need to go back out and hit the package store?"

"I've got a bottle of Bacardi stashed away."

"*Had*," Shelby corrected.

"You drank it?"

Shelby shrugged. "Mojitos go really good with Jerry Springer."

"I can't believe anyone with your IQ watches that crap!"

"It's highly entertaining...not to mention culturally enlightening."

Nikki shook her head. "If that's true, I'd rather stay in the dark, thank you very much. C'mon. Let's get this pathetic tree inside, although with all my stuff packed up, I'm not sure what we'll decorate it with."

Shelby grinned. "Don't worry. I bought a bunch of Christmas thongs on clearance."

———

"I'm so sad," Nikki whispered tearily into her phone. "I tried every flight but it's impossible. I *really* miss you, Wade."

"Me too, darlin'," Wade replied. "More than you know. I can't wait to show you just how much. We'll make up for all the lost time when I see you."

"You promise?" Nikki asked.

"Yeah. I promise."

"How are you going to make it up?"

"You really want me to tell you?"

"Yeah. In explicit detail, but maybe I should take this conversation into the bedroom first."

"That might be a good idea," Shelby replied, rolling her eyes and upending the empty bottle of Captain Morgan.

The doorbell rang. Nikki stared at her watch with a scowl. It was almost midnight. Who would be dropping by at this time of night? The bell chimed a second time. She covered the phone and hissed to Shelby who was sprawled across the sofa watching a marathon of *A Christmas Story*. "Get it, will you? I'm kinda busy right now."

Shelby protested, "But this is the part where he gets his tongue stuck to the flagpole."

When Shelby still made no move to answer it, Nikki jerked her head toward the door. "All right already!" Shelby muted the movie before heaving herself up to answer the bell.

"I'll be counting the days," Nikki continued to Wade.

"That so? Well, I'm counting the seconds now. I'm hoping it's not more than thirty before you answer the door."

"What?" Nikki bolted out of her chair. "Are you saying—"

Shelby flung the door open. "Well, boy howdy, Nikki! Just look at what Santa dropped off!"

Wade stepped through the doorway, tipping his hat with a mile-wide grin. "Merry Christmas."

"Wade!" Nikki shrieked, shoving Shelby out of the way to leap with simultaneous laughter and tears into his open arms. He picked her up and swung her around, almost knocking over the thong-covered Christmas tree. "How did you get here?" she asked, raining kisses all over his beloved, beard-stubbled face.

"Camped out for two straight days at the airport waiting for anyone to no-show on any flight headed south. I only got as far as St. Louis and then had to rent a car and drive the rest of the way."

"I can't believe you did that! Or that you're really here!"

"I couldn't stand the thought of not being with you for Christmas, New Year's, or any other day to come."

"Oh, Wade," she cried. "I don't even know what to say!"

He flashed his sexy grin. "Say yes."

"Of course! Yes! Yes! A thousand times yes!" She suddenly drew back with a puzzled look. "Yes to what?"

"You didn't think I came empty-handed did you? A guy who shows up at his girl's place on Christmas Eve had better be armed."

Nikki's heart almost stopped when he plucked a velvet-covered ring box out of his shirt pocket.

"Oh my God!" Shelby's jaw dropped. "A ring? He brought you a freaking ring!"

Nikki swallowed hard. "But we never even talked about this. I thought we were going to wait a while to see…" She stared at the box, afraid even to touch it.

He opened the box to a gorgeous emerald-cut diamond surrounded by glittering baguettes. Nikki stared down at the ring through eyes blurred with joyful tears and then back at Wade.

"I'm not getting any less certain about us." He paused, searching her face. "Are you?"

"No," she cried. "It's been agony being away from you these past weeks."

"Me too. I know we didn't talk about this but it just felt right to me. We don't have to rush into it if you don't want to, but you'll let me put it on your finger, won't you?"

His eyes held a look of uncertainty, of vulnerability, that she'd never seen in him before. Did he actually think she'd refuse it? With her throat too tight to speak, Nikki stuck out her hand with an emphatic nod. Wade took it in his with an audible sigh of relief and then dropped to one knee.

"You've got to be kidding." Shelby grimaced. "Are you for real?"

Wade's grin returned, even broader than before, displaying his perfect white teeth and a mind-erasing dimple. "Humor me, Shelby. I'm an old-fashioned kinda guy."

Wade's expression immediately sobered when he took Nikki's left hand in his. "I had this all planned out. I was going to ask you this question on New Year's Eve, after a bottle of wine and a nice romantic dinner, but once I bought the ring, I knew I couldn't wait. I've already wasted enough time in my life. Now that I know what I want, I don't want to waste another minute."

"Me either," she whispered.

His eyes of crystal blue bored into hers. "Then will you marry me, Nikki? Will you be my best friend and my lover for real and forever?"

Nikki watched in breathless amazement as he slid the ring past her knuckle and firmly onto her finger. She gazed at the shimmering diamonds thinking this was the most sublime moment of her entire life. "I still can't believe this," she murmured.

"That's not the answer I was hoping for, sweetheart."

"How about this?" She clasped his face between her hands, kissing it all over with wild abandon. Wade soon took command, toppling her backwards over his knee for a long, deep, heart-clenching kiss, releasing her from it slowly, reluctantly.

"Can I take that as an affirmative?" he asked.

"Yes, Wade." Nikki stroked his perfect face feeling like her heart would burst. "I'll be your best friend and your lover. For real and forever."

Read on for an excerpt from
Rough Rider

Casper, Wyoming

SEATED ON THE TOP RAIL ABOVE THE BULL PEN, JANICE watched with growing impatience as the final riders finished. Unlike most of the girls she'd grown up with, can chasing had never held her interest. Sure there was good money in it, but she just didn't see the challenge in running circles around barrels.

Bulls, on the other hand, massively muscled, notoriously unpredictable, and sometimes dangerously aggressive, were her passion. She'd been raised with cattle, had fed bawling calves from the earliest time she could remember, but bucking bulls provided her family's real living.

While the final scores were announced, and the barrels cleared from the arena, Janice hopped down from her perch. Time to get back to work. Although she could have used some help tonight, there was none to be had. Ready or not, she was Combes Bucking Bulls' new chute boss. Janice walked the length of the pens, inspecting the animals and watching for any sign of trouble as the other stock hands prodded and loaded their animals into their respective chutes.

There were at least two dozen riders already surrounding the bull pens. Some were shooting the shit, and others were immersed in their preparations. Janice looked casually over the group for the one cowboy who made her pulse race. He was one of the early draws, but Dirk Knowlton hadn't made his appearance yet.

Although he'd never looked sideways at her, Janice had followed Dirk's rodeo career since high school when they'd competed on the same team. He'd ridden rough stock while she'd competed in breakaway roping. She'd always enjoyed working with ropes and livestock. Roping required speed, skill, and near perfect coordination between horse and rider—practical skills that were invaluable on a working ranch—and Janice was nothing if not practical. She'd been real good at it too. Probably could have gotten a scholarship or even gone pro if her family's needs hadn't kept her tied to the ranch.

In the end, she'd gone to work full time for her father, and Dirk had won a full scholarship to Montana State. She'd run into him on occasion since then, mainly during branding season when all the ranches helped each other out, but he'd never taken notice of her then either. He'd been too wrapped up in Rachel Carson. Along with half the boys at Twin Bridges High, he'd only had eyes for Rachel. Gangly Janice had never stood a chance against the pert, blue-eyed blonde.

Since graduation she'd only occasionally run into Dirk, usually no more than a hat tipping at the ranching co-op or the stock sale, but now that she was working the rodeos, their paths had once more crossed—not that it made any difference. Little had changed. Rachel was still the rodeo queen, leading the grand entry glittering with rhinestones, while Janice looked on from the rough stock chutes, mired ankle-deep in manure, and smelling

like the livestock. Even now that she'd finally filled
out in all the right places, she was either completely
tongue-tied or jabbered like an idiot whenever Dirk
came around, which was every day for the past week.

With her heart lurching into her throat, Janice
watched as the cowboy of her dreams swaggered up to
the holding pens. It wasn't just his rugged good looks
that made her palms sweat, there was something about
Dirk, besides his long and lanky physique that put him
head and shoulders above the rest.

He was clad in ass-hugging denim with leather chaps
flapping, white Stetson shadowing his ice-blue eyes, and
rigging bag slung over one broad shoulder. She watched
him throw his rope over the coral panel in preparation
for his ride.

Now or never, Janice. He'll be called up any minute.

With her heart hammering, she inhaled for courage
and licked her lips with a tongue that suddenly felt as
dry as sandpaper. "I watched you on Outlaw Josie Wales
in the second go 'round yesterday," she blurted.

"Why thank you, ma'am." Dirk tipped his hat with a
mile-wide grin.

"You about spurred his head off," she continued. "It
was one of the best rides I ever did see."

Grady Garrison leaned over from his perch on the
adjoining pen and spat a wad of dip. "Good thing pretty
boy scored so high on the broncs cause he sure as shit
won't make the cut on the bulls."

"That so?" Dirk paused in prepping his rope, his ice
blue eyes meeting Grady's for only a second. "Funny, as
I recall it just last week in Red Lodge I made the whistle while your ass hit the dirt." He went back to work,

crushing the lump of rosin and wrapping his gloved hand around the bull rope.

Grady jumped down from the pen with narrowed, steely-colored eyes. "I'm still going into the short round with the high score. You're delusional as shit if you think to beat me." His shoulders were thrown back and his thumbs hooked in his belt loops—the ones that supported the huge Collegiate Champion Bull Rider buckle.

Any stranger who didn't know them as longtime rodeo buddies would surely think fists were about to fly, but Janice suspected it was just pre-ride posturing. Cowboys as a rule were ridiculously competitive. Still, she bit her lip at the tension of rising testosterone.

"Maybe you're right, Grady, but a closed mouth gathers no boots."

"What're you sayin'? You think I'm all talk?"

Dirk shrugged. "I think a lotta rodeo legends are made by a flannelmouth on a bar stool. So maybe you'll wanna put your money where that big fat mouth is?"

She wondered how far they'd want to take this pissing contest. Dirk was a decent bull rider, but the smaller and wiry Grady was one of the best. Unfortunately, like a lot of cowboys, he too often let his mouth run off, and his ego get in the way of his good sense.

"All right pretty boy. How 'bout the lowest score on the next ride buys the drinks tonight? And none of that cheap shit either."

Dirk stood up straight, rolled his neck and shoulders, and then extended his hand. "You're on."

Grady accepted it with a laugh. Janice breathed a sigh of relief. The announcer gave the final scores on the barrel racing and then broadcasted the imminent start of the bull-riding.

Grady puffed up like a fighting cock as soon as audience attention riveted to their end of the arena. "Now the real rodeo begins."

"Plenty of people watch the other events too," Janice protested. "The broncs are my personal favorite." She darted a glance to Dirk. "Classier than the bull riding."

"Bullshit," Grady scoffed. "You know as well as I do that the bulls are what eighty percent of these people come for. No one really gives a rip about all the warm up acts, though team ropin's probably the worst." He looked to Janice with an air of expectancy.

"Don't ask why, Janice," Dirk warned. "It's his worst joke—and the one he always uses when he's itching for a bar fight."

"Oh yeah?" Janice couldn't stifle her grin. "Why's that, Grady?"

Grady smirked. "Because team ropin's a lot like jacking off, sweet cheeks—kinda fun to do, but no one wants to watch it."

Dirk rolled his eyes and Janice shook her head with a derisive snort.

Grabbing her flank ropes and hook, she methodically moved down the row of massively muscled, shifting, snorting bovines. Janice spoke in low, calm tones as she handled each animal. She knew every bull in the circuit by name, and endeavored to handle each one with the care and respect they deserved. To her annoyance, Grady followed her, jabbering on about nothing, while she flanked her bulls. It was damned irritating how the cocky SOB refused to be ignored.

After finishing with Sudden Impact, Janice double-checked the bulls in the pens. When she returned, Dirk was armored with his Kevlar vest and standing on the platform above Magnum Force. "You the gunner?" she asked.

"Yup." Dirk nodded. "Drew this big bastard. New one isn't he?" He jerked his head toward the massive Brahma shifting restlessly in his pen.

"Yeah. He's new all right."

"What happened to that ol' sonofabitch, The Enforcer? Did you retire him?"

"Hell no. Daddy sold him. Pocketed a big chunk of change and still had enough left to buy two replacements that he found down at this shithole farm in Arkansas. Mag here is one of 'em." She nodded to the bull.

While her father had made a respectable name in stock contracting, she'd always felt his methods were a bit hit or miss. He'd struck it lucky enough times to stay in the business, but would never make it to the top because he was too quick to sell his best bulls for cash in hand. To Janice's frustration, he'd never focused on the business of breeding his own stock. They had the land and the know-how, so it seemed a wasted opportunity.

Janice, on the other hand, saw a future in bucking bulls. While traditional rodeo was dying out and struggling just to break even, the new bull-riding associations were packing 'em in, even in the big cities. It was the new "extreme" sport. Breeding the rankest bulls for the toughest cowboys was her dream—what she was secretly working toward. She just needed the right foundation bull. She'd already wondered if Mag might be the one. If he made it big on this circuit, she was determined to buy him out for breeding—no matter the cost.

"I detect a pattern here. Outlaw Josie Wales? Magnum Force?" Dirk chuckled. "Your ol' man's a real Clint Eastwood fan, isn't he?"

"Yeah. He's always named his rough stock after favorite movies but the primest of the lot are called after Clint Eastwood flicks. Be careful with this one, Dirk. I think Mag just might be the rankest bull we've ever had. He's no chute fighter, but once that gate flies open, he's unpredictable as hell."

"Oh yeah? If you've got any other secrets to share, I'm all ears."

Grady snorted and spat another black wad of dip. "You so scared of eatin' dirt that you're asking the stock hands for lessons?"

"Damned straight, Grady. Her father owns the bull and I'm one ride away from winning the overall."

"Shit. If you're so hard up for teachin', you shoulda just watched me ride that badass." He jerked his head at Texas Tornado, the notorious bull he'd ridden for a high score of eighty-six points.

"Your style wouldn't cut it with Mag, Grady," Janice interjected.

"Oh yeah?" Grady pulled out another chuck of wintergreen Skoal and stuffed it under his lower lip. "There ain't a bull in the world that can't be rode, sweetheart—"

"Or a cowboy that can't be throwed," Janice finished with a smirk of her own. Although one of the top contenders, Grady needed to be taken down a peg or two and Janice hoped Dirk would be the one to do it.

"And just how many bulls have *you* rode now, sweet pants?"

"None," she shot back. "But that doesn't mean I'm ignorant. Maybe you forget I grew up with these animals. I know when I load 'em what kinda mood they're in and most times how they're gonna act."

"That may be, but all bets are off once you're actually forking the SOB with the flank rope on."

Janice shrugged. "I'm just sayin' look out if you ever draw this one, Grady. Usually the bulls clue you in on what they're thinking, but not this one. When you assume he's gonna spin into your hand, he blows, or he looks like he's fading right and then ducks off left, or maybe takes a sudden nose dive and snaps his head like ol' Bodacious did. He's smart as hell and he'll set you up for a big hurt in a heartbeat. This bull's gonna rearrange a lot of cowboy faces in his new career."

"Then it's too bad Grady didn't draw him this go round," Dirk taunted his buddy. "Rearranging *his* ugly mug could only be an improvement."

Grady grabbed his crotch. "It ain't my face the buckle bunnies are after, pretty boy."

Janice ignored the vulgar exchange. "Mag's an ornery bastard if you yank a foot on him. Ride him too aggressive and I promise he'll eat you up. If you don't want to be the first one to kiss that bull, Dirk, you'd do well to spare the spurs."

Dirk attached the bell to the rope and gave her a crooked smile that revealed a deep left sided dimple. "I hear you loud and clear."

Every bucking horse and bull presented its own challenge and Mag was new and an unknown entity. A savvy rider studied his draw before his ride and talked to the stock hands. She was glad Dirk was willing to listen.

"Why all this concern about *that* dink?" Grady muttered, jerking his head in Dirk's direction.

"Maybe 'cause he actually asked my advice."

"How 'bout I give *you* some advice, sweet cheeks? Don't waste yourself waitin' around on Dirk. Everyone knows he has it bad for Rachel. They've been playing it hot and heavy for years. 'Sides, there's better cowboys willing to bear company with a sweet thing like you."

"Better cowboys?" She let her gaze flicker over Grady for a fraction of a second. "Like who?"

Grady grinned big, broad, and bad. "Why yours truly, of course."

"Really?" She cracked a smile despite herself. "Does anyone besides you and your momma share this grandiose opinion of Grady Garrison?"

"Oh yeah, baby doll. Ask any buckle bunny from here to Houston."

"That so?" Her smile instantly faded. "Then I ain't interested."

"Maybe I just need the right woman to make me wanna settle down."

Janice snorted outright. "What a crock! Does that line of bull really work for you?"

He grinned shamelessly. "More times than I could count."

"You're the one who's wasting your breath, Grady. I don't sleep around, especially not with horn-dog cowboys."

Ignoring her racing pulse, Janice double checked the flank while Grady hooked Dirk's rope around the animal's massive barrel. A moment later, Dirk climbed up and over the chute, then quietly lowered himself onto the bull's back. He warmed the rosin-coated rope before tightening it around his bull, and then tied himself on. He'd passed on a protective helmet to keep his white Stetson instead.

"Who said anything about mattress dancing?" Grady smirked. "I'm only offering you a drink after the rodeo—Dirk will be buying of course."

"I wouldn't be so sure."

"Then how 'bout another wager? One just between you and me?"

"What kind of wager?" She knew better than to commit to anything Grady came up with without hearing all the details first.

"If I beat his ride you'll go to the party with me after the rodeo."

"Isn't it a private event, only for the team members?"

"Yeah," he replied. "But I'm on the team and I'm inviting you."

"I'll think about it, Grady." Janice eyed the bull, hoping to hide the sudden flush in her face. Mag appeared deceptively docile, but there was a dangerous fire blazing in his eyes. Her gut told her the bull was gonna blow.

As the daughter of a stock contractor she'd seen more rodeos than she could remember, and more wrecks than she could ever forget, but no matter how hard she tried, she'd never become desensitized to the gory aftermath of any bull ride gone bad—usually resulting in lots of blood and mangled bones twisted at unnatural angles.

Up to this point, the finals had been surprisingly free of injuries, but the bull riding was where most of them

happened. The last seconds in the chute never failed to
send Janice's heart into her throat. She'd kept a close
tally of Dirk's points and knew just covering this bull
was all he needed. She hoped he wouldn't slough off her
advice about spurring. Her fingers closed tightly around
the cold steel of the chute panel as Dirk raised his right
arm and nodded at the gateman.

Straddling the rails above the bull, Dirk focused solely
on his routine. Releasing one foot at a time from the
steel rail, he stepped lightly onto the bull's back, testing
Mag's reaction and then easing himself into position behind the animal's massive shoulders. The bull snorted,
pawed, and then tensed, a dangerous shiver of awareness
rippling through the three-quarter-ton beast.

Wrapping his gloved hand around his rope, he gave a
few swift jerks up and down and then pulled the sticky,
rosin-coated rope through his hand in a suicide wrap.
Closing his fist, Dirk sidled his hips up closer to his hand
and then pounded his closed fist to cement his hold.

Although he'd spent plenty of time backing broncs,
nothing on earth compared to the addictive rush of a bull
ride. The sensation of backing a bull was a heady shot of
pure adrenaline that coursed through his body, exciting
every nerve. Just like a junkie seeking the next "fix,"
hundreds of cowboys risked life and limb grasping for
the elusive eight second high.

It was balls to the wall every time the chute opened.

He inhaled deeply and then slowly emptied his lungs.
In these final seconds his senses were hyperaware.
Everything seemed magnified—the noise of the crowd

buzzing in his ears, the familiar smells of dirt, sweat, and cow shit. Dirk shut his eyes, and closed his mind to everything but the snorting mass of muscle and sinew under him. "Fuck Grady," he murmured. "This is between you and me, Mag. It's just us."

With his jaw set in fierce concentration, Dirk opened his eyes, raised his right arm, acutely aware of his own heartbeat, of the sensation of his blood pulsing through his veins, of the metallic click of the gate latch echoing in his ears, as he gave the nod to the chuteman.

The gate swung free to the last gong of AC/DC's "Hells Bells," and Mag exploded out of it like a derailed freight train. With his body jerking in all directions at once, Dirk countered the frenetic and frenzied fits of jumps, kicks, dives, and spins in the battle of domination with the bull.

With his right arm ever reaching for that precarious sweet spot of equilibrium, Dirk rose into his riding hand on each kick, and pushed his fist deep into the bull's shoulder on every rear, following the bull's lead in the deadly dance. Hell bent on hurling him through the air, the bull snorted and grunted with the jarring force of each buck and kick.

Heeding Janice's advice, Dirk held off plying his heel—at least for the first five or six seconds, but with only a second or two remaining, he raked his spurs upward into the bull's hide hoping to score extra points. Just as Janice had warned, Mag kicked up with a furious toss of his horned head that narrowly missed Dirk's face. Undeterred, he dropped his heels back into position for another go—but the buzzer sounded.

Dirk fisted the air to proclaim his victory, but a

millisecond later when he grabbed the rope tail to release himself, the bull dropped his head and ducked off into a hard right that threw his body hard left. And in the blink of an eye he was cast into the middle of a slow motion nightmare. Time seemed suspended as Dirk flailed for balance—completely at the mercy of a raging bull.

Mag bucked, leaped, and jackknifed in midair only to land in a clockwise spin that pitched Dirk over the bull's right side—into the well of the spin. He struggled to keep his wits about him and his feet on the ground long enough to free himself, but the bull had other ideas, hooking him with his horns, and tossing him into the air and onto the other side ... now the outside of the spin.

White hot pain seared through his arm and shoulder while Mag spun with enough momentum to turn Dirk into a horizontal propeller blade. Twisted the wrong way in the bullrope, his left hand had gone completely numb, while his right arm that he needed to free it, jerked helplessly in the air in rhythm with the bucking bull.

The first bullfighter appeared in the periphery of his vision, but with his feet dragging and scrambling for purchase, Dirk was powerless to help himself. With his attention now fixed on the bullfighter, Mag whipped around the other way to harrow the fighter across the arena like a super-charged John Deer.

Horses, ropes, and two more blurry bodies appeared, but true to his name, Mag was a force to be reckoned with—bucking, charging, and dragging Dirk helplessly along with his body flailing like a rag doll. Dirk's chest was heaving and sweat poured off his body in his effort to prevent his complete mutilation, but he was losing it fast.

"Hang on, cowboy! Stay on your goddamn feet until we shut this motherfucker down!" Grady's voice was the last thing Dirk heard before the bull's horns struck again, slamming into his head and then ramming his ribcage. Pain, blinding and deafening exploded inside him, wiping his mind and sucking him down into its black void.

———————

"Fucked that one up but good, din't ya, cowboy?" Grady's face came slowly into focus.

"Made the whistle, didn't I?" Dirk grunted back through the racking spasms in his ribcage. His head pounded like hell and it hurt like a sonofabitch just to breathe. He spat a mouthful of blood and then searched with his tongue for any missing teeth. Satisfied they were still intact, he performed a tactile survey of his face, squinting at fingers that came away smeared with blood. "Holy shit! How bad is it?"

"Coulda been a lot worse. Looks like the cocksucker only broke your nose. Don't sweat it though, pretty boy. It's an improvement." Grady grinned. "'Sides, chicks dig scars."

"Not Rachel," Dirk groaned. "She's gonna be pissed." That was for damn sure. They were supposed to have photos taken together at the after party for her Miss Rodeo America campaign.

"Talk about pussy whipped," Grady mumbled with a head shake.

"How many points?" Dirk asked, eager to know. It had been a hell of a ride. Roughest ever, but at least he'd covered the bull. The hang-up afterward wouldn't count against him.

"Eighty-eight," his buddy answered with a scowl. "But that motherfucking bull did all the work. He scored forty-nine of it."

A grin broke over Dirk's blood and muck-smeared face. "Beat your last ride by two points, didn't I? Looks like you're gonna be buying the drinks."

"I still have another go, but even if I don't out ride you on the next one, you owe drinks to the whole damned team for that dinked up performance."

"A bet's a bet, Grady." Dirk tried to sit up and hissed with pain.

"Hold on there, cowboy." A hand landed firmly on Dirk's shoulder. "Gotta check you out first."

"Says who?" Dirk tried to look up but a foam cervical collar restricted his movement.

"Says me. I'm Josh, the chief medic here. It's good that you've revived so quickly, but a loss of consciousness suggests a concussion. How do you feel?"

Pretty fucked up. "Fine, except my shoulder," Dirk lied. He knew for a fact *that* was screwed up, but the bone-jarring pain that jolted him with every breath told him he'd probably busted a couple of ribs too. He hoped he hadn't punctured a lung but wasn't about to volunteer anything that might put him on an ambulance.

Josh palpated his left shoulder.

"Sonofabitch," Dirk groaned.

"Looks like you've got an anterior dislocation. Have you ever had one before?"

"Yeah. Once. Long time ago."

"That makes repositioning the bone back into the joint a lot easier."

Dirk gritted his teeth. "Just do it, all right?"

"A few questions and we'll take care of it. What's your full name?"

"Justin Dirk Knowlton."

"What's the date?"

"June…" *What day was it anyway?* Dirk squeezed his eyes shut. It was right on the tip of his tongue. "Thirteen…*shit, no*…fourteen."

Josh's mouth tightened. "Where are we?"

Dirk gazed up at the stands again, blinking several times to force his vision back into focus. This one was easier. "The rodeo."

"Which one?"

"What the hell does it matter? They all look the same from down here." He grimaced. "They smell the same too."

The medic frowned and scribbled some notes. Grady squatted beside him with a muffled cough that sounded a lot like "Casper."

"We're at the Finals," Dirk blurted. "In Casper. Will you *please* put this damn shoulder back in now?" Dirk looked up into the stands where spectators leaned over the rails for a better look. He despised being on display all sprawled out in the dirt.

Janice had now joined Grady and a number of others crowded behind her to gawk. "C'mon," Dirk insisted. "Don't make me lie here like a jackass."

"Please, Dirk," Janice pleaded. "Just let him check you out and make sure you're ok."

"Look," Dirk protested, "my brain's not scrambled. I just need my shoulder put back in." He raised his right arm and ripped off the Velcro collar. "If you won't do it for me," he challenged the medic, "Grady will."

"It'd be my pleasure." Grady grinned.

Dirk reached a hand up to Grady who hauled him back to his feet, actions that incited a wave of spectator applause, whistles, and cheers. "Where's my hat?" Dirk demanded.

"Here." Janice handed him the dirt-covered Stetson with a look of mixed concern and disapproval. "Are you sure you should be on your feet already?"

"I'm standin', ain't I?" Dirk placed the hat solidly back on his head. "I've held up this show long enough."

"All right. All right," the medic grumbled in defeat. "We'll finish this up back in the med trailer."

Leaning heavily on Grady, Dirk staggered out to the mobile triage unit. Moments later, he was lying on the paper-covered exam table, bracing himself for the inevitable.

"Relax your left arm and don't fight me," Josh said. "This is gonna hurt pretty bad for a minute or two, but then it'll feel a whole lot better."

Dirk dropped his left arm by his side as instructed, grinding his teeth as the medic raised, rotated, and then jammed the bone back into place with an audible pop.

"It'll hurt much worse tomorrow. You'll need to wear a supportive sling for a few days. No drinking or riding of any kind for at least a couple of weeks."

"Weeks? Yeah. Right." Dirk laughed and then winced in pain. His left hand was swelling up like a friggin' balloon. He couldn't make a fist and hoped it wasn't destroyed. His ribs were probably cracked but there was nothing to be done for that and he wasn't about to stand for any more poking around when Grady was about to ride.

"I mean that about the drinking, Dirk. Especially tonight. The body responds unpredictably to alcohol following any kind of head trauma. The injury lowers tolerance and reduces cognitive function, not to mention impairing the brain's healing abilities." Josh's gaze met Dirk's and held. "It could even trigger a seizure."

"Right. No drinking. Heard ya the first time," Dirk replied.

Favoring his left side, he pushed up into a sitting position and then slowly stood, pausing only long enough for the world to stop spinning. He rolled his shoulder forward and then backward, finding his agony had been almost completely alleviated. "Thanks." He tipped his hat and made for the door.

"Hold on, cowboy," Josh protested. "I'm not finished."

"Then you'll have to continue without me. Gotta go now," Dirk shot over his shoulder. "My buddy's up next."

———~~~———

Dirk emerged from the med trailer on his own, albeit a little unsteady. Janice watched him out of the corner of her eye as she flanked the next two bulls. With his arms over his chest and one booted ankle crossed over the other, he leaned against the chute to watch the last two rides. It was a deceptively casual pose that might have fooled anyone who didn't know him, but she could tell by his pallor and shallow breathing that he hurt far more than he was willing to show. A moment later the medic brought him a sling, but he didn't put it on.

"C'mon, Dirk. Don't be a dumb-ass. Let me help you with that."

"Don't need it," he growled.

"Then why are you favoring the arm?"

He released it instantly from his chest with a scowl.

"Please," she cajoled. "No one's gonna think less of you for wearing the sling. Everyone saw how that bull freight-trained you."

"Need both arms. I promised Rachel I'd dance with her tonight."

"Then she'll need to make do with a one-armed two-step."

"No good. She's Miss Rodeo Montana and I've just won the All Around. The sling'll screw up the pictures. She's already gonna be pissed enough about my face."

"That's ridiculous!" Janice snorted but then grimaced at the truth of it. His face really was a mess with a split lip and a nose swollen to half again its normal size.

Dirk shrugged. "The whole PR thing is her gig. I won't ruin it for her."

"Then just take it off for the pictures."

His mouth compressed. "Thanks for the concern, Janice, but just let it be, will you? I already have a mother."

"Sorry...I just...well, you know..."

He cocked a brow. "No. I *don't* know."

"I thought maybe we'd become friends is all."

"A man can never be *friends* with a woman, Janice. Unless she's a troll, there always reaches a point when the guy starts thinking about getting' into her jeans. It's just how it is. You ain't no troll and I got a thing going with Rachel."

Janice looked away hoping he wouldn't notice the flames heating her face. "That's not what I...but you'd never…" She stammered at the idea that he'd ever think of her in *that* way.

"No?" His gaze tracked slowly over her and his mouth kicked up in one corner. "Think again, sweetheart. By the way, I've noticed Grady sniffin' around you. Be careful with him, Janice. He rides damn close to the edge sometimes."

"What do you mean?"

His mouth moved but the announcer's blaring voice drowned out his reply.

"Next up is last year's CNFR champion bull rider, Grady Garrison of Three Forks, Montana, coming into the short round on Rio Bravo."

Janice grinned. "Speak of the devil…"

"Yeah," he said. "And he's about as much trouble."

Janice grimaced. "Look, Dirk, I've been around long enough to recognize his type. Grady blows about as much hot air as a Chinook."

His gazed narrowed. "Don't be fooled. He does blow a lot of smoke but his bad boy *act* isn't an act, and he doesn't know how to keep his mouth shut either."

Her temper flared. If Dirk didn't want her, why shouldn't she go out with Grady? A drink or two was no big deal. "You didn't take my advice about the bull, why should I take yours?"

"Because you're a *nice* girl, Janice," he replied. "I'd hate for him to change that."

On those parting words, Dirk tipped his hat, and limped away to join some team mates, leaving a dull ache in Janice's chest. "That may be," she whispered to his back, "but it seems nice girls always finish last."

Grady's ride was the final event of the rodeo. He'd pronounced with his perpetual smirk that it was because they saved the best for last. Although Janice would like to have seen him pulled down a notch, he finished with another strong performance, riding and spurring his bull all the way to the whistle, and then dismounting with exaggerated panache for a final score of eighty-eight points.

With the final scores called, the spectators slowly dispersed from the arena. While the rough stock contenders packed up their gear, Janice fell back into the dirty and mundane routine of sorting and penning her bulls for the next haul. Dirk had joined the others behind the pens where the cowboys exchanged good-natured ribbing and swapped stories about their respective rides.

"So you coming or not?" Grady surprised Janice from behind.

"Where?" she asked.

"To the party."

"Oh, that. I said I'd think about it if you *beat* Dirk. You didn't. You tied."

"That may be but I damn sure rode better than him, and you know it. Hell, it was the bull that made *his* ride. I had to spur the shit out of the dink I drew to get anything out of him."

Janice grudgingly acknowledged that Grady had milked the most out of his ride. Rio was a highly respected bucking bull, but he was approaching retirement.

"Let me on *that* badass motherfucker"—he nodded to Mag—"and you'll see a *real* ride."

Cowboy Boots for Christmas

The first book in the Burnt Boot, Texas series

by Carolyn Brown

New York Times and *USA Today* Bestselling Author

—∿∿—

All he wants for Christmas is peace and quiet...

After two tours in Afghanistan, retired Army sniper Finn O'Donnell believes his new ranch outside the sleepy little town of Burnt Boot, Texas, is the perfect place for an undisturbed holiday season. But before he can settle in, an old friend shows up looking for protection and a place where nobody knows her name.

But that's going to take a miracle...

Callie Brewster must relocate to protect her young nephew, Martin, and the only person she trusts is her old Army friend, Finn. Burnt Boot seems like the perfect place to be anonymous, but it turns out a small town with big drama is no place to hide...

—∿∿—

"Brown has the touch for creating a Western that many readers would like to be real." —*RT Book Reviews*

For more Carolyn Brown, visit:

www.sourcebooks.com

How to Marry a Cowboy

Cowboys & Brides series

by Carolyn Brown

New York Times and *USA Today* Bestselling Author

—⁓—

She's running from her past

Mason Harper's daughters want a new mama in the worst way, and when a beautiful woman in a tattered wedding gown appears on their doorstep, the two little girls adopt her—no ifs, ands, or buts about it. Mason isn't sure about taking in a complete stranger, but Lord knows he needs a nanny, and Annie Rose Boudreau stirs his heart in long-forgotten ways…

And he's the perfect escape

Annie Rose is desperate, and when a tall, sexy cowboy offers her a place to stay, she can't refuse. After all, it's just for a little while. As she settles in deeper, her heart tells her both Mason and her role as makeshift mama suit her just fine. But will Mason feel the same way once her nightmare past catches up with her?

—⁓—

"Brown continues her streak of satisfying contemporary Western romances…" —*Booklist*

For more Carolyn Brown, visit:

www.sourcebooks.com

The Cowboy's Mail Order Bride

by Carolyn Brown

New York Times Bestselling Author

—⁓—

She's got sass...

Emily Cooper promised her dying grandfather that she'd deliver a long-lost letter to a woman he once planned to wed. Little does adventurous Emily know that this simple task will propel her to places she never could have imagined...with a cowboy who's straight out of her dreams...

He's got mail...

When sexy rancher Greg Adams discovers his grandmother Clarice has installed Emily on their ranch as her assistant, he decides to humor the two ladies. He figures Emily will move on soon enough. In the meantime, he intends to keep a close eye on her—he doesn't quite buy her story of his grandmother as a mail-order bride.

A lost letter meant a lost love for Clarice, but two generations later, maybe it's not too late for that letter to work its magic.

—⁓—

"While the romance is hot, there is an old-world feel to it that will bring out the romantic in every reader, leaving them swooning and wishing they had their very own cowboy."—*RT Book Reviews*, 4 Stars

For more Carolyn Brown, visit:

www.sourcebooks.com

How to Handle a Cowboy

The first book in the
Cowboys of Decker Ranch series

by Joanne Kennedy

His rodeo days may be over...

Sidelined by a career-ending injury, rodeo cowboy Ridge Cooper feels trapped at his family's remote Wyoming ranch. Desperate to find an outlet for the passion he used to put into competing, he takes on the challenge of teaching his roping skills to five troubled ten-year-olds in a last-chance home for foster kids, and finds it's their feisty supervisor who takes the most energy to wrangle.

But he'll still wrangle her heart

When social worker Sierra Dunn seeks an activity for the rebellious kids at Phoenix House, she soon learns she's not in Denver anymore. Sierra is eager to get back home to her inner-city work, and the plan doesn't include forming an attachment in Wyoming—especially not to a ruggedly handsome and surprisingly gentle local rodeo hero.

"Realistic and romantic... Kennedy's forte is
in making relationships genuine and heartfelt as
she exposes vulnerabilities with tenderness and
good humor."—*Booklist* Starred Review

For more Joanne Kennedy, visit:

www.sourcebooks.com

How to Kiss a Cowboy

Cowboys of Decker Ranch series

by Joanne Kennedy

This cowboy is living a charmed life

Winning comes naturally to bronc rider Brady Caine. Ruggedly handsome, careless, and charismatic, the rodeo fans adore him and the buckle bunnies are his for the taking. He's riding high when he lands an endorsement deal with Lariat Western Wear that pairs him up with champion barrel racer Suze Carlyle.

Until one wrong move changes everything

A stupid move on Brady's part lands Suze in the hospital, her career in tatters. Now it's a whole new game for both of them. Brady is desperate to help Suze rebuild her life, but he's the last person she wants around now. Suze's got plenty of grit and determination—learning to trust Brady again is a very different matter.

Praise for Joanne Kennedy:

"Joanne Kennedy's heroes are strong, honest, down-to-earth, and sexy as all get out." —*New York Journal of Books*

For more Joanne Kennedy, visit:

www.sourcebooks.com

Acknowledgments

Anyone who has read my historical romances knows that I always make a sincere attempt to bring an element of realism to all of my stories. While this might seem easy in a writing a contemporary series, I don't think I ever could have done it without Kail and Renee Mantle of Montana Horses in Three Forks, Montana. My brief taste of Montana ranching was invaluable in helping me to understand the people and the real life struggles and helped to bring my vision for this series more vividly to life. Thank you so very much, Kail and Renee, for your generosity and friendship. I will treasure both always.

I'd also like to express my sincere appreciation to my two beta readers, Jill and Lee Anne. It was no small thing for me to leap three centuries. Your support and encouragement have been a true blessing.

Last, but certainly not least, I wish to offer my sincere thanks to my editor, Deb Werksman, for giving me the opportunity to foray into contemporary romance, and to the wonderful editorial and creative staff at Sourcebooks for all of their contributions.

About the Author

Victoria Vane is an award-winning author of smart and sexy romance. Her works of fiction range from historical to contemporary settings and include everything from wild comedic romps to emotionally compelling erotic romance with a trademark dash of wicked wit.

In addition to reading and writing, she is an avid equestrienne. She loves the mountains and resides in the upstate region of South Carolina. Look for more of her sexy new contemporary cowboy series coming from Sourcebooks in 2015.